THE BATTLE OF THE THRONE

THE COSMIC WORLD OF OLYMPUS

JOSEPH BELL

For more information, or to book an event, contact :
Email : TCWOlympus@gmail.com
Web: http://www.thecosmicworldofolympus.com

Book design by Joe Mansir
Cover design by Joseph Bell

ISBN – Paperback : 979-8-218-31640-2
First Edition: November 2023

Contents

Dedication

To my beloved wife Ivy who not only embraces the untamed wanderings of my imagination but also, when needed, gently guides me back to solid ground. To my precious children, Ethan and Livia, may you always cherish the youthful spirit within and delight in life's simplest treasures. This story is for you.

Joseph Bell

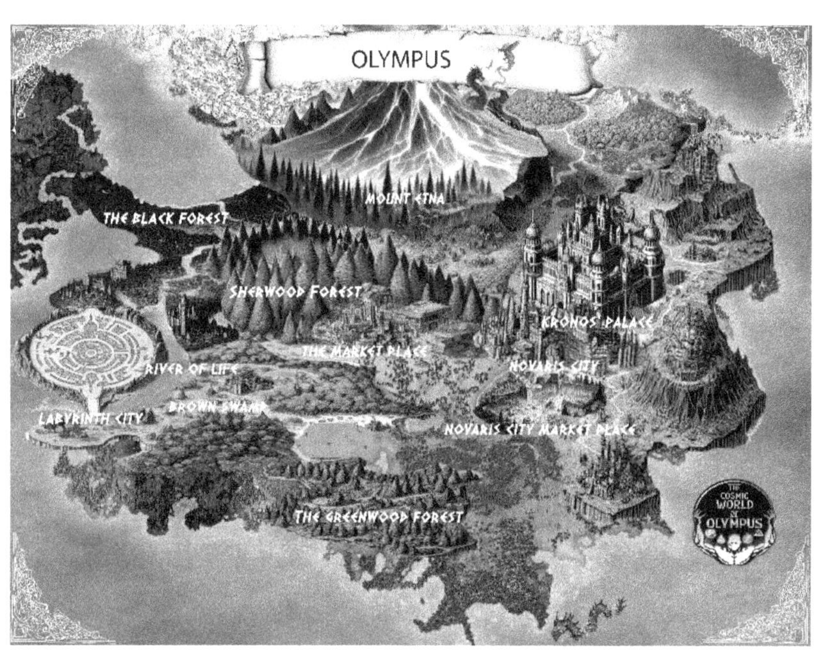

OLYMPUS
MOUNT ETNA
THE BLACK FOREST
SHERWOOD FOREST
KRONOS PALACE
THE MARKET PLACE
RIVER OF LIFE
NOVARIS CITY
BROWN SWAMP
LABYRINTH CITY
NOVARIS CITY MARKET PLACE
THE GREENWOOD FOREST
THE COSMIC WORLD OF OLYMPUS

Chapter One: Birth From Ashes

The air was thick with ash and pain. A poisonous cloud gathered like fog and swirled over the ground, obscuring the village at the base of the mountain. People ushered their animals into their homes and locked their windows tight even as sweat ran in rivulets down their backs. "It's coming," mothers whispered to their children, husbands to their wives. Their brows knotted with fear and their voices trembled. "She's coming."

Through this village, silent and newly fearful, a woman staggered. She clutched her swollen belly and leaned against the side of a house, gasping air as though it were fresh and cold. Her dark skin had a gray cast and her hair, a rainbow of black and gray and white that fell to her waist, was damp with sweat.

The ground rumbled as she heaved against the wall. She must keep moving. She must walk until she could walk no more. She made her way up the dirt road toward the mountain. She wore a simple crown of stone and a dress of greenery that flowed over her body, with leaves that fluttered in the wind and cradled velvet-soft flowers as they bloomed at her hips and shoulders. A wave of shimmering heat blasted through the town; the leaves browned and curled. The woman gasped. The magma beneath the planet's crust ebbed and flowed in time with her contractions.

She wasn't ready to give this child up to the world. Right

here, right now, he was hers alone. As soon as she birthed him, all that would change. For this child was destined for greatness, beyond all the monsters and gods she'd birthed before. She tried to hold on to each moment, to each swell of pain. The ground buckled, but she didn't stumble.

She'd gotten a mile from the village when Mount Etna roared for her son. Fire spewed into the air and ash fell over the valley like snow. Lava spilled over the top of the mountain and flowed in a river toward the houses below. Gaia had always stopped the lava from reaching the village before; now she threw her head back and screamed as a contraction took hold.

Over the next four hours, smoke filled the sky, turning it black as the birthing bed. Gaia staggered up the mountain and did not stop even as the tough grasses shriveled to a crisp. She ascended to bare, smoking rock; she ascended as orange-red lava flowed over her feet. And every time a contraction came, both the mountain and the woman convulsed and screamed, until the people of the village were unsure where one's pain stopped and the other's began.

At last she staggered onto a rock that jutted from the mountainside. It was black as pitch, smooth as glass. She collapsed onto the stone. Her skin was streaked with soot and every breath rasped. The contractions were coming faster now, and stronger than ever. She could go no farther. It was time.

She lay on her back and breathed deep. The air was searing, here, and filled with poison, but she paid it no mind.

She rested her hands flat against her stone bed, and she pushed.

The mountain rumbled. Gaia's eyes, blue as a clear summer sky, stared into nothing. She pushed again, and a river of lava cascaded down the side of the mountain.

She pushed a third time and the mountain exploded.

The top of Etna was engulfed in a crown of fire. Lava splashed against her bed and flowed like blood toward the valley. Errant sparks kissed the red-tiled roofs of the village. The woman – or was it the mountain? – pushed one final time, and from the womb of the world he came.

He was gray as ash and slick with magma. His eyes were shut tight, but his mouth opened wide. He howled. The wind whipped hot and frenzied.

He floated down the river of lava, still screaming, until two dark hands lifted him gently from his fiery cradle and brought him to his mother's breast. He latched immediately. As he sucked the wind died down and the lava slowed its descent. Gaia breathed deep, and at her relieved exhale, fire turned to stone mere feet from the edge of the village. At her second breath, the mountain began to speckle over with bright green moss. A light breeze dispersed the ash cloud and for the first time in a full day, the people of Mount Etna saw flashes of azure sky.

Now that the danger was over, Gaia looked her son over. His breath was hot against her chest and he snuffled as she checked his hands and feet and head. He was perfectly formed. As the breeze cooled, his gray skin cracked and flaked, as though he were made from the mountain that birthed him. And perhaps he was. Gaia ran her fingers over his skin, brushing away the ash to reveal olive skin that matched her own. As her hand found his cheek, he opened his eyes. They were red as the heart of Olympus.

Gaia held her son close. Her greatest creation yet.

All Gaia's children were special in their own way, but this one was destined to be something more. His brothers—she knew there would be more brothers—would look to him as a natural leader. He would guide them and steer them. He would save the world, or he would destroy it.

It was a hard road to travel, and much of it would be travelled in secret. But a cataclysmic event would hardly go unnoticed by the boy's enemies. If he was found while he was still vulnerable—

There was no *if.* The boy could not be found.

Gaia lifted her hand and began to weave it through the air. In the wake of her fingers, fine volcanic ash trailed and spun into a long thread. Then it knit itself into a silken gray cloak, just large enough for an infant.

The child slept. She gently wrapped him in his fine new cloak. Her dress rippled, growing a mossy sling to hold him tight against her body, then she got to her feet. Wiping soot from her still-damp forehead, she set off over the mountain. By the time the villagers at the base of Mount Etna were brave enough to venture outside, all signs of their goddess were gone, save for a carpet of narcissi at the bottom of the mountain and a high, thin wail on the wind, the latent memory of a child's cries.

Most people called it, 'the mountain.' It dominated the skyline, trickling smoke, snow dusting its rocky summit. Travelers who came to the city of Solara on the plains asked about the mountain, and always received the same answer: people did not go there, because people did not return.

This wasn't entirely true. The mountain was surrounded by steep rock formations that jutted from the ground like spikes and made the slope difficult to reach, but resourceful and experienced climbers could manage. From there, climbing the mountain was simply a matter of perseverance: trekking up a slope that had no discernible path and was slick with moss, careful not to fall into one of the holes that riddled the mountain's side. Some of these holes were large enough to swallow a man; others merely sufficient to break an ankle.

But there were some who went looking for the caves of Etna. The right caves led a traveler through a maze of caverns—some natural, others hewn from the rock by some ancient hand. Gaia now made her way through these caverns, holding her son to her chest. At first she traveled in darkness, trusting her feet and her heightened senses to guide her. Gradually she saw little slivers of light, shivering on the volcanic walls. She followed that light as it danced and grew. When she came to the first torch, she nodded and took it. Hopefully, refuge lay here for her boy.

She followed the twisting tunnels until she felt the first blast of warm air and turned a corner to find herself at a ledge. She took a careful step forward and looked down on the city that sprawled around her.

The black rock had been carved into houses that stacked, one on top of the next like a child's block tower. Walls, walkways and roofs ran dense with moss and ferns that flourished in the hot and humid environment. Steep stairs twisted around the mountain and flowed with life as people made their way up and down. At the base of those stairs, the city became a maze of streets and shops teeming with people. Gaia gazed on it for a few wondering moments, taking in the fire-red feathers of the Phoenixes, brilliant scales of the Dragons, the bright clothes of the Giants. Dwarf mail glinted and flashed by the light of over a thousand lanterns that drifted, held aloft by magic. A russet Griffin swooped past her to land on a nearby ledge. Tunnels led around the sides of the mountain, branching like the veins of a leaf, leading to smaller towns and living spaces that catered to the more unusual creatures that called Etna home.

When she looked up again, the Dragon was there.

His scales were bluer than the midday sky, and his eyes dark as jet. His wings were the size of a small house. His talons were as long as Gaia's hand, and cruelly hooked to grasp both the stalactites of Mount Etna and the goats that Dragons plucked from the mountain's outer slope. Two wicked horns curled at the top of his head, and his snout and beard were tinged with gray, showing his age.

He dipped his head – no mean feat as he beat his wings to stay aloft. "My lady," he said in a rumble like thunder. The stink of fresh blood was on his breath.

Gaia gave him a half bow in return not pleased to be recognized so immediately. The Dragons must have realized what the cataclysm of Etna meant and been on the lookout for her. "My greetings, Ankor. May prosperity smile upon your tribe. I hope I find you well."

"You find me troubled," said the great Dragon. "We would speak with you."

He let himself drop, baring his spine. It was lined with dark spikes. Gaia took a spike with one hand and slid onto his back, putting the other hand around her son. It was unusual to be offered a ride on a Dragon, and Gaia murmured her thanks as she mounted.

They soared up. Ankor let out a blast of fire that singed the air around them, then tucked his wings and dove through an opening barely large enough to fit him near the top of the mountain. Gaia kept her head low and her child close. Ankor twisted through a tunnel and came out into another cavern, half the size of the great city.

This cavern had no hanging lights, nor shops at its base. It was lit only by Dragon fire, and decorated with shed scales in various vibrant colors. They decorated Dragon-carved nests, hewn from the rock and stabilized with short walls built from the blackened bones of their meals. One craggy cliff, higher and grander than the rest, glittered with flashing scales and the eyes of five more Dragons. Ankor ascended and they made space for him in the middle.

He dropped his neck and Gaia slid to the ground, silently blessing the solid stone beneath her. Then she turned and bowed to each Dragon in turn. She was the mistress of Olympus, but these mighty creatures commanded respect. They lowered their heads in turn, touching their wings to the ground in deference. They were all gray at the nose, and some at the wingtip – these were the Elder Dragons of Etna.

"We would ask what brings you to our mountain home," said a female with scales the color of moss and horns that spiraled to wicked points at the top of her head.

Gaia hesitated a moment. Then the tendrils of her child's sling unwove, and she turned him gently to the Elders. "This is my son," she said.

The Dragons recoiled. One let out an angry lick of flame. Gaia pulled him close. "He has a great destiny," she said, her low voice ringing with portent. "And he is in great peril."

The Dragons exchanged glances. They seemed to understand her meaning. The green female spoke again. "And what would you ask of us, the guardians of Etna?"

Gaia hesitated, looking from face to face. The Dragons stared back at her, unblinking. It was difficult at the best of times to read a Dragon's expression. Their eyes were guarded, and an acrid smoke trickled from their noses. They liked their petitioners to be direct, but they felt no need to be open and direct themselves.

She drew herself up and pushed back her shoulders. "I am a Queen and a Goddess, and I would ask for your protection. I would ask that my son grow among you and learn the wisdom of the Dragons, the cleverness of the Griffins, the steadfastness of the Dwarves and the tenacity of the Giants. I would ask that you keep him safe and help him make Etna his home."

For a long moment, all was still. No one's expression changed. Then Ankor said, "We cannot."

He sounded regretful, but his words still stung. "Cannot?" she asked, more sharply than was wise. "Or will not?"

"Is there a difference?" An elder with scales the color of blood swung his thin head down to face her. "We will not, because we cannot. We are the guardians of Etna. We protect the mountain and all within it. You would bring great peril to our home. The mountain is no place for a boy to grow up. There are too many crevices and cracks, too many lava vents. We have no notion of how to take care of a wingless boy— especially one with such a destiny as him."

Gaia turned from one Dragon to the next. "You knew," she realized, running a finger down her son's back as he snuggled against her. "You knew I would ask."

"We suspected," replied Ankor. "And we regret our reply. Perhaps other tribes in the mountain would give you a different answer—"

"There are no others I can trust," she said sharply.

There was another pregnant pause. Gaia's feet dug into the ground, as if trying to root in the hard stone. With some effort, she shifted her stance. "He is entwined with this place, somehow," she said softly. "If it is not to be his home, then I'm afraid of what that truly means for Etna."

"That," said the green Dragon, "is a matter of fate and the future."

They dipped their heads again, stirring up a breeze that left Gaia's shoulders cold. A cape of white morning-glory flowers bloomed to cover her. "Are you certain you do not wish to take him? He may well be your savior."

"He may just as well be our destruction," said the red Dragon.

Gaia bowed in return, then climbed aboard Ankor again. There was no arguing with the Elder Dragons once they'd made up their minds. They were strong-willed and unbending, and to them to safety of Etna was paramount. More important, even, than the freedom of the whole world.

###

Ankor took Gaia and the baby boy down to the edge of the mountain, where a black river churned through the great city and out into the world. She boarded a river boat and thanked the Dragon under the gaze of a dumbstruck riverman.

"A war is coming," she warned him, plucking a rose from her dress as a token of thanks. "You cannot avoid it."

"Nor will we provoke it," Ankor replied, and took the rose delicately in his talons. Then he took to the sky, churning up a cloud of black dust.

Gaia gave another rose to the riverman as payment for their travel, and he poled them through the city. The scent and sound of civilization assaulted her: roasting meat, hot metal, stale beer. Sellers shouting their wares from the market, couples arguing loudly as they strode along the streets, Griffins snorting and Phoenixes cawing. More riverboats joined them until a throng of barges crowded the river from edge to edge. In the midst of this, Gaia sat still and upright, letting her fingers rub against the knotted wooden seat, watching as pale fish flashed in the water below.

They reached the edge of the city and the turmoil fell away like a discarded cloak. The cacophony of life was reduced to a burble as faint as the churn of the river as the buildings on the bank turned to warehouses, then lean-tos, then nothing. They passed under the final hanging lantern of town and headed into darkness, with only a single light suspended from the edge of the barge to guide them along the black river. The scent of sulfur filled Gaia's nose.

They poled into a tunnel and the water picked up speed, tilting slightly downward. The riverman moved his pole deftly, angling them off sharp edges and away from the sides of the tunnel as the boat wobbled around a series of pin turns.

Daylight pierced the tunnel like a sword, and the riverman dug his pole into the bottom of the river. They slowed their progress, drifting closer to the mouth of the cave, until they came to the edge of daylight. He tossed a rope around a little pole that stood on a ledge, a natural disembarking point, and pulled it fast. The boat rocked. Gaia stood and allowed him to hand her up to the ledge. Then she thanked him again, and watched him pole back up the River before heading into the light.

She had hoped to give her son an extraordinary and protected life in Etna. With the Dragons' rejection, she had but one person to turn to. It was both bitter and sweet that she knew he would not refuse her.

She traveled along the River until she reached the edge of the Brown Swamp, then set off north and west. She moved on foot, calm and confident, and the path she walked blossomed with grass and wildflowers. It gave her enemies an easy trail to follow, but Gaia doubted they'd discovered the boy quite yet. These flowers would wither in the dull Swamp in a matter of days, their sweet scent turning rotten, their petals browning and drooping. She was safe until she got to the forest. And the forest, being her heartland, would conceal her.

Mother and son traveled for three days. He nursed as they walked; she stopped only to rest and to drink the nectar of the surrounding flowers. She did not worry about the creatures of the Brown Swamp; she was a goddess, and the animals here knew better than to trifle with her. Instead she accepted a tribute of honey from the bees and an honor guard of serpents who slithered ahead.

When she came to the forest, she wove herself a cloak of grass that covered her dress and pulled the hood over her head. She was coming into the realm of men now, and she wanted to travel in secret. She set off on a small game path.

The path soon widened. Gaia strode past trees that could

not be encircled by three men holding hands, with broad leafy canopies and branches as thick as her body. Bright poppies, cheery marigolds and dangling bluebells dotted the forest floor, and sunlight fell like rain through the leaves above. Birds warbled the news of the day from branch to branch, and nearby a stream chattered and teemed with little green and brown frogs. As if sensing the change in his world, her bundle shifted against her skin, cracking open one eye to look out at the forest before tucking his nose against her chest once more.

The dirt path turned to stone and the first houses began to appear. Some of them had been built right into the trunk of a tree, while others perched in the branches like birds, with little rope bridges running from room to room, from house to house. The road bent to follow a sparkling river that wound lazily through the heart of the city, and shops began to appear along the river's edge. The mill and brewery were equipped with water wheels, and wide barges docked all along the river's edge, spitting out men to load and unload wares. The city at the heart of Sherwood Forest was as metropolitan as the one within Etna, and as she followed the road Gaia saw a number of familiar shops: the potion maker's, the book binder's, the milliner's, the blacksmith's. All were suffused with a greenish-gold light, the peculiar and enchanted light of Sherwood. A few people stopped to look at her as she passed, but the people of Sherwood were used to strangers passing through—and this woman was hardly the strangest of them.

Gaia walked until she found a smaller path, leading away from the center of town. She followed the road until she found a red door set into the trunk of an enormous oak, carved with the motif of a bearded man shrouded in leaves. She knocked three times upon this door, then let herself in.

The yeasty smell of rising bread dough greeted her, mixed with the scent of woodsmoke and meat. Gaia found herself in a small front hall with a mat and two pairs of boots lined neatly against the wall. A wood-hewn staircase led to the upper floors. From above, a distracted male voice called, "Raven! Someone's at the door."

Gaia heard a rhythmic chopping from the kitchen. "And?" a woman's voice called back.

"And go answer it, I'm in the midst of—" The man made a frustrated sound.

"These onions won't cut themselves," she said irritably.

"I've spared you the trouble," Gaia said, and began to ascend the stairs.

She heard the sound of a knife *thumping* into a chopping board, then hurried footsteps. As she came up to the next floor, she saw a spacious room with chairs and rugs and a cheerful fireplace, enchanted to protect the tree. A dining table sat off to one side. Next to the dining table was a door, and in the doorway was a black-haired, pale woman with a sharp gaze. "Gaia!" she exclaimed, her sharpness giving way to a broad smile. "We weren't expecting you—we hadn't received a note—" She stopped, and her face stormed over. "Ethan! You didn't receive a note, did you?"

Gaia heard a thundering on the stairs, and a moment later Ethan was there. He was broad-shouldered and tan from a life in the sun, with brown hair and a beard sprinkled with early gray. Even indoors he wore a leather jacket and a crimson scarf around his neck. In three strides he had crossed to Gaia and wrapped her in a large but careful hug.

"Of course not," he said over her shoulder. "I'd have told you if I had."

"If you'd remembered," Raven corrected him, crossing her arms. She wore a sturdy white shirt and black vest, more suited to trading in town than breadmaking.

Ethan released Gaia. "I assure you, it's as surprising to you as it is to me. And I take it that *this* is the reason for your visit?"

He gestured to the lump against her breast. Gaia's dress loosened enough for her to bring the baby out. He shifted. His face screwed up.

"He's perfect." Ethan slid one broad hand under the baby and brought him in to his chest. The boy's wail quieted. He looked at Ethan with wide, dark eyes.

"He's taken with you," Gaia said, a hitch in her voice.

Raven noticed it and gave her a sharp look. "What's this about?"

"It will take some explaining," Gaia said. "May I tell you over dinner?"

###

Dinner was bread and meat for Ethan and Raven, and a fresh bed of greens and flowers for Gaia. The infant slept on a little pillow lined with rugs and blankets. Gaia did her best to explain the situation.

"And this boy's destiny is to restore balance and overthrow Kronos?" Ethan looked over at the little sleeping lump. "How can you be so certain?"

"I know his destiny. Just as I will know the destiny of all my sons," Gaia said. "But in order for him to fulfill it, he must be raised away from the public eye. Hidden."

"And that's where we come in," Ethan guessed. Gaia nodded.

He picked up a wing of fowl and took a bite, pondering as he chewed. "We're rather simple folk. We can't teach your boy much in the way of politics or ruling."

"You will teach him to be good and kind," Gaia replied. "You will teach him to be practical. He will learn to hunt, he will learn to help, and he will learn to do what's right."

"It's quite an undertaking." Raven frowned down at her food. "We've never raised a child before. Why should we raise this one?"

It was a sore point for them. Raven and Ethan had long wanted children of their own but had been unable to conceive. "Ethan is the leader of the Cross of the Iron Phoenix. Surely the chance to raise your greatest weapon against the tyrant is reason enough," Gaia said.

"Children aren't weapons," Raven replied, mouth pinching.

Gaia looked over at her. "This child *will* have a purpose. To deny it would be to do him a disservice." She leaned over and put a hand on Raven's arm. "This is why I wish for it to be *you.* You will always remember that he is a boy, and he needs a mother's love." Her face drew serious. "It is something I cannot give him. Not without endangering his life."

"I—well, Raven and I will have to discuss it," Ethan began.

"We'll take him," Raven said.

Ethan leaned back, surprised. But a smile played at the edge of his mouth, a joy that he struggled and failed to contain. "You are certain?" said Gaia, though she was hardly surprised.

"I know you want a boy," Raven told Ethan.

"I want as many boys as I can have." Ethan stopped trying and let his grin break out, lopsided and rakish.

"And I always knew you would make a good father. If this boy is so important, then it's important he grows up well. But I have some conditions." She crossed her arms and gave first Ethan, then Gaia a stern look. For a moment all was silent, save for the chirping of starlings outside the window and the rustle of the leaves.

"I don't want him growing up with some great destiny hanging over his head. I want him to grow up like a normal boy. He will be loved and treated like one. If it truly *is* his destiny to lead the Resistance and bring Kronos down, then his destiny will come to him. These are my terms."

"I…Of course." Ethan sounded a little dazed.

Raven turned to Gaia, raising an eyebrow expectantly.

Gaia inclined her head, as much of a bow as she could give over the dinner table. "I came to you because I trust you. Be the mother I cannot be."

An understanding sympathy filled Raven's eyes, and she relaxed enough to take Gaia's hand and squeeze it. "I will."

Gaia had met Ethan when she'd saved him from an accident in the woods some years before. She hadn't known, then, that he was fomenting a rebellion against the tyrannical ruler of Olympus, and the friendship she'd fostered with Ethan and Raven had been a rare one. The Dragons might have been able to teach her son political intricacies and complicated magic, but Ethan would raise him like a boy, and this would be better.

As long as he could protect him, too.

The child stirred and began to flail his tiny fists. Ethan hurried over and scooped him up while Raven went in search of some milk to give him. From the fabric of her dress, Gaia spun a rose of deep maroon and scooped a dewdrop from its heart. "Feed this to him when he needs milk," she said. "It will give him the nutrition he needs."

Ethan let her tip the dewdrop into the baby's mouth. He smacked his lips and quieted. Ethan held him out, but Gaia shook her head and willed her tears not to come. "He should get used to you," she said. "And I must not tarry. I want to be far from here when Kronos learns what I have done. He cannot follow the trail to you."

Ethan nodded. "I understand."

From outside the forest began to glow a soft and gentle

green as the sun went down. The enchanted trees would illuminate the paths of the city for several hours yet. It was time for the Goddess to go.

Raven reappeared and tickled his bare belly. "What's his name?" she asked.

Gaia refastened her cloak. "Hades," she said, pulling the hood over her head.

Chapter Two: Genesis Of Life
Three Years Later

In the midst of the Black Forest, in the metropolis known as Labyrinth City, Gaia prepared to give birth to another son.

The city rumbled and rattled. Vendors that had set up their stalls against the high brown walls that lined the streets of the Labyrinth hastened to pull their tarps down and clear their wares. Some abandoned their stalls entirely, fleeing the city before it could come crashing down on them. The city marketplace, normally crowded with spice and carpet sellers, with wizards and doctors and food carts, lay empty and silent, as though the people of the city had disappeared and left only ghosts behind. In the deep of the night the moon cast a silvered glow over the streets, amplified by abandoned torches set into the walls.

Gaia stopped at the edge of the market square and cast a terrified glance behind her. Kronos' men were hot on her tail tonight, and even the ground's tremors could not throw them. She cupped her belly and whispered, "Soon."

The city streets were twisting and thin, all lined with the same brownstone that confused travelers and led them deeper into the maze. And this was only the upper level: beneath her feet, the labyrinth continued, winding down and down to the lower levels of the city, to the sewers and tanners and other unsavory types. And, eventually, to the dangerous home of the Minotaurs.

If she were going to survive this night, she would need the Minotaurs.

Gaia took the nearest staircase down. At the beginning of the night the air had been full of shouts and cries as people packed what they could not spare and fled into the forest. Now it was still, devoid of any sound but the crackling of the torches, her own labored breathing, and her footsteps, determined and uneven, as she made her way deeper into the maze.

And, like an echo, footsteps that followed.

She focused on her feet, counting on them to lead her down. From somewhere far away, water dripped onto stone. The air was musty and damp. The stones bucked as another contraction took hold. Under cover of the rumbling ground she moved when she could, casting out vines that wrapped around corners and pulled her forward. The air grew thicker, staler, and as she moved down new, strange smells began to permeate it: musk, fur, blood and bone. She was getting close.

Her pursuers knew it, too. Their footsteps pattered as they started to jog. They were being thorough, checking every alley and dead-end, but there were more of them and they could work as a team to find her.

She made her way down six steep steps, leaning against the wall to steady herself. The light here was dimmer, torches placed further apart on the walls. A snuffling snort bounced off the high walls, sending cold skittering down her spine. "Timotheus," she gasped as she contracted again. "I would beg a meeting with Timotheus."

Someone shouted behind her. Footsteps pounded on the stairs. Then she heard a scream and the crunch of bone. Her pursuer went silent.

She didn't dare turn around. There was a sound like something heavy being dragged along the floor. Then a hot breath wafted over her, stinking of rancid meat. "What makes you think that Timotheus would meet with you?" rumbled a deep voice.

"He will," Gaia said, clenching her fist until her nails cut into her palms. "The mother of Olympus would beg a boon of him."

She heard a wet crunch. "I think I have already done you a favor," the Minotaur behind her said. It slurped something. "But I will spare you to walk the Labyrinth, and I will tell Timotheus you are here. If he wishes to find you, he will."

"May your horns be sharp and your bones strong," Gaia replied, a common Minotaur blessing. She did not wait for him to reply. She rounded a corner and limped onward. Her breath rasped and echoed, and every time she had another contraction the Labyrinth trembled around her.

She paused as she let another aftershock subside, and in the stillness she heard it: more footsteps. And they were close.

She pushed away from the wall and tried to run, panic overtaking her. She could not let herself be taken. Her pursuer ran, too. She turned blindly, trusting her magic and her senses to guide her. She turned left, then right, then right again—

And came to a small door at a dead end.

She hesitated for a moment. She might be bringing

danger into someone's home. Then a contraction hit, and she flung the door wide.

The room looked as though it had been prepared specially for her. Torches glowed on the walls, suffusing the room with a glowing warmth. A bed lay in the middle of the room, dressed in plain linen bedclothes and surrounded by pillows and rags. A steaming bowl of water sat at the ready.

There was a door on the other side. Gaia stumbled toward it. Then pain erupted at the base of her scalp. She fell backward, yanked by her hair. She let out a short, sharp scream.

The man who'd grabbed her was small and pale, dressed in dark brown and black to blend in with the Labyrinth at night. His face was smeared with blood, his mouth twisted in a sneer. His knife flashed like fire as he held it up to her throat. Gaia stilled.

"My master wants to speak with you," he said in a peculiar, hissing voice. He grabbed her arms and forced them behind her back, pulling her flush against him. He stunk of unwashed man and too much wine. "I'll be taking you to him. But *only* you."

His knife moved down to her belly. Gaia screamed, thrashing, and the world thrashed with her. The man lost his footing and they fell in a tangled heap. She started to kick, fighting to free her hands, but his grip was tight and he bound her wrists with three quick loops of a rope. One of her vines flung the knife away. He growled a curse, ripping it from her shoulder. One hand wrapped around her throat.

A shadow fell over them. The man made a strange gurgling sound. A hand the size of a serving platter reached past Gaia and a moment later the man was being lifted into the air.

The largest Minotaur in the Labyrinth walked over to the door, the man dangling from his hand like a wriggling sack. Timotheus disappeared through the door, closing it behind him. Gaia heard a *crack*, then a thump. Then the Minotaur ducked back inside. He knelt before her. "My lady," he said.

Gaia raised her head to acknowledge him. Then she was wracked by another contraction.

Timotheus's broad brow furrowed. His head was more bull than man, with heavy brows and a short snout, and a face covered in fine brown fur. Two horns angled away from his head, capped with gold. But his eyes held a human intelligence, and his hands were soft as he helped her lay down on the bed.

"Had you sent word, I would have met you at the edge of our territory. Our midwives have retreated from the quake, but it would be my honor to assist the birth."

Gaia could barely nod. It wouldn't be long now. As she pushed she felt her son crown, and at another push a thin wail filled the air. The ground split with a sound like thunder and a coppery taste filled her mouth. Timotheus slid his enormous hand beneath the baby, to support his head and neck as he emerged.

The child was dark as soil. As he was placed in his mother's arms, he blinked eyes as green as summer leaves. A true child of Olympus's soil, Gaia thought. She put her hand flat on the ground as a second shock ran through the Labyrinth. She breathed deep, and whispered reassurances to her son, and slowly the world stilled.

Timotheus handed her a silver knife. It looked like a toy between his fingers, but it was long and wicked in hers, and cut the umbilical cord easily. "I shall summon the midwives," he said. "They will return and care for you."

Gaia wiped sweat from her brow, smearing it with dirt. "I don't have the time to linger." Kronos' men had been too hot on her heels, and while she had confidence that Timotheus's Minotaurs could take care of any intruders, it pinpointed her last known location rather exactly. And if Kronos thought the Minotaurs had harbored her, he would raze Labyrinth city. Besides… "There will be another."

"A twin?" Timotheus's bull-brown eyes widened in surprise. "All the more reason to call for the midwife."

"Not here." Gaia struggled to sit up. She handed her child over to the Minotaur leader. "I must find the water."

Timotheus cradled the boy. "But…why?" he asked. Gaia did not answer. It was a goddess's prerogative to make grand statements and maintain a little mystery.

"Lead me out of the Labyrinth," she said.

"You must rest," Timotheus objected.

Gaia wrapped her son in a cloak the color of soil. Then she bound him to her chest with vines that bloomed a pale, bell-shaped flower. She got to her feet and stood tall. "Take me."

Timotheus knew better than to argue with the mother of Olympus.

He led her with confidence, following some unerring sense or secret sign, turning, at times, in what seemed like a full circle. Gaia never doubted him. Once or twice they heard the soft patter of human feet; when Gaia asked about them, he smiled, revealing sharp yellow teeth. "If they are mere travelers, we may yet let them pass. If they are hunting you, they shall themselves be hunted."

At last he led her to a place where the air was not musty or tinged with sulfur. It smelled salty, and wet, and a chill wind whistled through the alleys of the Labyrinth and kissed her shoulders. Gaia felt the first contraction coming on.

Timotheus led them around a corner, then stopped. Ahead, a square of night air sat at the end of the tunnel. "I will go no further," he said.

Gaia unstrapped her boy from her chest and handed him gently to Timotheus. The boy's green eyes fastened on the Minotaur's glinting gold ones. "I will return for him," she said.

"And until you do, I will guard him with my life," Timotheus replied. He knelt again, and did not rise until Gaia had turned away and made her way down to the end of the maze.

Labyrinth city sloped up the mountain behind her, high-walled, full of shouts as people began to return and pick through the wreckage. Before her the blue-green sea lapped at the dark, stony shore.

Her belly heaved. She made her way down to the water. In the distance long ships rowed around, headed for the dock on Labyrinth City's other side. Gaia walked in the other direction. A spit of land protected a small cove there, hidden behind an outcropping. As soon as her foot touched the water, a cloud passed over the sun. At her second step, the wind picked up. Thunder drummed in the distance.

Gaia stepped into the cove and found a small tide pool amongst the jagged rocks. Here she squatted. She scooped up a palmful of water and used it to wash her face and dab at her neck. She sipped at it, savoring the sting of salt on her tongue. Heavy dark clouds swirled above her. The sea churned and roared as it pulled back from the shore. From high above, in the city, people screamed.

Gaia pushed. The sky broke open and an enormous wave reared up, monstrous, slamming the mountain and the city. Water thundered down staircases and boiled through the high-walled streets. People ran for higher ground. And over all this, the scream of a baby rang loud and angry.

The wave withdrew, leaving him in the tide pool. His eyes were sown up and his brown little fists balled and flailed. Gaia lifted him gently from the waters and at her touch, he quieted. His eyes opened. They were as turquoise as the tropics. As his distress lessened, the turmoil of the sea abated. Gaia tucked him against her and let him suck.

A child of the land and a child of the sea. Twins with shrouded destinies. Gaia's path, on the other hand, was clear. Clear and heartbreaking. Kronos had been closer than ever to catching her. He must not get his hands on these children.

When she was ready she staggered to her feet, then walked back up the slope, toward the Labyrinth and Timotheus and her second son.

The boy with the maroon eyes woke. Outside, the gentle green glow of Sherwood forest proclaimed it night, and he lay for a few moments in his bed, watching fireflies buzz around his window. Their golden light soothed him. They were active tonight, swirling and swarming about the house. He barely had time to find it odd before he smelled a scent at once odd and familiar. It was flowers, but not the wild roses of Sherwood. It was a slightly spicy smell, a smell that spoke of faraway lands and plants he'd never seen before.

A sharp, brief *rap* sounded at the door. The fireflies scattered. Hades felt a rush of sensation that he could hardly name—*home, love, mine*—and then his father was hurrying down the stairs. Without thinking, the maroon-eyed boy slipped out of his bed and followed.

"—Can't keep them. And I can't stay." The woman's voice at the door made his heart twinge. "His men were on me until the Swamp, and something there was watching me, too. I'll have to create simulacra to throw them off the scent."

"Go." As the boy came down the last few steps, he saw his father close the door on a grass-green dress and a dark foot. His mother stood next to him, and by the set of her shoulders she was unhappy.

"Ethan…" Mother said.

"What else could we do? Refuse? We dedicated ourselves to serving the Cross. And that means serving her."

"Hush." Mother had seen him. She crouched, and only then did Hades see what she held in her arms. "Darling, what are you doing up?"

Hades did not reply. He moved forward and put a hand out to stroke the baby's cheek. One chubby hand caught his finger and his heart flipped over in his chest.

"This is Atlas," said Mother, smoothing the top of the boy's head. Her black hair fell in a curtain, protecting them from the whole world. "He's your brother."

Father crouched down, too. "And this is Poseidon. Your other brother."

He stared at them with eyes as wide as buttons. "Brothers?" He'd wanted a brother his whole life, and now he had *two*?

"They'll need a lot of help growing up. You'll have to teach them to be good and strong and brave. Do you think you can?" Father put a hand on Hades' shoulder.

Father was entrusting him with a *job*. A big one. Hades felt his chest swelling with pride. "I'll teach them everything! How to feed the pigs and shoot a bow and sling pebbles, how to run messages to the baker and how to sneak an extra cookie so we don't get caught—"

"Hades, you would *never*," said Mother sharply. She exchanged a glance with Father. He chuckled.

They made a bed on the floor for the babies, with a dozen blankets and a wall made of pillows to protect them. Hades nestled between them. His whole body fizzed with excitement. "I *will* teach you everything," he whispered. "How to be good and brave and strong." He took one brown hand and one black hand in each of his, and looked from brother to brother, so enraptured that he never noticed as his smiling mother closed the door.

Chapter Three: The Spark
Five years later

She ascended the mountain with purpose, face pale with the now-familiar pain. This would be her last son, born as storm and tempest ravaged the land. Rain stung her skin like tiny needles. The wind howled. Light danced in the clouds above. The storm had raged for two days, heralding the birth and driving people into their homes once more. Streets had flooded and lightning strikes had caused at least three fires. The only good thing to be said was that Kronos' men had lost her trail. She would be safe from them tonight.

Gaia took the rocky path toward the top of the mountain, slipping as the slope grew muddy. A goat on the side of the mountain bleated in panic and tried to leap for safety, but its hooves slid on the rocks and it went down the mountain in a cascade of shale.

The air was wild and fresh. Her dress tried to tear away from her body, but she knit it together again, furrowing her brows in concentration and baring her teeth at the storm. The Griffins and Dragons would be roosting indoors tonight. There would be no one to see her, no one to betray her.

The path disappeared at the top of the summit. Gaia gripped the rocky face of the mountain and began to clamber, slipping, scraping her skin on the rock and slicing her calf open. She did not stop, even when a mighty rumble of thunder coincided with the spasming of her belly.

At last she came to the highest point. Gaia tilted her face back and closed her eyes. This storm was for her baby boy, so let it come. Let *him* come. She raised her arms.

Lightning arced down like a thick rope, twining about Gaia's wrist. The thunder was immediate, so loud it seemed to break open the mountain. Gaia's face contorted with pain.

And then the lightning retreated. The wind calmed and the rain warmed. Droplets sizzled as they hit the lightning strike, a patch of scorched dirt at Gaia's feet. And lying in the middle of that patch was the boy. He was pale as the moon, with a full head of white-blonde hair that stood on end. His blue eyes twinkled with starlight. A little fizzle of lightning wound up one leg and into his hair. He hiccupped.

Gaia wrapped him in her cloak. The rain was a light drizzle that would clear in a couple of hours. The clouds, black as midnight when she'd ascended the mountain, were now a slate color, and already breaking up at the horizon. The air was thick with the smell of ozone.

The baby helped himself to the breast. He would be a willful one, Gaia thought, a force to be reckoned with. Like the storm that had birthed him. Emotional, unpredictable, wild. It would be a difficult road to walk, she suspected—but walk it he must.

\#\#\#

The maroon-eyed boy smelled the flowers before he woke. Now he was old enough to know what it had meant.

Ethan and Raven had always been honest about his adoption: that the three boys shared the same mother, and that she had asked Ethan and Raven to step in as their mother and father. Hades had been waiting for years for his birth mother to come back. He leapt from his bed and stuck his feet into his boots.

"Wha?" mumbled Poseidon sleepily.

"I'll be right back." Hades paused to squeeze his brother on the shoulder.

As he opened the door to the room they shared, his father hurried past. "Stay upstairs," he said in a low voice.

"Why?" Hades asked, but Father did not answer him. And, being eight, his curiosity was greater than his sense of obedience, so he followed Father down the stairs, treading lightly so as not to make any noise.

His father's broad frame filled the doorway and obscured whoever stood beyond it. Hades stopped at the bottom stair and inhaled, closing his eyes as the spicy scent of flowers hit him again. Love. Home. Mother.

"We'll take good care of him. Just like the others." Father was reaching out for something. "Please, come in. See the boys."

"I cannot. I cannot be seen here. Not ever again." His mother's voice was sweet and well-tempered, but laced with sorrow and fear. "I used every trick I knew to keep him off my trail this long. I can't risk him finding you. I can't risk him finding the boys."

"Raven will miss you—" Father began.

"I'm sorry," said Hades' mother—his birth mother.

He heard the patter of feet, but it took him a moment to realize what she was doing. He leapt off the stair and shoved past his father as the twins appeared at the top of the staircase.

"Wait, Hades! Come back!" Father cried after him. But Hades couldn't listen. His heart was full of a wild hope and need.

He spotted her green dress as she turned onto the road. It was empty at this time of night, glowing and full of the sounds of the forest. Foxes screamed, owls hooted, little rodents scratched at the trees. Hades pelted after her, toes digging into the dirt until he hit the stone of the main road. Then he skidded to a halt.

He turned to look behind him, then ahead again. But it was no use. The woman in the green dress—his birth mother—was nowhere to be seen. The street was empty but for a fox and a raven, both staring at him as though caught in some act of plotting.

A soft hand fell on his shoulder. His other mother knelt next to him. "I'm sorry," she said. "I'd have liked to see her, too."

Hades looked into Raven's eyes. Normally they were no-nonsense and skeptical of whatever scheme his eight year-old brain had concocted today. But now they were full of kindness and love. "Will I ever meet her?" he asked.

"One day, perhaps." She put an arm around his shoulder and stood up. "Her fate is not for me to say."

Turning him around, she guided him back to the house,

where his father stood, flanked by Poseidon and Atlas. He held another lump in his arms.

"Well," Mother said dryly. "You always said you wanted as many boys as you could have."

Chapter Four: At First Sight
17 years later

"Again." Hades stepped back and took up a defensive position with his sword. His maroon eyes flashed a challenge.

His youngest and most beautiful brother ran a hand through his blond hair and rolled his pale blue eyes. "You said it was the last time three times ago."

"That was because I thought you'd get it. Come on." As though he wanted to be here, listening to his brother grumble and smelling the telltale mix of sweat and leather that accompanied every practice. He wanted to be at the market.

Zeus ran his hands along the wooden staff with distaste. It was a simple weapon, unadorned and chipped from years of practice. He'd always loved the flashiest things: engraved throwing stars, ornamental claws he could slot over his fingers, swords with ornate handles. In short, things that were easily recognized and hard to buy with Cross funds. "I just don't see the point in practicing so much hand-to-hand combat. I mean, look at this." He flicked his wrist and a knife flew through the air. Hades jerked to the side to avoid getting his nose sliced off. "Oops. I was aiming for the chest. My point is, no one's going to get near enough to touch me."

"*Yaaah!*" screamed Poseidon, as if on cue. Their second youngest brother leapt from the underbrush that surrounded their practice clearing and swung a sword half the length of a man. Zeus' eyes widened comically and he stumbled back, tripping over his own feet. The staff barely came up in time to deflect, and by that time Hades was moving forward. He swung, stabbed, parried a sloppy rejoinder from the staff. Zeus' eyes darted from one brother to the other as he backed away, trying to keep distance between him and them.

And he hadn't reckoned on Atlas. Their largest brother had the shoulders of an ox and muscles that could barely be contained by his simple white woolen shirt. He was armed with two short swords. The first slapped straight into Zeus' leather-clad back, flat side first. The second ended at his throat.

Zeus dropped the staff and put up his hands, glaring at Hades. "You cheated," he said. His chest moved rapidly up and down, and his perfectly straight nose glistened with sweat.

Hades grinned and sheathed his sword. "I was proving a point. A staff is a good weapon against multiple enemies. And if you do find yourself surrounded and unable to reach your knives…"

"Or better yet, out of knives," Poseidon added, grabbing his little brother in a headlock. Zeus squirmed free and skipped back.

"Well, give me a sword or something interesting," Zeus grumbled. He loosened his leather breastplate at the shoulders, revealing a thin strip of sweat beneath.

"You'll get a sword when you've mastered the staff." Hades checked the angle of the sun, feeling the pounding heat on the back of his neck. "Which won't be today." He had to meet Harper in the market to make an information exchange. Whether the information was real or another test of his father's, he couldn't tell, but he knew that no matter what, if he didn't make the exchange, Ethan would never clear him to move up in the ranks of the Cross of the Iron Phoenix. He'd been training since he was ten, and he was more than ready. And Ethan had yet to give him a real mission.

"Aren't you supposed to meet Harper at midday?" Poseidon glanced at the sky. "That's at least an hour from now."

"Better to be early than late," Hades said, trying not to squirm. He was terrible at lying, even at times like this when he wasn't really lying at all. He simply…wasn't sure why he was so anxious to be at the market. But his feet tingled with purpose, turning toward the city and the market square whenever he let his mind wander.

He turned, finally giving in to the pull, and his brothers fell in behind him as they always did. "How was my entrance?" Atlas asked as they walked.

"I didn't see it, I was too busy trying to keep my head on," Zeus grumbled.

"You were terrifying," Poseidon reassured him.

"This is so unfair." Zeus' voice was climbing up to a whine. "You all get swords, and what do I get?"

"We had to learn the staff too, brother." Atlas gave Zeus a pat on the back that sent him stumbling forward. "Everybody does it."

They found a side path that would take them to

Sherwood's main street, and the nature of their chatter changed. It was hardly unusual for men of Sherwood to practice weaponry and forestry—it was a dangerous place, after all—but Ethan's boys had to be careful. They couldn't let on that they knew anything about the Cross of the Iron Phoenix, much less that their own father was its leader. Kronos the tyrant had been pressing down on Sherwood with his iron boot in a bid to stifle any sense of freedom, but his attempts had been more or less fruitless, so far. If he realized just how many Cross members operated here, he may well burn the forest to the ground.

Market day was the perfect day to run covert operations. It teemed with people of all sorts as they haggled and traded and argued and laughed together. You could pick an important pocket, slip a note, or have a seemingly-innocuous conversation at the beer stand, all out in the open. And the chance of getting caught was part of the thrill. Of course, Hades wasn't much for conversation, especially with strangers, so he tried to avoid that part. But today's assignment should be a simple matter. And though he was the oldest son of a well-respected man in Sherwood, people tended to forget about him when he wasn't right there. It was a skill that was rare and couldn't be learned, his father always said.

The main road of Sherwood City could accommodate three carts standing side by side, all paved over in clean white stone lined with grass. Trees stood along the road like sentinels, and in between each tree was a colorful stall selling spices, cloth, meat, wool, tools and more. In the upper canopy of the trees, rope bridges connected standing shops like the brewer or the blacksmith. Everything was draped and painted and *loud* for market day. The smell of bodies and beer and meat filled the air. In the middle of the square, a low stage sat free, ready for musicians or traveling players that sometimes came through town. It surrounded Sherwood's sacred tree, a moss-cloaked oak that, no matter the season, was always crowned with fire-hued leaves.

Hades kept an eye out for Harper. His friend should be easy to find; he usually stood head and shoulders above everyone but Atlas. He'd been given his own command three years ago and had made himself infamous for patrolling the wood and 'redistributing' the wealth of Kronos and those sycophants who prospered under him. At first, Hades had been sick with jealousy. He'd slowly come to realize, though, that he couldn't do what Harper did. He may be a leader of his own brothers, but he was hardly a leader of men.

"I don't think he's here yet," Hades said as they found the pungent cheese tent. Harper and Hades always met by the cheese tent.

"That's because we're *over an hour* early. Like I said." Poseidon rolled his turquoise eyes. Then his eyes lit up. "Ooh, goats!" He strode off.

Zeus watched him head over to the goat girl and lean down to scratch a goat on the head. "*Goats*? A hundred beautiful women around, and he wants to pet a goat?"

"It'll keep him out of trouble. Unlike you," Hades said.

He'd lost count of how many punches he'd taken for his little brother after Zeus had broken the heart of yet another maid. It was good to have a brother who didn't start fights. It was also rather sweet—Poseidon had a refreshing innocence to him, a joy of simple things like petting animals or mending cloth. He wasn't the best fighter among them, and he didn't have much of a head for strategy. But Ethan always spoke of him when he spoke of why they fought.

"I'm going to look at arrow heads," said Atlas. "Broke a few shafts last week." He shouldered past Hades and headed for the blacksmith.

Zeus heaved a sigh. "I guess I'll go see what Genni's up to—"

"No you won't," Hades replied sharply. Genni's father had come around last week, ready to give every man in the house a black eye. It had taken many promises and cups of cider to get him to leave.

"Fine. Then I'll have a beer." Zeus started toward the beer tent.

Hades' hand shot out and latched onto his shoulder, steering him away from the tent. "Also no."

Zeus shrugged free irritably. "You realize you're my brother, not my father."

"You're sticking with me." Hades turned and started to walk. Normally he'd stay near the cheese, so as to see Harper as soon as he arrived. But today, something seemed to be tugging him forward. A feeling in the pit of his stomach, a strange brand of excitement that promised that this could be the best day of his life.

And the worst day of his brother's, from the way Zeus was groaning.

He spotted a cart with an *Herbs and Spices* sign hanging haphazardly from one corner. *There.* The feeling in his belly grew warm. "Come on," he said. "Mother wanted more Swamp thyme."

"But we always buy it from Old Myrtle…" Zeus protested.

It was as though a hook had fastened to Hades' ribs and was reeling him in toward the cart. He went up and waited as the customer in front of him completed a complicated order, sending the harried-looking plump proprietress back and forth from the shelves to the counter. The stall was dark and smelled of the tea Mother always made them drink when they felt ill. Zeus yawned loudly.

At last the customer had packed his wares and set off, and Hades stepped up to the counter.

And there she was. The whole reason he was here.

The first thing he saw was an olive-colored hand reaching to tilt a spice jar back onto its shelf. Her fingers were slender, nails well-trimmed. Her raven hair cascaded in a smooth wave down her back. She then noted something down in a notebook, tucking her hair behind one ear to reveal full red lips as they curved into a brief smile. Hades felt his jaw go slack.

This. This was why he was in the market today. Not to pass notes like a schoolboy. Not even to buy materials for his parents and the Cross of the Iron Phoenix. The world around him seemed to drain of color and interest, leaving only her, wreaking havoc on his senses.

She looked up and their eyes locked. Her eyes were as dark as her hair, liquid pools of infinity that drew him in. Her lips parted, as though startled, revealing a sliver of white. His sharp intake of breath was a cold shock to his lungs, and he felt each hair on his arm as it rose in anticipation. His heart forgot how to beat—then made up for it in double time. He couldn't break that gaze. He couldn't even blink.

A figure moved in front of her and leaned on the counter. It was a woman—the girl's mother, presumably. She had the same tan skin, and her hair was shining and straight, though streaked with gray and largely hidden beneath a kerchief. Her mouth was thin with disapproval.

"Can I help you?" she asked, in a tone that plainly said she hoped she couldn't.

"Uh." Hades' mind was circling the girl the way a moth circles a torch. All he could think of was her small, pointed chin, her swanlike neck. The way her plain blue dress made her look like a jewel.

"We'd like some swamp thyme," Zeus cut in smoothly. He nudged his brother. Hades cleared his throat and nodded. "Quarter pound should do it."

The woman at the counter gave Hades a look that could freeze a wildcat, then turned to her shelves. "Persephone, go check the ledger. See how much saffron's left."

"But we haven't sold any..." Hades' heart twisted again.

Her voice was as clear and musical as a stream. As the woman glared, her daughter tucked her head. "Yes, Mama."

She ducked through a door at the back of the cart, dipping her head so that Hades couldn't catch her eye again. When she was gone, the proprietress slammed a jar of swamp thyme down on the counter and began to measure it out on scales.

"What in the world was that?" Zeus muttered, glancing at him.

"I…" Hades swallowed. His mouth was suddenly dry. He had no idea.

A broad, tanned arm snaked around his shoulders and Harper Oliver O'Donovan squeezed him in a half hug. His other hand cupped Hades' chin, squeezing it. "*That* is a glorious expression, my brother," he said. "Were you trying to catch flies?"

"In a manner of speaking," Zeus joked. Hades kicked his calf.

"Swamp thyme." The lady at the counter twisted the paper packet closed. "Two bits. Or if you've got eggs, we're interested."

Hades fumbled at his belt until he found a clipped copper coin and handed it over. She examined it, nostrils flaring, then tucked it into an apron pocket. "Thank you for your business," she said, a clear dismissal.

"What're you doing here, anyway? I thought we were meeting by the cheese as usual," Harper said.

Just then, Persephone popped her head out from the side

door. "We still have six ounces of saffron," she said. But she wasn't looking at her mother. She was looking at him, doe-eyed and curious. Hades felt the tips of his ears go hot. The edges of her mouth were turning up. Was that good?

"Frogseed next," her mother snapped, and she jumped. "Next customer!"

Zeus prodded Hades. Hades turned, dazed. Her eyes were so full—of life, of interest, of mirth. He felt as though he could read her whole story in those eyes.

"I see what we were doing now," said Harper, grinning and jolting Hades back into the present. "Found ourselves a skirt."

"Don't call her that," Hades snapped before he could think better of it. He blinked in surprise. He never got angry at Harper, his best mate. He cleared his throat. "It's disrespectful."

"Yet you've never had a problem with me saying it before." Harper stretched his massive arms over his head, flexing his muscles. Scars crisscrossed his arms, pale against his sun-kissed skin, the souvenirs of many fights and heists as he stole Kronos' coin and dispatched his guard. He had a neatly trimmed beard that glinted red and gold in the dappled sunlight of the forest, and a nose that twisted slightly to the side, the relic of a brawl. It added to his rugged charm, a charm he was all too versed in using. "She is a beauty. And here I thought your one true love was the Cross." He grinned, showing off even white teeth. "So. Who is she?"

"Persephone," Hades replied.

"And?"

And…that was it. "Her mother runs the herb and spice shop."

"And?" Harper gestured for more information. "How did you two meet? What kind of drink are you going to get her later? When are you seeing her again?"

Hades rubbed at the back of his neck. Harper laughed in disbelief, a loud boom that cut through the general chatter of the market and had people staring. "Did you even speak to her?"

"Speaking's hard," Hades muttered resentfully.

Harper slapped him on the back hard enough to send him reeling. "All this time you've been my friend, and you never learned to talk to girls? I'm disappointed. Not in you, in myself. I've been a truly awful teacher." He faked a grimace.

"It's a wonder your whole life is deception, since you can't act to save your life," Hades grumbled.

"That is hurtful, and unfair, and I forgive you because you are clearly addled by love. And I'll even do you a favor, brother." Harper clapped him on the shoulder, then moved his arm down to perform their special handshake. It was complicated and allowed Hades to slip the necessary message from his sleeve into Harper's fist. "I'm going to teach you to woo."

"That's…not necessary," Hades replied. Harper and Zeus were cut from the same cloth, interested in the pursuit of the girl more than the girl herself. But Hades didn't want the thrill of the chase. He wanted the woman who lay at the end of it.

Harper grinned, and Hades' heart sank. He recognized that grin. It was the grin Harper had given him when he'd forged a plan to break into Ethan's stock of hard cider. It was the grin he'd had right before he'd planned to rob a three-cart, guarded caravan with no backup. It was the grin of mischief and bad ideas. "Oh, it's necessary. I will teach you to woo this Persephone…by wooing her myself."

Chapter Five: Brotherly Love

"I don't like it." Zeus crossed his arms as he hung back near the weaver's stand. The market frothed around him as people bartered and squabbled. From here he had a good vantage point of the herbs and spice stall. It had been two weeks since Hades had first seen his stall girl, and as the summer had bloomed, so had the market. The air was full of friendly calls as people hailed back and forth and argued good-naturedly with stall proprietors. The smell of sour beer hung in the air, mingling with that of roasting meat.

"Don't like what?" said his best friend, Leda. She took a bite of a crisp green apple. She'd recently returned from the hunt, and she smelled of fresh sweat and deer's blood. "Don't like that he's about to get another girl, and you're on a dry streak?" She spat an apple seed on the ground.

Harper squared his shoulders and walked casually up to the stall. From here Zeus couldn't hear what he said, but whatever it was made the proprietress break out of her perpetual frown for a moment. Off to the side stood Hades, bouncing from one foot to the other.

"He's making a fool of my brother. Offering to teach him to woo girls by wooing the only one he's ever wanted?" Hades had always been a little too serious for his own good, especially where women were concerned.

Leda shrugged one shoulder. She wore a green linen shirt and a leather vest, as if plain clothes could make her look less like the perfect icon of womanhood. Unlike Harper, her dark skin was flawless. Because 'only idiots let themselves get cut,' as she liked to say. "If Hades wants something, he should claim it. Maybe he should learn to stand up for himself." Leda didn't know the meaning of the word insecure.

"He's never been good at standing up to Harper O'Donovan," said Atlas with a scowl. He gestured angrily with his beer, sloshing a pale frothy liquid over the top of his clay cup. "Whenever Harper had a grand scheme as a boy, it somehow turned out to be Hades' fault the moment Dad got involved."

Down at the stall, the old woman disappeared into the back, leaving Harper alone. He lifted his chin and spoke, and from the depths of the stall she appeared. She was beautiful, Zeus had to admit. Beautiful enough that he'd have tried something himself if he'd seen her first. But he hadn't, and he had no interest in going after women his brothers sought to love. Zeus had few hard limits, but that was one of them.

He recognized Persephone's professional smile. She had to be nice to her customers, nothing more. No interest so far. Harper leaned on the bar, showing off his slightly unbuttoned shirt and the chiseled chest beneath. She said something, and whatever he said in reply made her laugh for real this time, tilting her head back and exposing her delicate throat. When she looked at him again, her eyes were warmer.

"This is bad," Poseidon said from Leda's other side. And when Poseidon said it was bad, it was. Poseidon's great skill was seeing the best in any situation, so if he was getting nervous, there was good reason for it.

Come on, Zeus thought. *Get in there.* If it had been him, he'd have stepped in ages ago. Every moment Hades left Harper alone with Persephone was another moment he'd lost. But he didn't realize that. His eyes were downcast, and a muscle was twitching in his jaw. He was angry and trying to control himself. Poor Hades was always trying to do what made others happy. He needed to stop thinking about O'Donovan and start thinking about himself.

"How bad is this, really?" Leda asked. "I mean, if it were me, I'd have punched O'Donovan in the face already." She shook out her hand as though reliving a memory. She had, in fact, punched O'Donovan once, during Outlaw training. Dad had responded by giving Leda lone assignments from that day forward.

"Okay, the next move is the arm touch," Zeus replied. "If she leans into it, that means she's interested."

Harper rolled his ample shoulders, then reached over to touch her briefly on the arm. Persephone's smile didn't flicker, but she did step neatly to the side, arranging some jars on the counter.

"Well, well," said Leda.

A flock of older woman sailed in front of them, discussing the price of shear-sharpening down at the blacksmith. When they'd cleared away again, Harper had moved to stand directly in front of Persephone. His broad back obscured her from their sight, and as she moved he angled to follow, effectively pinning her.

"But she didn't respond to the arm touch," said Poseidon.

"That's it." Zeus squared his shoulders. He turned and picked up the battered practice staff from where it lay behind him. He'd been getting better, determined to graduate to the sword. Maybe today he'd get the chance to prove himself. "He's gone from shooting his shot to being a pest."

"And he's an ass," Atlas rumbled.

"A snake," Poseidon added.

"A snake's ass." The almost-twins grinned at each other.

Leda finished her apple and tossed the core into the trees, where a happy squirrel would drag it back to the next. "No fighting in the marketplace," she said. Her light brown eyes ran the length of Zeus' staff and she pursed her full lips.

"We're not going to fight. We're simply going to show Harper the error of his ways and escort him home," Zeus replied.

"Well, do it without me. I don't need to be banned." She turned and headed off, hips swaying as she made her way through the crowd. People parted for her without realizing, letting her slip lithely through to the edge of the woods.

Poseidon nudged him. Zeus realized he was staring. He shook off his momentary distraction. "Right."

Atlas led the way. Zeus strode confidently behind him. If anyone was a match for Harper O'Donovan, Atlas was. Their boots scraped on the dusty stones of the marketplace, tapping out a battle rhythm until they were directly in front of the stall.

"O'Donovan," Atlas said, a low challenge.

Harper half-turned so that he could look Atlas up and

down as he leaned against the side of the stall. Behind him, Persephone's dark eyes widened. Her smile fixed in panic.

"What's going on, little man?" he said. He shook Atlas' hand, muscles bulging as he tried to crush the other man's fingers. Atlas gave as good as he got, setting his jaw.

At last Harper let go. Shaking out his hand, he nodded to Zeus. "Didn't see you there." He turned back to Persephone. "You know he's the shortest recruit I've ever had?"

Zeus' hackles rose at the jab. He flared his nostrils and took a deep breath. He was doing this for Hades. He didn't need to get sidetracked by second-rate insults he'd heard before.

"You can back off," Atlas said. "I don't think the lady's interested."

"I'm just selling herbs," Persephone said quickly. She held up a packet of something purple as if to prove it.

"And I'm just telling her a story. About the last time I went foraging for Dragon's breath. Stumbled on a slaver's caravan, didn't have any backup, took them on alone." He flashed Persephone his most dazzling smile. "Herb gathering can be dangerous, that's all I'm saying. You should really take a guard."

His eyes flicked to the side, and Zeus followed his gaze. Hades was biting his lip so hard that a trickle of blood wound its way to his chin.

Atlas noticed it, too. His own lip pulled back in a snarl. But Harper's smile grew more mischievous, and even more dazzling, and he leaned in towards Persephone. His voice dropped to a low purr. "I'd worry about someone as beautiful as you out there all alone…without someone to keep you safe and warm…"

"That's it," Atlas snarled. He stepped in, trapping Harper between himself and the cart. "She doesn't need *your* services."

Harper cocked his head. "And who's services does she need? Someone who's not even brave enough to say hello?"

Atlas' hands curled into fists at his side. Zeus tightened his grip on his staff. "Walk away."

Harper smiled again, and this time his smile wasn't mischievous or charming at all. It was a challenge.

At that moment, Zeus realized they were surrounded.

"Trouble, boss?" said a voice from behind him. He turned. Harper's lackeys, dressed as he was in poorly buttoned shirts and leather breeches, stood in a loose ring around the brothers. They dubbed themselves the Outlaws, and Harper O'Donovan was the Hood. They were all brawny, the sort of men who had boulder-lifting contests and thought a good night out always ended in a bar fight. They were also universally loved in Sherwood. Beyond the ring of men, a wide space had cleared as the other market-goers had backed up to watch, disapprove, or keep out of the way. The sun felt suddenly hot, as though even it judged.

"That's a good question, Johnny," said Harper. He arched an eyebrow at Atlas. "Do we have trouble? Or can you take a joke?"

"Is that what this is? A joke? Who's laughing?" Poseidon

cut in.

Harper snorted. "I'm laughing. Because it's hilarious. And I'm going to laugh myself all the way to the beer tent, where I'm going to buy my new girl a drink."

Atlas turned dark with fury. Behind them, Persephone said, "Oh, I'm not—"

Harper held up a hand. "Hush, darling. We'll sort out the specifics later." He swaggered forward to bump Atlas with his chest. "You're in my way."

He was looking over at Hades again. Zeus' brother had gone scarlet with rage, but when their eyes met, he quickly looked at the ground.

Harper wouldn't back down until he got a real rise out of Hades. But Hades was intent on keeping himself under control. Zeus saw only one solution.

Luckily, Atlas seemed to agree with him. He pushed Harper back, perhaps a little harder than necessary. Harper slammed into the side of the stall, making it rock. Persephone's onyx eyes widened.

"Watch it," Harper snarled. He wasn't smiling anymore.

"You watch it," Atlas snarled back.

Two of the Outlaws moved for Atlas. And in that moment, Zeus realized why the staff was so important.

He snaked it out, tangling up the feet of one Outlaw who tried to move behind Atlas. Then he jerked it back, straight into the midriff of an Outlaw who'd been moving around behind him. The Outlaw fell back with a grunt. Someone swung for him and he dodged out of the way. Poseidon's fist swung out of nowhere, catching the Outlaw in the jaw. The fight was officially on.

Zeus swept one man's feet out from under him, blocked a kick, and made another man double over. Poseidon moved lithe as a fish, jabbing and punching as he dodged the less graceful swings of his enemies. As Zeus prepared another swing, someone grabbed the end of his staff. He turned to deliver a punch—and found himself face to face with Hades.

"What are you doing?" His brother's face was twisted with horror. "Cut it out, *now.* Poseidon, stop this."

An Outlaw punched him in the shoulder, hard. Zeus caught his arm and twisted it behind his back, and Poseidon took the opportunity to give him a double blow to the stomach. Zeus let the man drop.

"You have to stop this." Hades dodged a swing and put his hands up. "We can't be fighting in the market square! I'm ordering you to stop!"

Atlas and Harper squared off, fists up. Harper swung first—and missed. He barely avoided Atlas' follow-up jab but ducked under a heftier swing and caught Atlas in the stomach. He grabbed Atlas around the neck but had to let go when Atlas elbowed him hard in the ribs.

"You know what makes a man look really good for the ladies?" Harper said. He dodged back. "A fistfight in her honor."

"This isn't about her honor," Atlas spat. He feinted forward, then to the side. Harper blocked his swing with a grunt. "It's about *his.*" He swung again, and this time his fist connected solidly with Harper's face.

Harper went down. Two Outlaws rushed over to help him up. He glared at Atlas as he spat a red-tinged glob onto the street. "If it's so serious, why doesn't he cut in himself?"

"Atlas, back down," Hades said.

"Because he doesn't know how to stand up to your snake ass," Atlas snarled. "And for some reason, he thinks you're worth protecting."

Harper looked at Hades, lip curling with content. "So what is it, lover boy? You going to stand up to me? You going to make a move?"

"That's enough." The gray-haired proprietress shoved two Outlaws out of the way. "You, big one. Back away."

Harper smirked as Atlas stepped back. "I'm so sorry, Una," he said.

"Keep your apologies," she snapped. "I know your type. The world is a game for you, isn't it? You probably think it's *fun* to put my livelihood in danger by tussling near my shop. It won't be you cleaning up broken glass and throwing away months of gathering and drying work."

The smile slid from Harper's face. Zeus felt his own mouth turning up at the corners. So much for Harper getting away with everything.

As if she could sense amusement, Una spun. "And what is so funny to *you,* young man?"

He swallowed. "Nothing?"

The next fifteen minutes were spent on the scolding. Una scowled, shook her finger, and used the words 'poor old widow' so many times that Zeus came up with an idea for a drinking game. His legs grew stiff from standing straight and still for so long. Atlas stood rigid and proud next to Harper, who looked no less rigid, but a great deal more sullen. Poseidon looked excited. It was probably his first fight, Zeus thought. He wouldn't be smiling near as wide when their parents found out about the scuffle. His mother's voice rang in his head: *You shouldn't be attracting attention to yourselves.*

The Outlaws did their best to look chastened, but Zeus knew they'd be plotting vengeance as soon as Una turned her back. Unless Harper told them to drop it, the brothers would be watching their backs for a few weeks.

And Hades wasn't paying attention at all. His eyes flicked from side to side and he kept tilting his head, looking for *her.* He became so engrossed that he didn't notice Una until she was a mere inch from his nose.

"Are you listening to me, young man?" she snapped.

He jumped and stiffened. "Yes, ma'am," he said, somehow contriving to look past her.

She leaned back and crossed her arms over her ample bosom. "Then what did I say?"

"That you're too old to be breaking up fights between common thugs, and we're too old to be thinking with our egos," Hades rattled off.

Zeus raised his eyebrows. She *had* said that.

Una wrinkled her nose. "Hmm," she said, and moved on.

She slung a few more insults their way, then sent them

off, finishing with, "And if I ever see you at my stall again, you'll get a broom handle about the head and shoulders until you've gone." Then she flapped her hands, sending them all on their way.

Zeus leaned on his staff as he limped to the side of the square in a pocket of cold air. Someone had gotten him in the calf, and he'd only noticed when he'd been forced to listen to Una's impressive lecture. The other market-goers turned away from him, or shot him disapproving looks. Market days were truce days, everyone knew that. He sat against a tree stump.

"I told you." Leda reappeared, handing him another apple. "Your father's going to be incensed."

"He's been angry with me before." Zeus shrugged and took the apple. It was crisp and sweet and perfect. Ethan would say that Zeus had disappointed him today, and that he had to keep a low profile, and that they didn't need any enemies. It was the same speech he gave whenever an upset ex-girlfriend came around. "It'll be a bigger shock for Poseidon. I'm not sure the last time he was told off for anything."

"Dad's told me off lots of times." Poseidon came toward them, looking suitably chastened.

Zeus snorted. "Like when?" He waved Atlas over and let his big brother clap him on the back. "Well, we defended our own, and that's what matters, isn't it?"

Atlas grinned. His knuckles were split from where he'd punched Harper, but he was in decent shape otherwise.

"That's what matters. Where is the man of honor, anyway?"

Zeus scanned the crowd. Hades was difficult to spot at the best of times—he had a special way of blending into the scenery. But then Leda murmured, "Well, at least he found his courage," and Zeus followed her gaze.

"Oh no," he groaned.

Chapter Six: Timeless Love

He'd faced down men with swords and polearms. He'd slipped intelligence to a contact under the gaze of traitors and informants. He was an apprentice under his father's leadership to the Cross of the Iron Phoenix, the biggest resistance infraction on Olympus.

So why did it feel like talking to one girl was harder than any of that?

The sounds of the market were fuzzy to his ears, as though all the chatter were as insignificant as the buzzing of flies. As Una left the herbs and spices stall, Hades forced his feet to move. They carried him as if in a dream, and in his hazy befuddlement he remembered nothing between the moment he got up and the moment he found himself in front of her.

Persephone sat in the sweet-scented grass behind her mother's stall, sharpening an herb knife. Her deep red lips formed a moue as she concentrated. Hades swayed as a sudden nausea boiled in his stomach. What if she turned him down? What if he'd fallen in love for the first time with someone who thought he was foolish for fighting and never wanted to see him again? Maybe he should go, and return next week when the incident was likely to be forgotten.

He started to turn, but the movement caught her eye. She looked up at him.

Her eyes rooted him to the spot, as though he'd been

struck by magic and turned to stone. They were inquisitive and interested. A little mirthful and a little sorrowful. Her mouth smoothed into a slight smile.

"Yes?" she prompted gently, in a voice more musical than any birdsong.

He kicked down his instinct to flee like some small rodent, and cleared his throat. "Sorry about that. My friend, you know. And my brothers." His own voice sounded rough and coarse by comparison.

She laughed, and he went weak at the knees. "The people of Sherwood seem rather passionate," she said. "I guess this is your home?"

He hesitated. He wanted to tell her both yes and no—his parents had related to all of them the story of how their mother had brought them to the forest, leaving them in Ethan and Raven's safekeeping. But Father had always said it was a secret.

Persephone shifted a bit and patted the grass beside her. Hades' mouth went dry again. "I…grew up here," he said. "Yes."

"You're so lucky. I grew up in the Swamp, which is dull and brown. No one wants to live there, so I didn't have any friends."

"Impossible," Hades said before he could stop himself. Persephone arched one perfect eyebrow at him. "I mean, everyone must want to be friends with you."

She laughed again. "You're funny," she said.

Una's voice rang out from the front of the cart.

"Persephone? Where are you?"

Persephone's eyes grew wide. "Oh, she'll be so angry if I'm talking to you," she whispered.

"Sorry." Hades tripped over his feet in his haste to rise. "I'll go. I shouldn't get you into trouble—"

"*Persephone!*" Una hollered.

"She's in a really bad mood." Persephone's brow furrowed. Then her lips curved wickedly and she shot him a mischievous glance. "Come with me."

She grabbed Hades' hand. Electricity shot through him, lancing his heart and making him gasp. Before he could get ahold of himself she was running, and he was running with her, feeling the warmth of her fingers as they twined through his and hoping wildly that she never let go.

They left the edge of the road and crashed into the woods. They stumbled over roots and slipped on slick moss. "No, this way," Hades said on instinct when she tried to pull him to the right. He took them left, instead, across a tiny stream and deeper into the trees. They ducked under houses and scurried beneath bridges, keeping to the shadows. Persephone giggled.

Hades slowed when they passed the last houses in Sherwood City. He knew where he was going now. He'd been an Outlaw for a couple of years and he knew the forest like he knew the inside of his own house.

He led her over a network of roots so thick it might as well be a road. Her hand was soft as velvet in his, and he hoped she'd never let go. At last he came to his objective, and pulled her around a massive tree to reveal a clearing full of blue cornflowers bobbing in a gentle breeze. The air here was fresh and free of woodsmoke, full of birdsong. Persephone's breath caught and another shard of feeling lanced through his chest.

"It's beautiful." She bent to brush one elegant finger along the top of a silk-soft flower. "How did you find this place?"

"I found it back when I was Harper's lieutenant."

She looked back at him. "That arrogant one? Who's obviously in love with himself?"

Hades laughed. "Yes, the arrogant one. He is a little in love with himself. And he's my best friend, aside from my own brothers. We trained together." He stopped and tried to get a hold of himself. He didn't know where Persephone's loyalties lay. Even if his heart told him she was too pure to be in the thrall of a leader like Kronos, he knew what Father would say. *Play things close to your chest.*

But Persephone didn't pry. "It must be nice," she said wistfully, dropping gracefully to sit amongst the cornflowers. She tilted her face up and let the sun slant across her cheekbones. "I never had any brothers or sisters. What's it like?"

Hades found himself telling her everything. Of the schemes they would pull, of 'trading' missions they nearly botched. He kept things vague—he knew how disappointed Father would be if he went about spilling Resistance secrets— but he got around it by telling her of his brothers' harebrained schemes to build their own secret tree house, or the time he'd been on an operation and gotten caught in an inn without any clothes and an angry gang leader going from room to room, looking for him.

"What did you do?" she asked, breathless. She leaned in. They were not quite touching amongst the cornflowers.

"I got my contact to rent a hay cart. One dive into the cart, one long ride into Sherwood, and one embarrassing family reunion later I was free. I still itch at the very thought of straw." He scratched under his arm. Persephone hid her laugh behind her hand. Without thinking, Hades pulled it away. Her smile was too beautiful not to share with the world.

The smile flickered. His fingers tightened around hers reflexively and he swallowed. *Don't let go,* he told himself. Bolstered by this sudden courage, he lowered their hands together, creating a link between them in the grass. Persephone's ink-colored eyes rested on their twined fingers.

Maybe Harper had done the right thing after all. It wasn't nearly as impossible as Hades had imagined, talking to this beautiful creature. Rather, he was worried about what would happen when they *stopped* talking.

"I wish I had a large family," Persephone said. "My father died when I was young, and my mother never remarried. I'm all she's got. Even if I had the chance to go out on strange trading missions—" here she looked at him slyly, as though she knew they weren't trading missions at all—"I'd never take it. I need to stay with her."

"Taking care of the people we love is as noble a cause as any," Hades said, squeezing."

"Even if it can feel a little stifling? Even if you have to be home by dark—" Persephone gasped. "Home by dark! What time is it?"

The light in the clearing had gone from the brilliant white of midday to the long gold of the afternoon, and now the trees glowed with the colors of sunset.

"Dinnertime," Hades said, struck with a sudden idea. He should ask her to dinner—bread and cheese and mead in the marketplace was simple fare, but delicious.

"Oh no." She leapt to her feet. "I've been gone far too long. I only wanted to help you escape." She bit her lip. Hades had to stop himself from leaning over and easing it out from under her teeth with his thumb. "She'll be so worried. Do you think we can go back?"

"Of course," Hades said, pushing his disappointment down. Persephone had duties of her own. He could respect that. Surely she'd let him take her to dinner another day.

Now that they weren't trying to stay hidden, the easiest way back was to find the main road to town. Hades led them north. They kept talking as they walked: him about the pitfalls of having three rowdy brothers, her about life in the Brown Swamp. She insisted it was boring at first, but once she opened up about it, Hades found it fascinating. They didn't have wights or will o' wisps in the forest, and while he'd had to shake plenty of spiders out of his boots, he'd never had to fish out an angry adder.

They were nearly at the road when Hades stopped and held up a hand for silence. His whole body prickled over with foreboding. A moment later he realized why: the birds were silent. As were the frogs, and even the insects. It was as though life had fled this part of the forest.

And if life had fled, that meant something dangerous. A cold that had nothing to do with the wind brushed at the back of his neck.

"What is it?" Persephone whispered.

Hades frowned, concentrating. He heard a distant and unmistakable rumbling. "Someone's coming up the road."

"More caravans, late for market weekend?" Persephone suggested.

Hades shook his head. The market was as busy as ever. Creeping up to the edge of the road, he pulled Persephone close and stood behind a large elm. She peered out past him, one hand right over his heart. "Do you think they'll see us from here?" she asked.

"Doubtful," he said in what he hoped was a confident tone. In reality he was hoping she couldn't feel how hard his heart was pounding.

The rattle and rumbling of carriages grew louder, and suddenly they were there. Great black coaches, pulled by black horses the size of houses, who stamped and snorted steam as they trotted by. Grim-looking men sat at the front of each coach, armed with a whip and a sword. Hades counted as they went past: one, two, three, four—

He hissed as he saw the fifth coach, and the chimera that sat next to the driver.

The creature stood at twice the height of the average man,

with a chest as wide as a bull's and broad shoulders sculpted with muscle—muscle he'd earned hewing down opponents of Kronos and his regime. The chimera's skin was the color of a stormy night. Below the waist a thick serpentine tail coiled and lashed against the edge of the coach. At the end of the tail was something much like a hand, five-fingered and adorned with three-inch razor claws.

Above the waist the scales continued, rippled and rough as tree bark, all the way up his human chest to the bottom of his face. Bovine horns curled from his forehead, ending in steel-capped points. His yellow eyes gleamed with malice as he flicked the whip, urging his horses on.

"Typhon," Hades whispered.

"You know him?" Persephone asked. She trembled, as many did when faced with this brute.

Hades nodded, wrapping one arm around her before he could think better of it. Her trembling subsided a little. "Typhon is Kronos' emissary for Sherwood," he said in a low voice. "He 'keeps the peace' here. Usually, that means he comes in, roughs up a couple of people, and burns down a house or two to remind us who's in charge. And he takes whatever he wants from the market."

Persephone paled. "Mama…we have to go."

Hades nodded. "But we can't take the road. Typhon can claim we were trying to sneak up on him."

He'd tried to best Typhon once, back when Harper was the newly elected leader of the Outlaws, the so-called Hood. As the Hood's right-hand man, he should have dissuaded

Harper from going after Typhon. Instead, he'd analyzed the brute's weaknesses and the best spots along the road to take advantage of that weakness. They'd sent Typhon running and made him look like a fool.

But a month later, he'd come back in force. He'd closed down the market and burned the mayor's house to the ground. Fifty young men and women had been abducted as 'tribute' to Kronos. And it had been Hades' fault.

"You're not in this job to make mischief with your mates, or win personal glory," his father had shouted when the storm that was Typhon had passed. "You were supposed to tell Harper no. You were supposed to be the one looking at the bigger picture. Not just how to bring the one brute down, but what would happen when you did." The next day, Hades had been reassigned. And now he avoided Typhon whenever the chimeric beast came to town. It was easier that way.

"We'll be a little longer. I'm sorry." But it would keep her safe, so it was worth it. Hades took her hand again. He didn't think he'd ever stop reveling in how smooth her palms were. Her fingers twined through his, fitting neatly in the gaps. As though they'd belonged there, always.

They kept parallel to the road, sneaking between the trees until they found a smaller street. They straightened their clothes and linked arms, as though they'd been taking a casual stroll. By now twilight had turned the sky above a deep purple, and the famous green glow of evening enveloped the trees. The first of the fireflies flickered.

The market was silent. Vendors had rolled down their

tarps and closed their wagons. The meat cart's coals still smoked, but the meat itself was gone. The market's patrons had probably retreated the moment Typhon showed up. Nothing was left now except the lonely whistle of the wind.

At the edge of the herbs and spices stall, Persephone squeezed Hades' elbow and crept forward. Crickets stopped chirping at her approach. She slipped into the cart. A moment later, she was out again.

"She's asleep." Persephone grinned. "I'll catch an earful tomorrow, but right now…" She peered around the side of the cart. "I was working all day. Do you think it's safe to see the market? Even if it's all closed?"

Hades nodded. "Typhon and his crew have probably settled in the inn by now. They'll be getting roaring drunk. We won't have to worry about them until tomorrow." He offered her his arm again. "Might I offer a tour, my lady?"

Her cheeks turned a delicate shade of pink, but she fluttered her eyelashes. "I would be overjoyed," she said.

He took her first to the weaver, showing her the sturdy cloth of his shirt and boasting about the fine linen tablecloth he'd bought for Mother with his first real wage. Next up was the blacksmith, where he drew his sword and parried a few invisible foes for her benefit. At the beer stall, he extolled the virtues of Sherwood mead. "Even outside of Sherwood, if you get mead, you get it from Sherwood. The lavender's my favorite. I'll bring you some tomorrow—I mean, if you like."

"I'll probably be pinned to my post all day," Persephone groaned. But she was giving him that sidelong look again, and smiling. "But you can bring some by. I'll keep a distraction on hand for Mama."

Hades saved the stage for last. It was small, more of a platform, and build around their sacred tree. Hades sat on the low platform and Persephone sat next to him.

"The tree never loses its leaves," Hades explained. "When people get married, they say their vows under the tree. New babies are presented to it. We have a few sacred trees in Sherwood, but this one is the most sacred. It brings the city together. We announce all our big news here. And the mayor used to read his decrees out here, until he made an unpopular one about grain tax and we threw vegetables at his fine suit."

Persephone giggled. "It's wonderful. We never had anything like a stage in the swamp. We don't even have a marketplace in the swamp." She looked around the market with longing.

"You can come to ours anytime," Hades offered.

"If Mama makes enough money at the market, we will," Persephone said.

"Then I guess I'm buying your entire stock tomorrow."

He hadn't meant to say it aloud. When he realized what he'd done, he flushed all the way down his neck. Persephone had ducked her head. She was trying not to laugh, he realized.

He tucked a finger under her chin and lifted her head. Their eyes locked. His heart thundered in his ears and his hands shook. But he couldn't stop himself. Her eyes were mesmerizing, an infinite onyx pool, and he wanted to fall into them forever. He found himself leaning forward, willing to drown, and their lips met.

She exuded a soft warmth and she smelled of pomegranates. Her eyelashes fluttered against his cheek as she leaned in, opening her mouth to his kiss. He wrapped one arm around her back, pulling her against him, and her small gasp made his heart hitch. All other sounds in the forest faded. The rustle of the trees, the screaming of the frogs, the lonely *who* of an owl. The world seemed to drop away, leaving him floating, with only her to keep him tethered.

Hades wasn't sure how long he pressed up against her. He was lost in her sweetness. Then a bird screamed overhead, cutting through their reverie and making them both jump. Persephone giggled, tucking a lock of shining hair behind one ear. In the gentle glow of the night she was luminous. All except for her eyes, which still threatened to draw him into oblivion.

He was leaning in for another kiss when a rowdy shout came from one of the inns. He flinched. Persephone touched his arm, sending a bolt of electricity through him. "What's wrong?"

Typhon. "We should get you home," he said, not without regret.

She swallowed and smiled through obvious disappointment. "Of course. I don't want Mama to wake up and realize I'm still not there."

She thought he was brushing her off. Hades stumbled to his feet and offered her his hand, tripping over his words as she took it. Her every touch, her every glance reduced him to a simpleton. "When can I see you again?" he said.

Her smile went from false to exhilarated. "We'll stay through tomorrow, but likely leave once the market closes."

"Then I'll come. Tomorrow afternoon." He didn't know how he'd be able to focus on training with the thought of the kiss invading his mind, and the hope of another one muddling his thoughts.

She turned her face up to the sky. The stars twinkled like tiny eyes. "If Mama lets me set foot outside of the stall ever again."

He wanted to run his lips down that swan neck. He cleared his throat in an effort to control himself. "You can work on that in the morning. And if she doesn't listen to you, we'll have to find another way. I can spirit you out a side door while my brothers distract her."

Persephone laughed her high, tinkling laugh, and his whole body burned with longing. "I think your brothers have done enough damage to my poor mother's nerves."

Hades squeezed her hands and her laugh petered out. She gazed at him, lips slightly parted, eyes deep and inviting. "I will come tomorrow," he promised. *And the day after, and the day after that if you'll have me.* For now that he'd met this woman, he wasn't sure he could ever let her go.

Chapter Seven: The Element Of Surprise

"Again." Zeus raised his staff. Hades wiped the sweat from his head with a kerchief and tucked it in his pocket. The sun was high, the trees were verdant, the wildflowers vibrant. The whole world was brighter, the scents of the flowers stronger, the song of the birds more musical. And it was utterly distracting Hades from his work.

No. *She* was distracting him. For in every birdsong, he heard her laugh, and the sweetness of every flower reminded him of her. The glow of the sun was nothing compared to the glow of her skin.

He was, in short, a fool for love.

"You're letting us down, brother," Atlas said, pointing his short swords at Hades. "You let him slip through twice. Get your head in the game."

"He can't." Zeus laughed. "I know that look. He's afire. How else would he have gotten Mum and Dad to go easy on us?"

Hades stared at his sword, noting the shine of the steel in the sun, the crisp and sharp edge of the blade. Then he took a deep breath. "I'm ready," he said.

Ethan and Raven had been waiting up when he returned last night. They'd invited Hades to explain exactly how all their children had come home with bruises and a formal warning from the marketplace. Hades had done his best to be fair with the explanation—condemning Harper for coming on too strong, and his brothers for taking the bait that had been intended for him. He'd admitted that he'd gotten to the end of his temper, too.

Raven and Ethan looked at each other. They could have whole conversations with their eyes, and for the first time in his life Hades felt a pang of longing at the sight. They knew each other so well, inside and out. He wanted that with someone. He wanted that with *her.*

"Thank you for your honesty," Raven said at last, reaching over to squeeze his hand. "You've always been a level-headed one and disinterested in violence, so we hoped you'd provide us with a good explanation."

"But we do wish you'd thought a little more before allowing your brothers to make fools of themselves, and Harper, too. We rely on our reputation in Sherwood as much as anything," Ethan said. "If people start to think the Hood and his Outlaws are a bunch of swaggering buffoons, it could hurt all of us."

"I understand," Hades had said.

"And I hope you understand we have to punish you," Raven added. Hades dipped his head in assent. "You'll stay home from the market tomorrow. You can clear out the attic and sand down the floor."

"I can't," Hades blurted. Raven arched an eyebrow at him, lips pursed. It was her, *excuse me?* look. Her boys knew better than to talk back to her, especially when discipline was being enacted.

Embarrassment seared the back of Hades' neck, but he

knew he had to speak now or lose it all. "She's leaving tomorrow. Persephone. The girl we were fighting about. If I don't see her, she'll be gone." And she'd think he'd changed his mind, or only ever considered her a potential conquest.

Ethan and Raven exchanged another look. Then Ethan put a hand on Hades' shoulder. "You don't normally get like this over a girl, son."

Hades swallowed and looked from his father to his mother. "When did you know?" he asked. "That Mum was the one for you?"

Ethan looked at Raven with an easy fondness. There were years of love behind that look, a life of ups and downs, of arguments and reconciliations. "It was the moment I saw her," he said. "She was training, a new recruit of the Cross of the Iron Phoenix. She was so fearsome that even the training master was afraid of her. And then someone got a hit on her, she hadn't been protecting her flank—and she laughed. It was that moment that got me. She knew how to fight, and she knew how to learn from her mistakes. And I wanted to make her laugh like that for the rest of my life." He leaned over and kissed Raven. "It took her a good while to realize the same about me, but she did."

Love could strike in a matter of moments. With a look, with a word, with a smile. "I want to make Persephone laugh," Hades said.

Persephone, Raven mouthed. Now they had a name. "Are you really sure she's the only one? You know how your brother gets," she told him. She still had a steely glint in her eye, as though she suspected him of lying to get out of chores or the like.

Hades' first instinct was to say *yes.* Persephone *was* the one. But he forced himself to think things through. His mother never asked questions without reason. And it was true: Zeus had a new forever love each week. It was dizzying, trying to keep up with him.

Hades spoke slowly, trying out his words as he said them. "I don't know," he admitted, and though he hated himself a little for saying it, he knew he had to. "We only spent yesterday together. But…I've never felt this way about anyone else. And I think I have to see where it goes for myself."

There was a long pause. Then Ethan clapped his hands together. "Well, then. How about a new deal? You can take tomorrow as normal. Train with your brothers, go to the market. *Don't* cause trouble. And on Monday, you can do the attic instead of your normal duties. Agreed?"

"Agreed." Hades stood and drew his father into a tight hug. "Thank you," he said.

"Sometimes a man has to follow his heart," Ethan said.

Hades turned to his mother next. Raven kissed him gently on the cheek. "Love can be a difficult lesson to teach. I hope it makes you happy."

Now Hades glanced up at the sun, willing it to be further up in the sky. A moment later he was doubled over, panting for breath. Zeus had taken advantage of his distraction to give him a hit to the stomach.

"No fair," he rasped.

"Terribly fair." Zeus easily blocked Atlas' double slash and used the back end of his staff to trip up Poseidon. "When an enemy's distracted, I should use the moment to take him down. I wonder who I learned that from?" With a clatter, Poseidon's sword flew into the air and hit a rock. Zeus skipped back a few paces, keeping out of Atlas' reach. Atlas snarled and lunged, but their youngest brother had evidently learned a thing or two. He landed a flurry of blows on Atlas' midriff, belly and shoulder, and as the big man bent over, a sharp jab to the back sent him down.

Zeus tapped the staff on the ground. "I'm starting to like this thing," he said. His eyes blazed and crackled with mirth.

"As soon as I get my breath back, you're dead," Atlas groaned from where he lay face down.

"Good show. Good use of the staff." Poseidon clapped Zeus on the back. "Well done, brother. I think you're better with that thing than I am now."

"And that means I can train with a sword now, right?" Zeus prompted.

Hades ignored the request and set them to drilling, then lost a series of one-on-one bouts with each brother. Normally he was a strong fighter. He could outlast Zeus' patience, defeat Poseidon with sly moves and footwork, and slip dexterously through Atlas' defenses. But today, he couldn't think. His mind kept going back to those onyx eyes, those pomegranate lips. The fall of her dark hair and the way it shimmered as she shook it out of her face. The feel of her fingers had imprinted on his arm. His whole head was a haze, such that he barely avoided an overhand slice from Poseidon's sword.

"All right." Atlas stepped between them smartly. The sword had glanced off Hades' leather breastplate, but the crack to his shoulder throbbed. "A wise man once told me that you either focus or die in a match. You've had enough, brother."

Hades grinned. "You called me a wise man."

"You are when you aren't being a moony idiot," Atlas replied. "And Poseidon, you should have stopped after the last bout. You know that."

Poseidon sulked as he put his training sword away. "I was winning, for once," he grumbled.

"It isn't exactly a fair fight. Look at the poor fool," Zeus shook his head and took a drink from his canteen. "This is why you should have had a fling or two, brother. You'd know how to act around a girl."

"She's not a girl," Hades replied before he could stop himself. He did manage to swallow the second half of his sentence. *She's a goddess.* He took a drink from his own canteen, letting the sweet, cold water cascade down his chin. He loosened his breastplate. Sweat made his shirt cling to his back. Maybe meeting Persephone after training was a mistake. Unless she liked the idea of a man getting sweaty and muscular.

Hades poured the last of his water over his head. Maybe he could shock some sense into himself.

He did a few more drills and watched his brothers square

off against each other, until it was finally time to break. They put away their kit and Hades changed into a fresh shirt, then they headed into the marketplace.

"No funny business," Hades said. "Promise?"

"What if Harper shows up to steal your girl again?" said Poseidon.

"She's no mere girl. Now promise me."

The brothers grumbled their assent.

The marketplace was even more crowded today as people took advantage of their last chance to buy certain goods for the month. Every little path was stuffed with carts that sold herbs, meat, medicine, jewelry, and more. Hades approached Una and Persephone's stall but hung back, pretending to be interested in an ivory comb at a neighboring stall.

Persephone caught his eye and flashed him a smile that left him blind to the rest of the world. She'd been waiting for him, that much was clear now. She leaned over and murmured something in her mother's ear. Una looked up then, and her eyes were much colder as they settled on Hades. Unsure of what to do, he gave her a little wave.

She looked back down at the jar she was wrapping for a customer, then to Persephone. Whatever she said sobered the smile on Persephone's face, and Persephone nodded seriously. Then Una flapped a hand, and the smile was back. Persephone kissed her on the cheek, then trotted out the back door, pulling her apron off to reveal a dark blue dress that made her skin glow. Hades put the comb down and strolled up to meet her, trying to look collected.

"I'm glad to see you made it," Persephone said.

"It was a near thing. Poseidon nearly chopped me in half in training," Hades replied. His shoulder twinged. "And you? Your mother didn't lock you in the cart for being home so late?"

"She almost did, but she changed her mind. And that's something she never does, so we should get out of here before she changes it again." Persephone laughed and tilted her head back to grin at the canopy.

Hades fought to control his galloping heart. "What would you like to see?"

"The best of everything."

"Done," Hades replied, and hooked his arm through hers.

They made their way through the crowd, listening to people haggle over wares. Hades pointed out all his favorite stalls. He brought her an apple from a special tree that grew only in Sherwood. Its skin was an emerald green, and its flesh a bright pink. "It's tart!" she exclaimed as she bit into it.

He got them both a meat pie from a vendor near the edge of the market, and the lavender mead he'd promised her. Persephone wanted to talk about everything: the strange fruits she saw, birds like jewels in little silver cages, rings made of silver ribbon and strung with diamonds like stars. Hades hesitated at the ring stall, but Persephone was gone a moment later to hold up an ornate herb knife and ask his opinion on whether her mother would like it. He nodded to the jeweler and hurried over to her, mentally berating himself. He'd known the woman for a day, he couldn't buy her a ring. He'd promised his mother that he would take things slow.

"She'd love the knife," he said. It had been forged in a herringbone pattern of dark and light steel. "Allow me."

He paid for the knife against Persephone's protests. Then he took her to a stall full of flowers and bought her a rose to tuck behind her ear.

He was so wrapped up in the softness of the petals against her skin, in the way her tongue looked as it darted over her lips, that he forgot to keep his wits about him. He didn't realize that all sound had dropped away from the market until they rounded a corner and he bumped into a wall.

Hades fell back. He knew the market like the back of his hand, and there shouldn't be a wall here.

Then the wall spoke, and he realized his mistake.

"Well, well." Typhon crossed his scaly arms. His bullish eyes glinted with golden animosity. "What have we here? A couple of lovebirds, strolling my territory?"

He looked Hades up and down, lip curling to reveal two large canines. Then his gaze moved on to Persephone. The look he gave her was much more appreciative, wandering down her form, noting the swell of her hips and breast beneath her dress. Persephone paled. Hades heard a distant roaring.

"You look like a sweet sack of sugar," Typhon rumbled. The sounds of the market became even more distant. Hades felt adrenaline surge through his veins. How *dare* this brute speak to anyone in such a way? "Give us a twirl. Let's see what you've got."

Persephone took a step back. "We're sorry to bother you, sir," she said, casting her eyes down. Her bright vivacity was gone, and in its place was a stiff, dull terror. Her arm tightened around Hades'.

Don't make trouble, his mother's voice echoed in his mind. He was already on thin ice from yesterday. He should have been paying attention, he should have avoided Typhon; he shouldn't have been so *stupid*—

Typhon gripped her chin between fingers the size of sausages. "I gave you an order." Behind him, a few goons chuckled. They were men, bulked with muscle and armed with knives and sneers. "Twirl."

Persephone swallowed.

Red lapped at the edges of Hades' vision. Before he realized what he was doing, he stepped forward. "Whose territory is this?" he said, knocking Typhon's arm away from Persephone.

He'd surprised Typhon, and the arm came away easily. "Excuse me, twerp?" Typhon growled.

"Whose territory is this? This is the Sherwood marketplace, and it is owned by no man or beast. It is the city's, and always has been by charter." Ethan had made Hades memorize pages and pages of tedious laws and ordinances. It was finally coming in handy. "You don't own anything." *Not even yourself.* Everyone knew that Kronos held Typhon's leash. "You can stop your bullying now, and go about your day."

Behind him, he heard Persephone gasp. The goons

around Typhon had stopped sneering and had their hands on their knives. Typhon himself stared.

Then he threw back his head and howled with laughter.

His lackeys followed suit. Behind them, a leather stall pulled its shade down as the proprietor guessed what was coming next. Typhon laughed good and long, pounding a fist against his chest. The air was filled with hooting.

Typhon stopped and held up a closed fist. The sound cut off abruptly. The chimera leaned in. "I own your life, little man," he said softly, and it took Hades all of his courage not to step back. Typhon's breath was as rank as rotting meat. "Do you know why? Because my might trumps your right. I'll have you on your knees, begging for your life. And then we'll see what you think I can and cannot do."

His fist came in fast, and Hades' training kicked in. He ducked low and darted to the side. He took the opportunity to land a punch on Typhon's unprotected side and the chimera bellowed, more from surprise than pain. He twisted around. Persephone let out a short, sharp scream.

"Stay back," Hades warned. She couldn't get herself into danger. She couldn't get into his head, not for this fight.

"Little man's a fast one," Typhon chuckled. One of his lackeys started forward, murder on his face, but the chimera held up a commanding hand. "*Don't* dare. This one's mine."

He slid forward, fast as lightning. A lot of large men sacrificed speed for power, but not Typhon. His tail lashed, and Hades had to leap to avoid it in addition to ducking the blows from the chimera's fist. He delivered a kick to Typhon's ribs that bounced off the ridged scales, and another punch to the chimera's chest that the creature easily absorbed. Slipping around Typhon's back, he jabbed hard with an elbow, slipping between two scales. Typhon roared and spun.

The next fist caught him by surprise. He jerked back, but not fast enough. It glanced off his chin and sent him flying. He hit the dirt with a *thud* that knocked the air from his lungs. Then he rolled ungracefully away from Typhon's whipping tail and scrambled to his feet before the beast could hit him again. As he fought to regain his breath he moved in a wide circle, keeping plenty of space between them.

Typhon's goons were shouting. "Get him, boss!" "Knock him dead!" "Teach him a lesson!" Hades tried to ignore them. Then a woman's bold voice shouted, "Hit the beast where it hurts!"

Typhon was momentarily distracted. He whirled toward the crowd of onlookers that had gathered to either side of the little street. "Who said that?" he roared. "Who—*oof.*"

Hades tackled him full in the stomach. They went down. Hades landed a blow on his nose, another on his chin. His knuckles were bloody, and he wasn't sure whose blood it was. Rage pumped through him like his own blood. Rage and something more, a power like adrenaline, rushing through him, desperate for an outlet—

Typhon's tail hooked around his leg and flipped him over. He hit the ground with enough force to knock his breath from him and speckle his vision with black. Typhon loomed over him. One giant hand closed around his throat and the chimera got to his feet, hauling Hades up with him. Hades kicked and sputtered as his feet left the ground. Typhon was slowly squeezing the life from him. He scrabbled at Typhon's arm, trying to break the hold, but chimeric beasts didn't have the same weak points as humans, and Typhon was unaffected by Hades' meager efforts. He got to his feet, squeezing. He slammed Hades against the side of the leather cart. Hades' vision swirled. Typhon's other fist slammed into his stomach. Then his ribs. Something wet and coppery slicked the inside of his mouth.

No. He wouldn't be defeated. He wouldn't be left bloody and begging for his life. He wouldn't watch Typhon terrorize Persephone, nor anyone else. They deserved to walk through the market together. They deserved to be free of people like him.

They deserved to be free.

Something switched inside of him. His vision cleared, and everything came into sharp focus. Persephone stood behind Typhon, hands over her mouth, eyes wide with horror. As he watched, the horror changed to wonder—then astonishment.

His hand found the strength to curl into a fist. He knocked Typhon's arm away from his neck. Odd, he thought, looking at his closed fingers. They were…glowing.

He punched Typhon in the chest with a sudden surge of energy. The chimera's eyes grew wide as his feet left the ground and he flew backward. Persephone darted out of the way. Typhon sailed through the air, through a clump of trees, and hit a fruit stand. The stand splintered under his weight and fruit went flying. The beast sprawled in a sticky mess. His head came up, and he looked at Hades in wonder—and fear. Then he collapsed.

The crowd roared its victory.

From the corner of his eye, Hades saw Typhon's goons start forward, but someone threw half an apple that bounced off a shining silver breastplate. "Don't you dare," a woman shouted.

"Yeah, clear off!" said a man. More fruit followed the apple.

A few of the goons tried to press on, but as cabbages were added to the mix they exchanged a few hurried words and scurried away. "This isn't over," one of them snarled at Hades, but his words felt fangless. As Kronos' men rounded the corner in retreat, the cheer doubled.

Persephone was standing in front of Hades. Her fingers brushed over his face, his side, his bloody fingers. "You're hurt," she whispered.

Hades smiled at her through a split lip. "I've had worse." He wasn't sure that was true, but it didn't matter. Her smile was all the healing he needed.

The crowd surrounded him then, slapping his shoulder and shaking his hand. "Never seen anything like it," was uttered more than once, and Hades was fielding half a dozen offers of beer before he could draw breath. The crowd swarmed back toward the main square and Hades and Persephone were swept up in their ranks. To fight it would be like fighting the tide.

Persephone leaned in. Her eyes still shone with wonder. "How did you do it?" she whispered. "He's twice your size. And you just…"

"I know. And I don't know," Hades confessed. "I…felt something. A power. It's like it was always there, waiting for me to discover it."

Her hand slid down his arm and her fingers twined through his. "Let's get out of here?"

Hades nodded. His side was starting to throb. If he was lucky, his ribs were just cracked.

Persephone held tight to him, watching for her moment. When she found it she tugged and they slipped down an alley, away from the turmoil. Then she hesitated. Hades took the lead, drawing her through the back maze of city streets, away from the market and its clamor. People might look for him at first, but everyone would assume he was somewhere else, and soon those beers he was promised would be drunk by whoever had bought them.

At the outskirts of Sherwood City lay an old guard tower, long abandoned after Kronos had torched it out. Hades came here to think sometimes. He'd always kept it as a sanctuary for himself, but today he wanted to share it with her. He stepped over the remains of the stone wall and turned to lift her by the waist, gritting his teeth as his ribs screamed.

The inside of the tower was cool and covered in a springy carpet of grass. He sat down against the wall as the fatigue hit him at last.

"Wait here," Persephone squeezed his hand, then retreated. He heard her clamber over the wall. A few moments later she was back with a full canteen and a kerchief. "Let's get you cleaned up."

She soaked the kerchief and began to blot his face. The skin was already turning tender and puffy. Her nose wrinkled every time he gasped. "Sorry."

"It's all right. Thank you."

"Thank *you*." She paused, studying him unhappily. She chewed on her bottom lip, considering, then nodded. "Typhon…stopped at our stall earlier today. He said some things…I think that's why he singled us out."

Rage flushed through Hades. Rage and that new, foreign feeling. "What did he say?"

"Nothing a girl isn't used to hearing." She smiled at him, but it was a tired smile. "But I'm sorry. He said he'd be back at our stall later, so Mama thought it smart to send me away, and then…It's my fault he hit you."

Hades caught her fingers as she moved to blot his face again. He met her gaze and squeezed her hand gently. "It's Typhon's fault, not yours. He thinks he owns the forest and everyone in it. He thinks he can do what he wants. Well, he got what was coming to him today."

Without really thinking, he drew her in. Her lips were cool against his mouth. She slid onto his lap like she'd always belonged there. Her fingers twined in his hair and she pressed against him—

"Urgh," he groaned as she leaned on his injured ribs.

"Oh!" she pulled away in horror. His blood was smeared on her mouth and chin. He couldn't help but laugh. Persephone blushed. "I'm sorry. I couldn't...You were amazing. I've never seen anything like what you did."

Hades looked down in embarrassment. He found himself smiling, though, absurdly. "I was only defending myself. My home. My...you." He coughed. "I don't know what happened, or why. I think..." A memory flashed in his mind, of a glowing woman in a green dress, surrounded by flowers. If anyone knew what had happened today and why, it would be Hades' birth mother. "I think I need to talk to my father."

Persephone sighed. "And I should probably go home to my mother. She was so angry last night. If she hears we ran into Typhon and you brawled again...well, she'd never let me see you again. Ever."

"Can't have that." Hades braced himself against the wall as he pushed to his feet. His own mother would have a salve for his cuts and bruises, and a more accurate prognosis for his ribs.

Persephone grabbed his elbow to support him. "Here." He fumbled at his satchel and pulled out a small paper-wrapped parcel. "Your mother's knife. I'd hoped to woo her with it, but...tell her it's from you."

Persephone took the package and leaned up to give him a quick, searing kiss. "Never," she said, smiling.

He took her back to the edge of town and told her how to get to the marketplace. Then he set off in the opposite direction, looping through dirt paths and hopping over streams to get home. He didn't feel like getting another wave of congratulations, or stopping to accept a free ale, or tell the story, which had certainly been blown out of proportion by now. And he didn't want to know whether Typhon had managed to get himself out of the fruit stall yet, or whether he was looking for revenge.

As soon as he got to his front door, he knew something was wrong. Everything was too quiet. There was always at least one brother outside, chopping wood or fixing the fence or lounging in the shade of their glorious oak home. He was used to hearing shouts from open windows as well. But everything was shut up tight.

Hades took a deep breath and let himself in. The smell of fresh bread wafted down the stairs, but otherwise all was quiet. He loosened his knife in its sheath. Did Typhon know where he lived? Had he done something to his family? If he had…that strange, powerful feeling swept through him again, giving him the energy to move swiftly and silently up the stairs.

His family sat at the table. They all looked fine. The room around them was as it always was – tidy and simple, adorned with sheepskins and plants. At the sight of him, his brothers' eyes widened. Hades looked down. He was glowing again. He hastily put the knife away. As he did the glow faded, until his skin was its usual grayish color.

Raven looked resigned. Ethan looked calm, expectant.

"What's going on?" he asked. His stomach twisted uneasily. Everyone looked so somber, he could only think of two possibilities: first, that someone they loved had died. That was unlikely, as Hades' whole family sat around this table. The other possibility was that Hades was in so much trouble he would be under house arrest for the rest of his life.

"Sit, son." Ethan didn't sound angry, but gentle. And so authoritative that Hades sat without thinking. Was it the Resistance? Were they folding? He looked at his father as Atlas, Poseidon, and Zeus did the same.

"My sons." Ethan smiled as though he'd told a joke. Hades and Atlas exchanged glances. They'd never known their father to be bitter about the fact that they were adopted. He cleared his throat and looked down at his hands. When he looked up again, his eyes shone with emotion. "There's something I need to tell you. Something we've kept from you for far too long." His voice was hoarse.

The brothers looked at each other. Raven sighed and reached over, taking Ethan's hand in one of hers, then reaching out to Zeus on her other side. Bolstered by her support, Ethan cleared his throat and spoke again. "Your fight, in the marketplace, Hades…you should have known before this. I have failed you in that, and I am sorry."

"You haven't failed me at all," Hades burst out. "I didn't mean for anything to happen. I wasn't trying to start a fight. I—"

His mother cut him off with a look. Hades looked down at the table. "Why don't you start from the beginning?" she said to Ethan. "The *very* beginning."

"Right. Well." Ethan took a long drink from his cup. "In

the beginning, there was her. Gaia. She is…not human. Rather, she is a being of Olympus, and for Olympus—a goddess, to some. And when she gave birth to each of you, she birthed you out of an element. Fire." He nodded to Hades. "Soil." He turned to Atlas. Atlas looked at his dark hands. "Water," He looked to Poseidon. "And Air." He gestured at last to Zeus. "Your birth mother bestowed a great destiny upon you all. But she knew that destiny put you in danger, so she sought me out. As the leader of the Cross of the Iron Phoenix, I'm practiced with fighting, with politics, and with hiding in plain sight. Gaia felt that each of you needed these skills, and a loving home in which to learn them. And now…you have learned what you can from me, and you are beginning to learn your birthright powers. The powers you inherited from her. She said each of you would discover them on your own, in your own time. And until then, it would be my job to keep you safe and your identities hidden. But we can no longer pretend that you are mere mortal men. Not after what happened at the market today."

"We have a destiny?" Zeus leaned forward, blue eyes crackling with interest. "What is it?"

"Do we all have powers?" Poseidon added. He held up his own hand, as though he could make it glow.

"I've put us in danger," Hades said in a small voice.

"No," Raven cut in swiftly. "This was always bound to happen. What you are doing is coming in to your true self. You are leading the way, Hades, as you always have."

She tried to give him a reassuring smile, but Hades

couldn't return it. His gut churned. "But Typhon...he'll report back to Kronos. He'll mention me. The whole of the Cross has just been put into their focus!" He shoved back from the table and started to pace. "We'll have to move. Harper's in danger, too. And Persephone—"

"Settle down, son," Ethan said firmly. Hades stopped, though he didn't sit. "It will take weeks at least for Kronos to act, and that's if Typhon admits his defeat. The chimeric beast is a symbol of strength and cruelty for his master. What will it say for him to go back to Kronos with his tail between his legs, complaining of a wiry boy with an ordinary physique? It's possible he may say nothing at all. Other people will convince themselves that they saw nothing, that the way you glowed was a trick of the light or the imagination.

"In the meantime, we'll take the proper precautions. You'll move out, and we'll work to conceal your house. But you'll keep training, and now, in addition to politics and weapons, you'll work on harnessing your powers." Ethan looked from boy to boy, face growing stern. "These powers are no ordinary magic. They're secret. I will arrange for a private training ground, and you *will not* work with them outside of that. The less Kronos knows of your abilities, the greater the surprise when the time comes to fulfil your destiny."

Silence fell over the room. Hades struggled to take it all in. He had powers? He had a grand destiny?

Zeus finally broke the silence. "What *is* our grand destiny?" he said.

Ethan paused, as if considering whether to tell them. Raven nodded to him, and he nodded back. "Your destiny is to dethrone Kronos."

There was another silence, this one shocked. Then Poseidon said, "*Noooo.*" A smile split his boyish face.

Atlas was less enthused. "Kronos has been ruling our whole life. He's been ruling *your* whole life. He doesn't grow old, he doesn't grow weak. How exactly could we defeat him?"

"You have the strength," Ethan said, and Atlas pushed his shoulders back proudly. "And we have been training for decades to ensure you have the ways. You have never shied away from a cause that is greater than you. Now you will not merely work with the Cross. You will not merely help it survive. You will make it victorious."

For a long while, no one spoke. Hades stared out the window at the canopy of leaves. He was dazed, and he wasn't sure why. He'd always known his father was grooming him to be the leader of the Cross of the Iron Phoenix. What was so different about it now?

Perhaps the fact that Ethan believed *they* had the fighting chance to change the world.

"When will the rest of us discover our powers?" Zeus asked.

"In good time, that's all I can tell you." Ethan reached into the middle of the table and broke off a piece of bread. As he slathered it with butter and honey, he said, "They are part of your journey to becoming heroes. To becoming what this world needs. Your powers will manifest when you are ready…and you must *promise* to keep them secret. From everyone. Wives, children, best friends." He shot Zeus a look, and Zeus busied himself with taking his own piece of bread. "In fact, this whole conversation is a secret. We don't discuss your destiny with outsiders. Lives are at risk if we tip our hand too early, so I need your word." His eyes met Hades'. "Promise me."

"I promise," said Hades, without hesitation. Who else did he have to tell? There was no knowing whether Persephone would want to stay with some odd glowing man who started fights with dangerous beasts.

"We promise," said Atlas and Poseidon in unison.

"I promise." Zeus' eyes shone with a new fervor.

Something stirred within Hades, then. A growing warmth that started in his belly and spread up through his chest. He looked from man to man. In this moment, these were not his brothers. These were warriors. Trained with the best, resolute in their purpose. Ready to do battle for the fate of the world, if their father was right. And he couldn't think of anyone he'd rather trust with his life.

"We won't let you down, Dad," he said. His voice was steady. The voice of a leader. "We will fulfill our destiny."

Ethan's eyes shone with pride. "I know you will, my sons. I have faith in you."

Chapter Eight: Strength And Beauty

Atlas sneezed as he entered the dusty old treehouse, earning a dirty look from the desk guard. Atlas returned it with interest. This was why he hated libraries. You got shushed for breathing too loud. If they didn't want people sneezing, they should try to dust this place once in a while.

Atlas would rather be almost anywhere else, but he could shirk his duties no more. He'd been training daily since the revelation of his birthright, hoping to trigger his own powers. So far, no luck. But he did have an important assignment: to befriend and turn a member of Labyrinth City to the cause of the Cross. He needed to brush up on the history and customs of that place. Time and tradition intermingled in unique ways in Labyrinth City; the claustrophobic streets and mix of Minotaurs and men made for complicated rules of social etiquette. He could blow his chance with the Cross' potential ally if he were ill-prepared. And so he studied.

He found himself the object of more scrutiny as he strolled between the shelves. His footfall was too loud on the wood floor, and his back was still damp with sweat from the morning's training. A librarian turned pointedly away as he went by, and he stifled the urge to shoot a rude gesture at her back. Well, he could find a book on Labyrinth City all by himself. He didn't need anyone else's help.

It took him a good half hour to find the section he was looking for, and another twenty minutes to find a book that looked useful. But at last, armed with a folio of maps and a five-hundred-page tome called *A Brief History of Labyrinth City,* he found a table and began to read.

The library murmured around him with the shuffling of pages and the whisper of patrons. His muscles ached, and the library was dim, and the lengthy descriptions of who built what part of the maze were so boring…

A book thudded on the table next to him, startling him awake. Cursing himself, he looked up at the source of his disturbance—

—and found himself entirely devoid of breath.

Her skin was pale as milk, and her hair a striking red-gold like the sun on a copper coin. Freckles dusted the bridge of her nose. Her shell-pink lips were pulled back in a smile, and she was directing that smile at him.

"You snored," she said in a low, musical voice. She glanced down at his book. "Not much one for history?"

"Not the history of the development of dumbwaiters," Atlas gestured to an illustration, fighting the urge to hide his face until he could smooth it of embarrassment.

She leaned in to look at the text. She smelled of fresh soap and lavender. "Think of what a breakthrough that must have been," she said. "In a city with nothing but stairs, the ability to transport goods from low levels to high, and so quickly? It must have been incredible."

"I didn't think of it that way," Atlas admitted.

"Are you going to Labyrinth City soon? Or do you have some other reason for being bored to sleep?" She smiled mischievously, eyes twinkling. She was teasing him.

The truth was classified. Atlas said, "I have some business with a merchant from Labyrinth City. I was hoping to make a good impression on him. Though I don't suppose 'Your culture makes me yawn' is a very good approach."

"It's all in how you phrase it. You spent so much time studying Labyrinth City that you only stopped to sleep," the woman suggested.

"I like it," Atlas decided. "Though I can hardly follow it with, 'tell me about those brutes in your basement.'"

She guffawed. It was loud and joyful and rather unladylike, and it was a captivating sound.

Apparently, Atlas was the only one who thought so. Someone leaned out from behind a shelf and said, "Shh!"

The woman rolled her eyes. "Come on," she said. "Let's borrow the books and talk about them somewhere more interesting." Without waiting for him to acquiesce, she scooped up the books and headed to the front of the library, where she checked them out from the grumpy front desk attendant.

Atlas took a moment to marvel at himself as he followed her. There were only two people in the world whose orders he obeyed: his parents', and his older brother's. Yet he trailed after her like a duckling. No, he trailed after her like a man enchanted. She might have been one of those dazzling will-o-wisps that Persephone kept going on about, the little lights that hid in the Brown Swamp and bobbed enticingly before travelers, luring them off their safe paths and into the murky water, to be lost forever. Only, she was much more beautiful than anything that might come out of a swamp. No offense to Persephone.

Atlas followed the woman outside. The sun caught in her hair and seemed to set it aflame. "You're not some fairy creature, are you?" he blurted. Then he mentally smacked his own forehead. He was no lady killer like Zeus, but he'd never fumbled and stumbled around girls like Hades, either.

She arched one perfect red eyebrow. "No," she said, pressing her lips together in an attempt not to smile. She failed. "I'm Ivy. Just Ivy."

"Ivy," said Atlas. The name tasted like spring on his tongue.

###

Ivy had lived in the forest all her life but only came to Sherwood City to trade or visit the library. It was an all-day trek from her family's remote home to town, but she said she didn't mind. "I'm used to sleeping under the stars. Besides, how else am I going to see you every week?" She batted her eyes at him as she sucked on the end of a pencil. Atlas almost choked. "How are Tuesdays?" They sat in the marketplace with another library book between them—this one on the agriculture of the lowlands. Atlas would be posing as a grain merchant on his way in to Labyrinth City and he needed to be able to answer simple questions in case any guards got suspicious.

Atlas coughed and scrubbed at his face in a futile attempt to get rid of his blush. "The next three weeks I'll be out of town."

"Doing what?" Ivy asked.

He forced himself to stop tapping the edge of the table. It was his tell—what he did when he was nervous and lying. "I'm transporting a few things. Fruit and such." He disliked lying to Ivy, but his father had sat him down long ago and told him about the downsides of the work. Only members of the Cross could know the truth. And if he wanted to recruit, he had to go through Ethan. He knew what his father would say if he brought home a girl he'd just met. He knew Ivy was different than anyone else he'd taken an interest in. But still, he had to be cautious.

"Well, four Tuesdays from now, I'll be here. And every Tuesday after that." Ivy smiled her heart-shattering smile. "How does that sound?"

Atlas found himself nodding, even though it was a promise he knew he couldn't keep. He was a field agent now. If this operation worked, he'd be taking regular trips outside of the forest to liaise with Cross contacts and smuggle supplies. Kronos had been suppressing an uprising in the southern district of Centennial City by restricting access to grains and goods, and it was imperative to get people fed. Centennial was the home to the largest marketplace on Olympus, which meant almost everyone relied on it. It was also a two-day journey from Sherwood, along roads regularly patrolled by Kronos' soldiers. These missions sounded simple when discussed around the dinner table, but they were potentially lethal and relied on outside supporters to give them good, up-to-date intelligence. And ever since Hades had started courting Persephone, Atlas had taken on more responsibility. It was obvious to everyone that his older brother would soon be married, and family would likely follow. Hades' duties to the Cross of the Iron Phoenix would be strategy and planning, and Atlas would be given the action. He preferred action to strategy any day, but it also meant dropping everything at a moment's notice if the intel they got was urgent.

Though maybe the idea of coming home to *her* would only sweeten the deal.

Atlas was late home: Ivy had spent long hours chatting about her house in the woods, and he'd been too charmed by her stories of chasing angry chickens all over the yard to check on the time. Dinner was underway as he came in, and as he kicked off his boots the smell of fresh and well-spiced soup drifted down the stairs. That meant Persephone was over for dinner. She always knew how to use her herbs.

Ethan raised an eyebrow as he sat, asking subtly if he'd been in trouble. Atlas shook his head slightly. Then he leaned away as Zeus took a deep sniff of his shoulder.

"What are you doing?" he said, in a voice that promised violence.

"You have a lady's scent on you," Zeus replied with the air of an expert. He crossed his arms. "Let's hear about it."

"Ooh." Persephone smiled and exchanged a knowing

glance with Raven. "It'd be nice to have one more around the dinner table."

Atlas stalked over to the soup pot and started to ladle soup into his bowl. "She's been helping me out at the library," he said gruffly. "Don't get all moony about it."

"*Ooh,* he's sour." Poseidon dunked a piece of bread in his soup and stuffed it in his mouth, talking around it as he chewed. "She must be interesting if she lured you into the library."

"She knows how to find the books, all right?" Atlas glared at Poseidon, but his warning looks had never worked on his almost-twin. "If my younger brothers weren't so immature, I might not have to visit so often, and I might not have caught her attention." Which would have been horrible. Maybe there was a benefit to having such irritating siblings.

"Well, whoever she is, I'm glad she's helping you." Hades pushed his empty bowl away. "After dinner, we need to go over the plan again. Tomorrow we're picking up the cart." The cart was a special one with a false bottom, owned by one of their contacts who lived on the outskirts of Centennial City. Grain would be smuggled into the southern districts, and two Centennial leaders of the Cross would be smuggled out. Kronos and his men had been on their tail for nearly a week, and it was only a matter of time before someone ratted them out.

"So, we're still on?" Atlas said. The soup was scalding, thick with potatoes and summer peas, and made from the bones of a chicken Hades had slaughtered a few days back.

"No other news from my contacts, so yes." Hades chewed on the inside of his cheek. "Tell me again."

Atlas did not groan, because groaning was for whiners and children, but he did chafe at being made to feel like a schoolboy reciting a lesson. "Two days down, enter the city through the south gate, one day for execution of the plan, then exit through the west gate and double back around. Two days back, as long as there isn't any trouble."

"And turn back if you get a bad feeling about the trip," Hades reminded him. "It's not worth your life."

Atlas wasn't sure he agreed. He was bringing food that might well save the lives of many people, and he was scheduled to return with two Cross leaders. Surely his life was a reasonable exchange?

But Hades and Ethan didn't see it that way. Ethan kept reminding him of his destiny. "You're no ordinary man, Atlas," he said whenever Atlas brought it up.

Hades was much more practical. "If you get your throat cut on the way in, then we're down three men, the cart, and the wheat," he'd reasoned. "What sort of trade is that?"

Nothing will go wrong, Atlas told himself. And even if it did, he was the best fighter of all his brothers, revered in Sherwood for his talents. Even Harper O'Donovan couldn't match him, and *his* fighting prowess was the whole reason he'd been chosen to lead the Outlaws of Sherwood.

Atlas tried to concentrate after dinner, but his thoughts kept straying to fiery hair and soft blue eyes. He should have said a proper goodbye to Ivy, in case things *did* go poorly.

Maybe he should leave a note. No, that was pessimistic thinking. He'd be back in a week's time with a sunburn and two new brothers for the cause. Besides, what would he say? *I'm not coming back, and I'm sorry* was rather the limit. He still wasn't close enough to Ivy to tell her the truth—even in the event of his death.

"Are you listening?" Hades cut through his reverie. His maroon eyes flashed with irritation.

"Of course," Atlas scoffed.

"What did I just say?" Hades asked.

Atlas rifled through the last few moments. "Um, something about checkpoints?"

"That was five minutes ago." Hades sighed and ran a hand through his dark hair. His fingers were stained with ink from writing out ledgers and notes and plans, though Atlas spotted a yellow bruise on his arm from where he'd taken a hit in training that morning. Hades somehow found time to do it all: run the Cross with their father, take care of his brothers, and be with Persephone. How did he do it?

"This is important," he said, and Atlas forced himself to pay attention. "If this run works, we can make regular trips down south and relieve the burden faced by those people. The Cross will get a good name and we can try to spread our network. Father insisted you were ready, but if you can't focus on one briefing—"

"I am ready," Atlas cut in, feeling the flush of anger. Hades was a mere three years older than he, yet he insisted on treating Atlas like a child.

"Are you?" Hades shot back.

"I'll take you for a round right now," Atlas offered. "Best of three decides who takes the assignment." He stood. Hades was a quick brawler, but Atlas had trained with him enough to know his weak points.

Hades threw his hands into the air. "This is what I mean! You can't get out of every problem with your fists." Atlas disagreed, but he didn't get a chance to say so before Hades continued. "Some things require finesse." He stopped and rubbed at his temple.

"I know this job. I've been practicing for months. And it's a supply run. Simple field work," Atlas argued.

For a moment, Hades said nothing. He closed his eyes and breathed hard through his nose. Then he said, "I know. I'm sorry."

The silence stretched. Atlas leaned over and put a hand on his brother's shoulder. Hades opened his mouth, on the verge of saying something more, but paused. He cleared his throat.

Finally, he croaked, "We've set a date."

Atlas' hand clenched reflexively around his shoulder. "For the wedding? That's good."

"It means it's all real. It means my responsibilities have doubled. I can see an assignment crystal clear in my mind's eye, but I can't follow through. And if I don't explain it correctly to you, if I don't make sure that you've been paying attention and *understand everything*—you could get hurt or worse. And it would be my fault. But I can't marry Persephone and then run off into danger myself. What if I left her alone, and with child? Do you see?"

Atlas did see. He owed it to his brother to avoid distraction. He owed a few years of his life to the Cross, before turning it over to the sorts of things that Hades worried about now. Love, children, family: it could wait. It *would* wait.

"All right." He pulled a stack of papers toward him. "Let's take it from checkpoints. I'm listening."

###

The supply run was a bore. With specialty goods loaded on the top of his cart, Atlas set off south, accompanied by a former Outlaw who was posing as his apprentice. The specialty goods were for Kronos' army; at the border, he traded jars of cherries in syrup for fast access through a checkpoint. He held his tongue as they checked his papers. They made vague and rather cliché threats in exchange for taking some of his cured meat, but waved him through without further trouble. He did his trade, bought a flea-infested room in a nearby tavern, then snuck out in the middle of the night to help his Cross comrades lift the false bottom of his cart and move the grain into a farmer's wagon. Two men in dark clothes and hoods hopped into the now empty cart, nodding their thanks as he settled the boards back over their heads.

"That was it?" his Outlaw apprentice moped as they made their way to the west gate, watching the dark streets of

Centennial City turn to the dull gray of pre-dawn. The apprentice yawned loudly.

"That was it." Atlas kept his voice neutral, though he was inclined to agree with his associate. He'd expected the life of a spy to be more about taking down lackeys in an alley and less about sitting around while officers discussed his paperwork. But he remembered Hades' words, and he thought about all the ways it *might* have gone wrong, and he knew that the smart thing was to be glad that the trip was boring.

He couldn't deny, he rather wished he could hit something.

The Cross leaders were welcomed into Ethan and Raven's home, and Atlas gave up his room so they could rest before finding their own living quarters and getting set up in Sherwood. Ethan clapped Atlas on the back. "We knew you'd have no trouble." Hades enveloped him in a quick, strong hug.

The next day Atlas was given a break from training and working as a reward. It was market day, so he wandered into town, eager to investigate some small daggers he could hide up his sleeve or in his boot. As he was fingering a soft piece of leather and considering the merits of a new belt, a pale, delicate hand landed on his arm. "You're back."

Ivy. His words tangled up like weeds as he turned to her. She was, if possible, lovelier than the last time he'd seen her. Her blue eyes held an impish quality, and her mouth was turned up in a secretive smile, like she'd broken it out specially for him.

Then he thought of Hades with his head in his hand, worrying about his soon-to-be-wife and all the responsibilities he had to juggle. Atlas had sworn to focus on the Cross, and that promise meant something. Lives depended on him now. He wasn't ready for this. He was a man of action.

That helped bring him back to his senses. He gave her what he hoped was a brief, friendly-but-not-too-friendly smile. "I'm back. What do you think of this?" He held up the leather.

Too late he realized he was probably flirting with her. She rubbed the leather between her fingers, biting her lip. "For what? It's too soft and impractical for outerwear; it'll get scratched and scuffed in the forest."

"You're right." He put it down and nodded regretfully at the tanner, who glared at Ivy as though she'd personally wronged him.

"I'm always right. And I'm buying you a drink. Come on." She grabbed his hand and started to march.

Despite his resolve to the contrary, he found himself following her. Even when he willed his feet to stop, they refused to obey. And letting go of her hand was simply out of the question. Her grip was strong, and he felt callouses at her fingertips, the mark of an archer's hand. "It's nine in the morning," he protested.

"I never said it was an alcoholic drink," she replied.

The late summer sun had already turned the market into a heat sink. Atlas sweated through his light linen shirt and squinted in the sunlight. The crowd parted easily for him—or maybe they parted for Ivy, who walked without hesitation.

She came to a little market stall where a man stood with containers of ice. "Cold tea," she said to Atlas. Then, to the vendor, she said, "Two sunrise teas, please."

The man put ice into two cups and added a bright orange liquid. Ivy handed him two coins before Atlas could fumble out his purse. "I can pay for my own tea," he said gruffly.

"I know." She smiled as she picked up the cups and held one out to him. "But I wanted to pay. Taste it."

Atlas raised the cup to his lips. It smelled like a sunrise, somehow: bright and fresh, like dew in the early morning. And it tasted even better, floral and cool with a hint of sunshine. Atlas closed his eyes, savoring the flavor as it washed over his tongue. When he opened them again, Ivy was still looking at him.

Oh, no.

"Well, thank you for the tea. I…must be going." He nodded to her.

"Where? I'll walk you there. I have the whole day to myself."

She was persistent, he'd give her that. He wasn't sure whether she was oblivious to the way he was trying to throw her off, or whether she was simply determined to ignore it. No matter what, he hadn't prepared a suitable lie, so he said, "Errands. But I'm sure you have errands as well."

She threw him a funny look like she thought he was being particularly stupid. "I came into town to see you."

His heart squeezed painfully. *No.* This was fine. Friends saw each other all the time. Zeus and Leda were always seen together, and that hardly made them a couple. "Well, I suppose you can come along and be bored."

And he truly meant to make her bored. But it wasn't easy, because Ivy herself was anything but boring. She knew most of the vendors by name and could tell Atlas everything about them—from how many children they had to what allergies they suffered. He found himself thinking that she would make a fantastic informant for the Cross. Maybe there *was* a way to recruit her.

"How was your trip, anyway?" she asked.

"Dull," said Atlas, and that at least was true.

"Really? You didn't see anything interesting down south?"

"It was dusty. Not many trees and not much of interest. And the swamp was wet. And the army is arrogant. And I'm going back in two weeks."

"I can't believe you traveled all that way, and this is what you have to say about it." Ivy threw her hands wide. "If I could travel…"

"What's stopping you?" Atlas asked before he could think better of it. But he found himself curious. Nothing had ever stopped him from doing what he wanted, not if he truly wanted it. Even Hades and Ethan only held so much sway over his stubborn mind.

Ivy made a face. "My father. He hates it enough when I come to market. He thinks the whole farm will collapse without me. It's just the two of us at home since my mother died, and I think he's worried I'll leave him all alone."

Atlas could understand that well enough. Being alone now and then was a blessing, with three brothers and members of the Cross traipsing through the house on a daily basis. But alone forever? Losing Ivy? "He sounds like a loving father, at least," Atlas said.

"But it's in the nature of children to leave their parents." Ivy kicked one sandaled foot at a pebble, sending it skittering down the street and bouncing off boots. "I shouldn't sit around waiting for him to die in order to live my own life. It should be my choice."

"Maybe it's your destiny," Atlas suggested.

Ivy's bright, loud laugh was tinged with anger, and a few people looked their way. "Come on." She grabbed his arm again, leading him to the edge of the market and through the trees beyond.

"Where are we going?" Atlas tried to tug free, but his treacherous body was again refusing to cooperate. Right now, the thing he wanted most was to be alone with Ivy—which meant it should be the thing he wanted least.

"Here." Ivy pointed to a tree swelling with apples. They were still unripe, though the size of Atlas' fist; when autumn came and they were ready to harvest, they'd be as large as his head and sweet-tart, perfect for pork and pies. Ivy drew a small hunting bow from her back. "See the one with the black spot?" She pointed.

Atlas found it, bobbing from a high branch in a slight

breeze. Ivy narrowed her eyes, drew back her bow, and released.

The arrow went straight through the apple, tearing it from its stem and knocking it to the ground. Ivy strode over to it and picked it up, then wagged it at him like a finger. "Still think I'm destined to feed chickens and milk cows for the rest of my life?"

Atlas found that his mouth was hanging open. He shut it with obvious effort. No one he knew—not his brothers, not his father, not his mother—no one could shoot like that.

Ivy came back over to him, then pulled out a knife to cut her arrow from the apple. "What do you think your destiny is? Is it to drive carts for the rest of your life?"

"No," Atlas said forcefully. She looked at him inquisitively, cocking her head. But he wasn't sure what to say next. He couldn't tell her the truth. "I'm…" he sighed. "I'm hungry." He closed his fingers into a fist to keep them from tapping against his leg. "What do you say we split a turkey leg?"

Ivy arched an eyebrow at him, clearly considering whether to let him off the hook. "A warning: I don't share turkey legs," she said, snagging his hand as she walked past him. "I get one all to myself."

Atlas laughed.

They found their turkey legs and sat on the ground with more sunshine tea. Atlas found he was liking it better than any ale, though perhaps that was the company speaking. Ivy eyed him over her turkey leg as they tore into the juicy meat. "You brought up the idea of destiny, but you didn't want to talk about it," she said.

Atlas wiped his broad hands on a handkerchief, gritting his teeth. He hated lying, especially to her. "It's…complicated," he said at last.

"Oh?"

"My destiny was foretold when I was a baby."

"It must be impressive," Ivy said. Atlas nodded. "And perhaps intimidating?"

"I wouldn't say intimidating," said Atlas, who had never been intimidated by anything in his life. "Constricting, perhaps. I have duties. To my family, to the…work, and to my destiny." He met her eye and said frankly, "It doesn't give me a lot of time for other things."

The mischievous glint dropped from her eye, and her smile sobered. "I see."

Atlas' stomach felt as though it was lined with lead. This was for the best, he told himself. What if Ivy had attached herself to him before realizing that she couldn't come first? She would grow to resent him, perhaps even hate him. And the idea of being hated by Ivy felt worse than letting her go. She deserved to be happy, even if it was with another man.

"I should go." He tossed his turkey bone into the woods, where a fox would find it and carry it off.

"Please, don't." Ivy stood quickly. "I understand. Let's just…talk. Run errands. If you can't tell me about your destiny, maybe I'll tell you about mine."

He didn't have the heart to refuse her again.

Ivy wanted to travel. For a time, she'd dreamed of joining a circus, wandering all over Olympus, doing trick shots with her bow. That was before she'd learned of the state of things outside of the forest. Now she wasn't sure that circuses existed anymore, and she disliked the idea of performing for Kronos' armies.

"They killed my mother," she said soberly, as they started the walk back to Atlas' house. He'd purchased a few items: wool for new socks, a belt, and two daggers no longer than his little finger.

"I'd hate them for that, too." He *did* hate them for that. It was one more reason they had to pay. "Did you live outside of Sherwood when it happened?"

Ivy shook her head. Her lovely face was drawn and serious, sadness layered upon sadness. "Typhon came by our farm. He was collecting taxes. Only, the winter had been rough. Foxes had killed most of our chickens and unseasonable cold had destroyed the fruit in our orchard. We hadn't been able to forage much to make up for it. And Ma was sick with goldenroot fever."

Goldenroot. It wrapped itself around root vegetables and trees and poisoned everything it touched. The last flare-up of goldenroot in Sherwood had been fifteen years ago.

"But goldenroot is treatable," Atlas said. If Ivy had only come into town, she would have gotten medicine whether she could pay or not. No one would have turned away a girl desperate to save her mother.

"We got the cure," Ivy's lip curled. "But when Typhon

saw that we didn't have enough to pay, he took it. Said the coin he got from selling it would take care of our taxes." She dashed tears from the bottom of her eyes. "It was a lie, of course. You can't sell half a bottle of Vitha tincture, it costs nothing in the first place. He just wanted to teach us a lesson. He wanted us to watch her die, all because we couldn't give him a few silvers in tribute."

Atlas' hands were shaking. Belatedly, he realized he'd stopped in the middle of the street. If Typhon were here now…well, Hades' beating would look like child's play compared to what Atlas wanted to do to him. Starting with shoving a whole fistful of goldenroot-tainted vegetables down the chimera's throat.

This. This was why they had to do something. If a hundred boring missions would spare the life of someone's mother, then it was action Atlas had to take.

Chapter Nine: Forever & Ever

Atlas traveled back and forth well into the autumn, stopping only when heavy rains turned the Brown Swamp into something resembling a Brown Lake. Perhaps it was for the best; Hades' wedding was scheduled for the midwinter festival, and his brother was on edge about everything. Atlas took over a few meetings with the Cross members they'd saved, taking note of what Centennial needed and how they could help once roads reopened, though that probably wouldn't be until spring.

Frost began to gild over the forest in the morning, creating delicate patterns on their windows and over the streams that wound through town. The markets started to serve hot cocoa and mulled wine. But Atlas didn't have time to savor them, nor see Ivy. He was overseeing the brewing of dozens of barrels of mead, negotiating with farmers for the purchase of a whole herd of pigs, and ensuring that the baker had enough flour to make a cake for nearly a hundred people. The ceremony would be held, as most were, in the main square beneath the sacred tree. Ethan himself would officiate, and the square would be stuffed with anyone who was anyone in the Cross of the Iron Phoenix. It was the biggest party any of the boys had ever seen, and Atlas' job was to get Hades to the altar without letting his brother suffer a nervous breakdown. He argued with suppliers, sorted information sent by informants, and got his brother to bed far too late every evening.

The wedding was worth it, though.

The square was strung with hundreds of candles the day of the wedding, and people crowded around the stage, dressed in their finest leathers and furs. Old friends greeted each other, and old enemies put aside their feuds for the day. Even Harper O'Donovan arrived looking sober and well-dressed, shaking hands and smiling his charming smile. When he got to Atlas, his grin turned roguish. "Just think. If we hadn't started a fight in the marketplace, none of this would have happened."

Atlas rolled his eyes. "You are the veritable doctor of love," he said.

"Love Doctor. I like that. Put it on my tombstone." Harper chuckled and moved away. Atlas snorted. He supposed that Harper *was* Hades' best friend, and had the right to be here. He wished Ethan might have contrived to send him out on a mission, though.

Snow fell in fat, gentle flakes, dusting the square and giving the trees a luminous quality, even in the day. The air smelled crisp and cold and perfect. As Atlas ascended the dais in the middle of the square, he spotted Ivy's telltale hair, crowned with snow. She wore a white leather coat lined with fox fur. Their eyes met and she shot him a dazzling smile that made his stomach flip.

He'd hoped that some time away would dim his feelings. He was wrong.

Hades joined them next, shaking the hand of each

brother. He was trembling, Atlas realized. "You can't be nervous," he muttered. Hades had practically been planning this moment since he and Persephone met.

Hades looked around to make sure only his brothers were in earshot. Then he leaned in. "What if she doesn't come? What if she's changed her mind?"

Atlas, Zeus, and Poseidon looked at him for a long moment. Hades blinked anxiously.

Then Zeus burst out laughing. He slapped his thigh and shook his head. Poseidon was chuckling, too, though he at least looked sympathetic.

Atlas could keep himself from laughing, but he couldn't keep the smile off his lips as he pulled his brother in for a hug. "She wants to marry you as badly as you want to marry her," he said. "Trust me."

"I want it to be over with," Hades muttered. "Maybe such a big ceremony was a bad idea."

"Are you sure about that?" Zeus inclined his head toward the back of the square. Atlas and Hades turned to follow his gaze. And there she was.

Her dark hair had been swept up into a crown and decorated with dried roses. She wore a wool dress of the palest white, draped with lace and lined with fur at the collar, sleeves, and hem. She held a bouquet of snowdrops. Her onyx eyes shone and her cheeks glowed with anticipation. Walking next to her was Una, dressed in a simple but elegant wool dress as well, trying—and failing—to look severe.

Hades' mouth hung open. He stood stock still. Atlas

gently guided him into place before their father. Una and Raven carefully helped Persephone up to the dais.

"Thank you for coming," Ethan said. "To all of you, but particularly to my son and his beloved." A laugh rippled over the crowd, and even Hades smiled at that, blushing.

"Family is the greatest gift a man can wish for. For many long years, my wife and I wished for a big family. And we were blessed with four sons. Every day, they taught us new lessons about family and love. And Hades always led the pack. His brilliance, his steadfastness, and his creativity surprised his mother and I every day. Throughout his life, Raven and I only ever wished for one thing: some daughters to round out our sons. And today, we gain a daughter. May you be steadfast with each other, creative together, and shine brilliantly on our lives. And may your children be as creative in their troublemaking as you were."

The crowd laughed again, and Atlas found himself chuckling along with them. But sadness lay beneath the mirth. It hadn't really struck him that Hades was leaving. Of course, he would. Ethan and Raven lived well, but their house was hardly large enough for a budding family.

Persephone and Hades exchanged rings and vows under the rustling, ever leafy oak. Ethan guided their hands together, then turned them toward the crowd. "You are bound to each other, man and wife," he said. His eyes glistened. "Honor each other."

Hades pulled Persephone in for a kiss. The crowd cheered, and no one cheered louder than Atlas.

###

His feet and fingers were freezing from standing still for so long, so when someone offered him a mead, Atlas took it gratefully. The party was in full swing: the pigs were roasting in their pits, guests danced to the lively tunes of four musicians hired for the occasion, and every so often someone in the crowd roared, "To the bride!" which was matched by an enthusiastic toast from everyone around. It was perfect.

Nearly perfect. Zeus was locked in an argument with Leda and Poseidon had lined up to arm-wrestle Harper. Atlas was alone.

"Hey." Her voice was soft but somehow cut through the crowd perfectly. Atlas turned to see Ivy resplendent in her white coat. She crooked a finger and he was walking forward before he could think about whether it was wise. "Good wedding."

Atlas looked around. The level of cheer was high, and the number of fistfights was low. "It is." He felt a swell of pride.

"It can do without you for a few moments. Come on." She turned and slid through the crowd.

"Wait, I—" he began to push after her. What did she mean by that? He couldn't abandon his brother's wedding. Not that Hades would notice he was gone. The bride and groom had been surrounded by well-wishers for the past hour, yet they could only gaze at each other. Surely Raven and Una would make sure they got something to eat.

Atlas caught up with her at the edge of the square. Ivy smiled slightly, nodded, and then started into the woods. Twilight was coming upon them, the long gray hour that was the most dangerous in the woods. It was easy, especially in snow, to catch your toe in a root or slip into a divot. The world was devoid of shadow and growing cold. Atlas' breath frosted in the air as he tried to keep up with her sure pace without slipping and breaking something.

"Where are we going?" he asked.

"My favorite place," said Ivy.

"I hate to ask it, but is now really the time?" But she didn't reply, and he couldn't stop following her. He never could.

Ivy led him through the woods to a small clearing. Quince trees clustered along one edge, bursting with red flowers. Yellow blooms poked bravely through the snow at their feet. Atlas almost felt bad about breaking the peace of the meadow with his footprints, but he followed Ivy right into the center.

She hadn't looked at him once since starting her walk, but now she turned to him. Her cheeks were rosy and her blue eyes were bright. "I love you," she burst out.

Atlas blinked. *Say something.* But her declaration had knocked all the air from his lungs. The best he could do was work his mouth like a fish.

"You have work. You have a destiny that scares you. And I know you have to focus on these things. But I can be with you, too. I can help you. I don't want to pretend that I can be your friend when I can't. I don't want to let you go. Maybe this is crazy, but *I* want to be under the sacred tree next." She pointed back towards the square. "And I want you to be there with me. I want to travel with you and try new things with you. Whenever I want to talk to someone, I only want to talk to you. Please, let me."

She stopped again and looked at him. Atlas tried in vain to corral his thoughts. They had scattered like field mice at her first volley of words. "I…"

He had to keep her safe. He had to keep her protected, from the scum who killed her mother and sought to keep all of Olympus under the same monstrous thumb. But he also needed her. From the moment she set her eyes on him, he'd been powerless to refuse her anything.

She was waiting for his answer. His mind raced. *I love you, too. I'll marry you. I'll go anywhere with you.* Could he truly make those promises? He'd sworn his life to the Cross.

He was taking too long. Ivy swallowed, hard, and a single tear slipped from her eye down her cheek. "Or, I can go. We can stop seeing each other. I just wanted to be honest about it all."

She tucked her head and tried to hurry past him. Luckily, Atlas' body knew how to act even when his brain did not. He caught her by the arm and spun her around. *I love you, too.* But he didn't say it. He swept her against him, and he caught her lips between his.

Fire spread through his body, warmer than any mead. She smelled like meadow and moss and honey. He lifted her off the ground and her arms wrapped around his back, pulling him closer and closer, scraping her teeth against his bottom lip. He stumbled. His whole world was moving.

Ivy pulled back and looked at him through shuttered lashes. Then her eyes widened. "Whoa," she whispered.

His whole world *was* moving. The ground buckled at his feet, sending out tremors that rippled the snow like waves. Grass sprouted around them, growing as tall as their knees in seconds. A dormant rose bush on the other side of the clearing exploded with green leaves. Buds unfurled to reveal roses of the palest pink, the color of Ivy's lips. At their feet, a tangle of strawberries ripened into a deep red. Flowers sprouted and burst with wild abandon.

"Your eyes…all of you." Ivy leaned back, gazing at him in wonder. "You're *glowing*."

Then she looked around at her meadow, and her mouth dropped open. It was a riot of purples and yellows and reds, a mix of spring and summer and autumn flowers.

She jumped from his arms and knelt. She plucked a strawberry the size of her palm and stared at it, then took a bite. Then she showed him the inside, red as a jewel. "It's perfect," she whispered. "What did you do?"

He'd come into his destiny. And he'd done it with her.

Hang his obligations. Ivy was a part of him now. "I love you too," he said, slipping his hand over hers. Her fingers were cold, but her smile was so warm. This was right. She was right for him. They could figure everything else out. "Come back to the wedding with me." He pulled her lightly to her feet. For once he was the one in the lead. And he would give her one perfect night before going back to his duties tomorrow. "I want you to meet my father."

Ivy's smile was nervous and surprised, and all the more beautiful for it. "Okay." She let him lead her through the trees.

Hades had found a way to balance his priorities. Maybe Atlas would leave the field, too. He'd been hoping to get more exciting assignments, but Ivy should take priority—

And then a brilliant, wondrous, terrifying idea took root in his head. "What if you could do everything you wanted? What if you could get revenge on Typhon and travel the world at the same time?"

Chapter Ten: The Moment Things Can Change

Persephone's fingernails dug into Hades' hand until they cut through his skin. She let out a strangled groan. Sweat stuck her raven hair to her face, and her normally smiling mouth was twisted in a grimace. She lay on the bed with her knees up. "That's it," the midwife said in a soothing tone, patting her knee with tan fingers. "That's it. Push."

Another contraction seized her. Hades stroked her hair. "Not long now," he whispered, hoping it was true. But the midwife's demeanor made him nervous. Her eyes darted from side to side.

They'd been waiting for this moment for months. Persephone had glowed the day she told Hades she'd missed her courses, and every spare moment had been spent building a nursery, a crib, a rocking chair for Persephone to nurse. Every waking moment for the last eight months had been consumed with daydreaming and preparing for their own little family. But now Persephone had been in labor for nearly twenty hours, and she was so exhausted she could barely breathe.

Her body seized again. "Push," shouted the midwife. Persephone screamed, clawing for Hades. But the midwife beckoned him. "You will catch the child," she said.

"What?" Hades' eyes widened in panic.

She positioned him, and with a final push, the baby boy slid into his hands.

But something was wrong. He wasn't crying. His face was blue.

"The cord!" the midwife cried. A glistening rope was wound around the child's neck. Without thinking, Hades gripped the boy by his ankle and raised him in the air. The midwife's knife flashed, severing the umbilical cord, and with a deft movement, she unwound it from his neck.

Hades' breath caught in his chest. This couldn't be. This couldn't be…

The boy's mouth opened and he let out a scrawny, toothless wail. It was the most perfect sound Hades had ever heard.

His vision blurred over. The midwife took the boy tenderly and handed him to his mother, who had flopped back against the mountain of pillows Hades had propped up to keep her comfortable. Persephone set the baby against her breast and gazed at him as he sucked.

He went back to her and sat on a stool beside her. He and the stool had become intimately acquainted during the long labor, but right now he was too tired to stand. He could hardly fathom what she must be feeling. "Are you all right?" Hades stroked her damp hair.

She brushed his tears from his cheeks. "I am now," she said.

Together, Hades and the midwife checked the baby's fingers and toes. He was perfectly formed, though he had an odd, pale ring of skin around his ankle where Hades had held him up. "Did I…?" he asked.

The midwife ran her deft fingers over the ring. "It looks like a birthmark. It's harmless, I'm sure."

She cleaned Persephone, then bustled about the room. It was strewn with clothes, cups of water, and crusts of bread. Hades sagged back on the pillows next to Persephone. "You did it," he murmured.

Persephone looked down at the thatch of dark hair. "I think he's asleep," she murmured. "Would you like to hold him?"

Hades slid his arm around his son and brought him close. His cheeks were bright red, a good sign after his scare. His eyes were screwed tightly shut, and his lips smacked, as though he were dreaming of milk. "Hello, little one," Hades whispered. Such a precious, tiny thing. And within that thing, the power to change a man's whole world. "I'm your Dada."

Persephone lay her head on his shoulder. This was perfect. In this moment, his life was utterly perfect. He breathed in deep, savoring the smell of his wife's sweat and his child's new skin. He reveled in the feel of her dark hair against his cheek. "What should we call him?" he asked.

Persephone blinked sleepily. "I always liked the name Achilles," she said.

"I love it," he whispered against her head. Achilles. A boy with a name like that would grow up quick and clever and strong. And most importantly, he would grow up safe. In a world where he didn't have to fear Kronos or any other dictator. In a world where Hades could dedicate himself to being a father.

The baby was starting to rouse for his mother again, but the midwife motioned for him to get up. "Take him out to meet his family," she suggested. "Let the lady rest."

Hades nodded and got to his feet. The midwife showed him how to swaddle the baby, reminded him to be careful, then opened the door and followed him out.

Ethan, Raven, and Una sat on one side of the sitting room in Hades and Persephone's new house. His brothers and Ivy sat on the other. They all looked a bit the worse for wear: Una and his parents had been here since Persephone's labor began, and Atlas, Zeus, and Poseidon had taken it in turns to go out for supplies and bread. As one, they leapt to their feet. Hope and anxiety shone on their faces.

Hades turned the baby toward them. "A boy."

His brothers cheered. Una and Raven swept forward to envelop him in a hug that made him stagger back. It was, if he recalled correctly, the first time in his life that Una had hugged him.

Ethan was next. "A boy." He grinned down at the little figure. He looked almost as dazed as Hades himself. "May he bring you all the joy you have brought to me."

Hades blinked back sudden tears. "Thanks, Dad," he said quietly.

Atlas was next, bending over the little figure, touching his large, dark index finger to the child's tan forehead. Ivy kissed Achilles's dark hair. Then Zeus came forward, eyes shimmering with excitement. "I'm going to be the *fun* uncle," he promised, tugging on one tiny foot. Atlas and Hades exchanged an alarmed look.

But one man had not come forward. Hades sought out his brother Poseidon—and then he understood. For his brother stood stock still, staring, as if in shock.

It was strange, thought a distant part of Poseidon's mind, how a man's world could change in a single moment. For example, Hades' life had been destroyed and rebuilt the moment he'd met his son. And now Poseidon's life had been blown away. From now on, there would only be a *before* and an *after.* Before her, and with her.

Her simple blue-and-tan midwife's uniform did nothing to distract from her beauty. She had a small, sharp face, with large curving eyes that sparkled with intelligence as she washed a few bloody rags. Her cheekbones were high and defined, giving her a look of rare elegance, and her full lips were pursed in concentration. Gold seemed to dust her pale skin, giving it an otherworldly glow. As he watched she stretched her back and pulled her hair from its messy knot at the base of her neck. Cascades of black fell to her waist. She moved with a quiet confidence, tossing the bloody water out of a window and draping the rags on a rack to dry. She must be tired, too—she'd been there for the entire birth—but she showed no sign of exhaustion in her movements. She was professional, and the new parents came first.

She began speaking to Hades in a low voice, then broke

off. Hades was staring at Poseidon. And now, so was she.

Their eyes met. Energy jolted from the soles of his feet up to the crown of his head. From outside he dimly registered the sound of rushing water and knew the river was high on its bank, though it had been low that morning and it had not rained. The woman's chest rose and hitched as her breath caught in her throat.

Some moments changed a man forever, and some revelations struck with such force that there was no room for error. This was Poseidon's moment. He moved forward, feeling half in a dream. But he was confident, too. There was no reason for fumbling shyness. This woman was part of his destiny, and nothing would change that.

"I'm sorry to interrupt," he said, and his voice was low and smooth and easy. "I couldn't help but notice you. My name's Poseidon." He held out a hand, palm up, inviting.

She pressed her fingers lightly to his. Her dark eyes searched his face, decoding him in an instant. Those lush lips parted in a smile. "Diana." Her voice was smooth as well, like the whisper of the wood on a summer's night.

Diana. His other half. He barely heard Hades clear his throat and move to the other side of the room. Conversation broke out again in a low murmur. Diana squeezed his fingers. "I have to get back to work," she said.

"I'll help you." She raised an eyebrow and Poseidon shrugged half a shoulder. It was the only natural thing to say.

"Interested in midwifery?" Diana said.

"Interested in you," he answered honestly. No point in

being coy. This was just the beginning. And judging from her smile as she turned away, Diana agreed.

"Two more weddings." Zeus kicked an acorn down the road with his well-worn leather boot. "Why is everyone getting married?"

Leda walked alongside him, eating an apple. The sight of her eating an apple had reduced lesser men to quivering blobs, but Zeus had known her too long for that. "It's rather what people do," she pointed out.

"Poseidon's known Diana for what, three days?" he grumbled. Sherwood City was at its usual level of bustle for a non-market day: people took their bread dough to the baker and their knives to the smith. Someone was arguing with the apothecary over the price of mallow extract.

"Three weeks," Leda corrected him. She was dressed in a loose shirt the color of sunflowers, with her bow slung across her back and a brace of rabbits in one hand. Their morning hunt had been successful—for her. Zeus had decided to try out his throwing knives, and he'd struck more trees than animals.

"That's *nothing.* I've been deep in love plenty of times, and have never felt the need to propose after three weeks. They should be waiting months, at least." Inwardly, Zeus shuddered. The idea that anyone would have such power over his life and emotions…poor Poseidon was a fool.

Leda shrugged and shot him a sidelong look as she flicked her apple core into the woods. A swallow darted down and began to peck at it. "Some people know," she said.

Maybe. Or maybe his brother was rushing into things and making a mistake. But no one listened to Zeus, the expert on ladies and love. Everyone said he was too young and too immature and didn't look at women like they were people, which was unfair and untrue. Zeus had plenty of maturity and respect for ladies. For example, he respected that not all of them wanted long-term relationships. And he respected their feelings a few months later, when he discovered they *did* want long-term relationships, and he broke things off before they could get too serious.

He made to smack Leda in the arm. She dodged and gripped his wrist in one dark, long-fingered hand, twisting his arm until he squeaked. "Careful," she said, fixing him with her golden stare. She blinked slowly. Had her lashes always been so long and thick?

"Sorry." Zeus put up his free hand in surrender, and she released him. "I need your help. Who should I take to the wedding? Probably a different girl to each."

"Maybe you should go with a friend," Leda suggested. "You might give someone the wrong idea."

She had a point. Girls got mushy at weddings. Ivy had practically *proposed* to Atlas at Hades' wedding, and they hadn't even officially started courting yet. Zeus ran a hand through his light hair and looked at the leaves, dappled with sunlight and waving in the wind. He sat on the railing of a stone bridge. Then he snapped his fingers as an idea occurred to him. "You can come with me."

"Hm." Leda drew herself up to her full height, an impressive almost-six feet. "I'll think about it."

"What do you mean, think about it?" Zeus spread his hands. "It's perfect. What's there to think about?"

"Well, I might get a better offer." Her red, red lips twitched as she tried to keep from smiling.

"Better than me?" Zeus scoffed, insulted. It was arrogant, but it was also true. "Come on. We can dance like idiots, have a cake-eating contest, guess who's next. I know for a fact there's no one else you'd rather go with."

Leda examined her fingernails. "Maybe," she conceded. "But what if a handsome stranger strides into town the night before?"

Zeus shrugged. "He'll take one look at you, be horribly intimidated by your beauty, your wit, and your height, and hide behind a tree."

Leda shoved him off the bridge.

The icy water took his breath away and he came up sputtering. Leda grinned at him from above. It did nothing to help him start breathing again, if he was honest. "Want to try that again?"

"No." He sloshed to the bank and sat, pulling off his boots and pouring out the water. He tried to pull his shirt away from his body with a grimace. He hated wet clothes and the way they stuck to him. Ah, well. The forest was still chilly in the shade this early in the summer, but he'd dry off fast enough if they stuck to the sun. "And let the record show that you're a spoilsport when it comes to honest friends."

She trotted down the bank and offered him a hand. He took it. "And you are going to be a terrible wedding date," she said as she pulled him to his feet.

Zeus grinned. "That sounds like a yes to me."

"For now," Leda said sternly, though her lips were twitching again. Zeus found himself distracted by them. "And only because I feel sorry for knocking you in the river. I didn't mean to push you so hard."

Zeus was used to *yes for now.* He knew how to turn it into a yes for good. He grinned. "I'll make you a deal. You can decide what I wear to the wedding."

###

"I never should have let you decide what I wore to the wedding," he grumbled. Around them the party was in full swing: every guest had a cup, the meal had been full of good meat with crackling skin, and good toasts with sweet mead and ale. Now the square had cleared for dancing. His white shirt frothed with lace at the cuffs. He'd already dipped one in ale by accident, and Harper O'Donovan had sneered as he swaggered by, "Nice handkerchiefs, kid."

Leda wore a pale pink dress that left her dark arms bare. The color set her eyes aglow. "You look good in it," she argued. "I'm doing you a service."

"How, exactly?" Zeus pretended to cry, dabbing at his eyes. "It's so beautiful." Leda punched him, sending him staggering across the stone square. But she was laughing, and it was probably the drink, but the sound made his heart skip.

To be fair, the ceremony *had* been beautiful. Ivy had worn a dress the color of her eyes, and her hair had been wound with red-gold wire. And she'd looked at Atlas the way no woman had ever looked at Zeus. He'd had his fair share of moony love looks, of girls who thought they wanted something that they didn't even understand. But Ivy understood Atlas. She accepted him. He'd seen that same look reflected in Diana's eyes as she'd danced with his other brother. Perhaps they'd only known each other for a short time, but they seemed to have no secrets, no new corners of each other to explore.

Zeus didn't really…understand that. And now, three ales deep, he could admit that it scared him.

There was only one person who really knew him, and she stood two feet away in a stunning dress, with her hair piled atop her head like a crown. She'd rejected three boys already today, and he wasn't about to be the fourth. He didn't even *want* to be the fourth. Did he?

"Anyway." He tried to cast his thoughts on something else. "Did you get a chance to talk to our new friends on the border?"

Their 'new friends' were spies Kronos had sent into the forest to gather information. Zeus was confident they wouldn't get it; the Cross was used to attempts to crack it. All the same, Ethan had sat his boys down and explained to them that they might have to move.

Leda gave him a stern look. "I did not, and neither did

you," she said firmly. Zeus did suppose it was a risky move to bring up rebellion talk in the middle of a public party. "But I *did* hear that Anna accepted a proposal of marriage."

"Great," said Zeus without much enthusiasm. Anna had once been convinced that she would marry him, and while he supposed it was good that she'd moved on, in his current state it only emphasized that everyone understood the idea of forever except for him. All he wanted to do in his free time was hunt rabbits with Leda and let her mock his aim, then see who could make a higher tower of bread rolls or fit more strawberries into their mouth at once.

"Here." She handed him a fistful of acorns.

"Where did you even get these?" he laughed.

Leda patted the pocket of her dress. "I thought you might need some entertainment to keep you in line. You're like a child, but the trouble you can get into is *so much worse.*"

Zeus held up an acorn. "And this is going to keep us out of trouble? All right. All right." He closed one eye and took aim. "Ten coppers says that I can get this in the Mayor's cup while he looks away."

"Ten? Deal."

The trick was waiting for the right moment. Zeus was impatient in many things, but he treated the Mayor like a mark, and Leda like a stern weapons master. And then—the Mayor turned to kiss his cousin on the cheek, and Zeus let the acorn fly. It soared in a perfect arc and splashed in the cup.

The Mayor never even noticed.

"Beetle dung," grumbled Leda. "All right, let's turn that

bet right back. Ten coppers say I can use this one to knock that ridiculous flower out of Aunt Meridia's hair." The old lady in question wore an enormous wool rose pinned to her bun. It was nearly as voluminous as her dress, which was so stiff it made its own creaking sound and knocked into people as she turned to greet this friend or that.

"That's going to take a lot of force and a lot of finesse," Zeus warned her.

"Hush. I've done as much combat training as you." Leda narrowed her golden-brown eyes. For a moment she was the very embodiment of the hunt, all razor-sharp focus and steady gaze. But she let fly too soon.

"Ow." Aunt Meridia's hand flew to the back of her head.

"Oh no." Leda clapped her own hand to her mouth.

Aunt Meridia whirled around. Without thinking Zeus grabbed Leda's hand and dashed off. Leda let out a surprised whoop and kept up with him, shoving through the crowd until they came to an empty street. Then they burst into a full run, feet slapping against the stones until they'd raced all the way to the edge of town and the road turned to a dirt path, winding into the depths of the forest.

Zeus stopped and leaned against a stone marker that declared the official border of Sherwood City. His heart was so strangely full that the only thing he could do was laugh. Leda was laughing, too, unrestrained, with her eyes tightly closed and her head tilted toward the stars.

She really was beautiful in the arch of her neck, the curve of her cheek. The thought stopped him cold. She'd always been beautiful, of course. He'd always known it. So why was he noticing it now? What made it so important?

She paused. She'd caught him looking at her. "What?"

"I just—how is it you always get me in the worst kind of trouble?" He held up his sleeves to demonstrate. The mad dash had been unkind to them, unraveling part of the lace at the cuffs. Twigs and small leaves were caught up in the edges.

"Because I know you." Leda straightened. "And I know the things that make you happiest are the things that bring you trouble. And at least it's a good kind of trouble, right?"

She smoothed down her dress, sweeping her arms elegantly, and Zeus felt his heart skipping again. *The good kind of trouble.* Was that what this was?

The night around them chirped as crickets and frogs sought mates of their own. The sound of the party was distant but distinct. The green glow of the trees cast odd shadows over Leda's dress, and her eyes glowed like lanterns. The air was thick with the scent of wildflowers and possibility.

"Leda, what would you look for in a marriage?" he asked before he could think better of it.

"I'm not going to marry anyone," Leda declared. Her face got an odd, shuttered expression like she'd thought about it and written it off long before.

"What would make you change your mind?"

She shot him an odd look, but leaned against a broad oak tree. "I suppose…if I married someone, I'd marry someone familiar to me. Someone I know wouldn't hurt me. Someone who would keep no secrets from me, and who would put my needs above his own. Someone who woke up every morning and thought of me first. And…someone for whom I would do the same." She shrugged. "I simply don't see it happening."

"I know you," Zeus blurted without thinking.

Leda shot him an odd look. She was like a lioness in this light, cautious and proud, dangerous. "Yes, you do," she agreed.

"…And I know you'll find someone," he finished lamely. "When you stop throwing acorns at old ladies and grow up."

Leda's smile was tired. Like she knew she had to but her heart wasn't in it. "It's how I see my future, Zeus." She ran a finger over her eyebrow and sighed. "I think I'll go home."

Zeus pushed away from the stone to walk with her, as they'd done so many times. But now Leda put a hand out to stop him. "You should go back to the party. Your brothers will want to celebrate with you." He doubted it, but he knew a rejection when he heard one. So he let her turn and walk away.

It stung more than he'd thought it would, coming from her. After all, this was Leda. They'd known each other forever. They'd never kissed, even for practice. She'd been a part of his family for so long that she was practically his sister.

A sudden gust of wind stirred his hair and his emotions. No, Leda wasn't his sister. She was one of the people who knew him best in the whole world. He told her everything, even the things he was too embarrassed or scared to tell his brothers. He'd confessed to her who'd snapped one of the Cross' swords because he'd stabbed a tree with it and was trying to withdraw the blade. He'd admitted to her every time he'd been interested in a girl, and every time that interest had waned. She knew he secretly hated his mother's kidney pie, and that he'd brushed poison ivy over Hades' trousers when he was fifteen and his brother had gone especially hard on him during training. She knew he wanted to be his father's top operative. And he knew everything about her—all her secrets, all the excuses she made to sneak over to his house when they were children, all the things she loved and hated. It wasn't fair. He felt the wind pick up, and a thick raindrop smacked his forehead. It wasn't *fair.*

It wasn't fair that he might be in love with his best friend, and she had just told him that she wasn't ever going to get married.

Thunder crashed above him. A sudden surge of energy flooded his veins and without thinking, Zeus held up his palm. The rain turned to a torrent, and the wind howled.

A ball of light appeared in his hand, white-hot and fizzing. Lightning. Zeus looked down. Beneath his shirt, his skin glowed.

He had come into his power.

He threw back his head and laughed. He threw the ball of lightning skyward. The clouds flashed and the boom of thunder deafened him. His destiny was calling. It had the voice of the storm.

Chapter Twelve: Control Issues

Zeus found Leda again a few days after the wedding. Or rather, Leda found him: she strode into the family yard as he chopped wood and flicked an acorn at his head.

He caught it without looking. The drone of bees and the heat of the summer sun had left him feeling lazy and thick, but the moment he heard her boots in the yard, the fog cleared, leaving an electric buzzing in its place. Anticipation. Longing. Fear.

"You still owe me ten coppers," he said, trying to play it cool.

She held up a jangling pouch. She was dressed for the hunt today, in green and brown, in wool and leather. "I knew you'd say that."

Zeus straightened and looked at her. Even when dressed for a day of labor, she was the greatest beauty in Sherwood. It wasn't her looks, magnificent though they were. It was the way she held herself, tall and proud, confident and unstoppable. Leda was a force of nature, and she knew it.

Well, he was a force of nature now, too. And he didn't want to play it cool anymore. Not with her.

"I want to show you something." He beckoned for her to join him, then started out of the yard at a brisk walk.

"I promised my father I'd bring him a deer, so you'd better make this quick," Leda said, lengthening her stride to catch up to him.

He wouldn't, but by the end of this, she wouldn't care.

He avoided going through town. He didn't need his father or any of his brothers wondering why he was shirking his chores—or worse, following him. Instead he stuck to the outer streets, passing small houses perched high in the trees, dwellings that were little more than huts for travelers. At last he found one of his favorite spots in Sherwood: a little square, surrounded by the remains of shops and adorned with a single dried-up fountain, carved in the shape of a shell. When Zeus was young, the fountain had flowed with water and he'd played many games of tag and ball here with his friends. Then the fountain dried up, some ten years ago, and people went elsewhere to get their fresh water. The shops moved. Grass sprouted between the flagstones on the square. Now all that remained was a few stones, the lone fountain and a small sacred tree, bursting with leaves and glimmering in the sunlight.

Zeus turned. "You know everything about me, right?"

Leda shrugged. "Yeah."

"But you don't." His body hummed with nerves, energy, and excitement. "I've been keeping something from you. But I don't want to do that anymore." Because her man would keep no secrets from her.

Leda blinked slowly and took a cautious step back. "Okay."

Zeus lifted his eyes to the sky. It was a deep blue, devoid of clouds. A perfect day for showing off his power. "My father made us swear ourselves to secrecy. I wanted to tell you, but he made me hold my tongue."

"A rare feat for anyone," Leda deadpanned, crossing her arms. "Zeus, what is this about? You're acting weird. You've been avoiding me for days and now you're spouting about secrets?"

Zeus clenched his fists. He was going about this all wrong. Why was it he knew what to say to every girl but her? "I…" He sighed. "I think I should show you."

He held out his hand, and he called on the power.

It answered him easily. Lightning danced over his hand in a web, tickling his palm. Leda gasped. "Is that—?"

"Magic," Zeus replied, and he couldn't keep the smugness out of his tone. "I can do magic."

Leda came forward, leaning in until her nose was mere inches from his fingers. She lifted her hand, then seemed to think better of it and tucked it behind her back. The orb of lightning glowed. "Since when?" she said.

"Since the wedding." She wanted truthfulness, and he would give it to her in full. "Since I realized I loved you."

Leda raised her golden-brown eyes. They were wide with alarm. Goosebumps broke out over her shoulders. A shadow fell over the square.

"My destiny was to come into my power and defeat the tyrant Kronos, once and for all," Zeus said, willing sincerity into his voice. She needed to see it not as a boast, but as the truth. "My brothers and I will use our powers to save this world. And you helped me discover mine."

Leda was shaking her head. She looked like the deer she'd

wanted to hunt today, panicked and ready to flee. "I…don't know what to say. You've never wanted me before."

This wasn't right. She was supposed to smile, to say she'd been waiting for this, to lean over him. To kiss him softly with her red lips. Then he would create a gentle rain shower and a rainbow to smile on her. "I've always wanted you," he replied, realizing the truth of it as he said the words. "Through everything, you've been the one I wanted to talk to, to sit with. You've been the most constant thing in my life outside of my own family. I don't want to chase a new woman every week. I want you."

Her brow furrowed in consternation. "I…I have to think about this."

He'd never seen her confused before. He didn't like it. She either crushed men under the heel of her boot or pretended they didn't exist. She didn't ask for time to think.

"Wait." He held up his free hand as she started to back away. "Let me show you this. I promised myself I wouldn't keep secrets from you."

He glanced up. A fluffy white cloud had passed over the sun. Perfect. He took a breath, then threw his ball of lightning toward the sky.

The answering thundercloud sent him to his knees. Then the downpour started.

The cloud had turned thick and black as night. Power surged around him, and he had only a moment's warning before lightning slammed down. Instinctively, his hand shot out and caught the bolt. It fizzed over his fingers. He threw it back skyward, just in time to catch another. Then another. He lunged for a third but he was too slow. It slammed down on the fountain and the shell cracked neatly in two.

"Stop!" Leda lunged for him, but he skipped back. His hands were full of lightning and he didn't know what would happen if she touched him. "Make it stop," she screamed over the crash of the storm.

"I can't," he shouted back. He shifted a bolt and raised his hand in a fist. If he couldn't catch the lightning, maybe he could will the lightning to come to him. He could bring it in one strike, and calm the storm. He looked up, and called.

The lightning answered with a vengeance.

It struck his fist with a feeling like pins and needles. His chest swelled with excess energy. Electricity fizzed from the soles of his feet, bursting through his boots and crawling over the grass and broken stones. The lightning burst from his closed hand. Leda had dropped to the ground and covered her head. Trees cracked and split as more lightning grounded on them.

He tried to bring his arms down. He tried to pull the storm into him. But the more he pulled, the more he glowed. He was raw power, he was unstoppable.

And in the midst of it all, Zeus felt…joyful.

This was the weapon he would bring to bear against his enemy. He would whip up the storm and the fire against Kronos, and when he returned to Sherwood a hero, Leda wouldn't have to think about anything anymore.

But Leda was terrified. She gazed at him with unbridled

fear, teeth bared against the wind and the rain and the sound. Her skin glowed red in the light of flames.

This wasn't how it was supposed to be. "Leda," he tried to say, but thunder rumbled, drowning out his words. Her mouth formed around his name, panicked. "Leda!"

Two strong, tanned hands grabbed Leda by the shoulder and pulled her back. Ethan. He gestured wildly. Leda nodded, bestowed one last, wide-eyed look on Zeus, and fled.

Zeus reached for her before he realized what he was doing. Lightning snaked from his fingers and at the last moment, he turned them skyward so that they sprayed the tops of the trees, crowning them with fire. The flash of it blinded him.

When his vision recovered, his father was there.

Ethan was already soaked from the rain. "*Breathe*," he was shouting. Zeus tried, but it was like pouring fuel on the fire. Every breath was electric. He could no longer feel his feet. He was losing the sense of where the storm ended and he began.

Something silver flashed in the light. Zeus felt a searing pain on his arm. Ethan leaned in, the hair on his head and beard rising. "Focus on the pain," he shouted.

The pain. The pain was entirely human. It stung and burned in a familiar way, reminding him of the scrapes and lashes he got in training. Blood dripped to the ground, so dark it was nearly black in the gloomy sky.

Ethan gripped his shoulders and squeezed, hard. He gasped. Rain washed down the back of his neck and hissed as it made contact with the fire around him. "Come on," Ethan said.

"The rain," Zeus gasped. "I have to stop it."

"Let the rain put out your fire," his father said in a cold, clear voice, and pulled him forward. He stumbled and his bare feet kicked loose paving stones. He'd burned the bottoms of his boots right off. Swathes of crisp brown grass emanated from where he'd stood. The fountain was nothing more than a pile of broken stones.

His muscles ached, suddenly, and he sagged. Ethan cursed, then Zeus felt himself leave the ground as his father lifted him.

This wasn't what had happened when Hades got his powers. It wasn't what happened when Atlas got his. "How did I do all that?" he muttered hoarsely. Now that he was out of it, he was exhausted, as though he'd run the length of the forest without stopping for food or rest.

Ethan stomped onto the road. Around them, Zeus heard screams and smelled smoke. The lightning must have been farther-reaching than he'd intended. "The real question is, what did your little display cost us?" Ethan growled.

Zeus didn't make it home before he passed out. He woke up sometime later in his own bed, wearing a nightshirt instead of his soaked clothes and ruined boots. His limbs felt as though they'd been packed with sand. When he tried to push himself up, pain lanced through his skull. He fell back with a groan.

"He's awake," said Poseidon's voice from beside him. His brother's hand squeezed his arm in relief.

"Bring him in," Ethan called from the main room.

Zeus opened his eyes a crack. The light was blinding. "No thanks." He made to pull the blanket over his head, but it was roughly pulled from his body. "Hey!" He curled up in a ball.

"You're lucky I offered to watch over you," said Poseidon. His normally chipper brother sounded like he wanted to hit something. And Zeus had a bad feeling about who he wanted to hit. "Atlas wanted to interrogate you while you were hanging upside down. Hades suggested parading you out in the buff. I'll help you get dressed, at least."

"You'd all regret it if your wives saw me in the buff," Zeus tried to jest. Poseidon glared at him. His jaw worked, but he said nothing.

With Poseidon's help he managed to change into a new shirt and pull on some trousers. His head still ached, but he'd managed to force his eyes open. He reached for a comb to run through his hair, but Poseidon put a hand in the middle of his back and shoved.

"I'm going," he grumbled.

"Don't start," Poseidon snapped.

His entire family waited in the living room. Zeus' heart dropped as he looked from face to stony face. He'd gotten his fair share of lectures, but one of his parents always strived to look understanding, at least. And his brothers usually found such things to be the source of amusement. But no one was laughing now. They all looked exhausted, sad, and scared. A pot of soup sat on the table, with bowls for each of them, but it was clear no one had touched the meal.

He wanted to sit, but he knew he couldn't. He looked to his father. "Is Leda all right?"

Ethan gave a deep sigh. "She is, no thanks to you." He folded his arms. "No one was harmed by your little stunt, though the fire damaged a lot of property. The square you were in will have to be completely demolished—" *not a lot lost there,* Zeus thought sourly—"and lightning struck all the way to the market. It set the sacred tree ablaze."

A knot of dread hardened in Zeus' belly. "Is it…?" He couldn't bring himself to ask.

"We're optimistic. The crown suffered great damage, and one of the branches had to be removed. Luckily, it's not so easy to destroy a sacred tree."

Silence descended for a moment. Zeus' stomach churned.

"What happened to your promise?" Hades said. He held baby Achilles in his arms. The gentle way he bounced the child felt at odds with the rage that radiated from him. "Your promise to keep our secrets? To train with us, and no one else?"

"I don't need a lecture from everyone, and I don't need two fathers," Zeus said, already tired.

"Yes, you do." This came from his mother, of all people. Her jaw was tight with anger, her lips pale. "You don't understand, Zeus. You don't have the *first idea* what you've done."

"Tell me, then," Zeus snapped. Atlas moved forward, raising a hand, and Zeus put his own up in surrender. This was his fault, he knew it. He had to take his punishment like a man. He took a deep breath and tried to make his voice neutral. "Tell me so I can make it right."

"You can't make it right," Ethan said. His face sagged, and for the first time, Zeus realized how much gray threaded through his father's hair. "It's too late for that." His shoulders stooped, as though they carried the weight of the world. He began to pace. "Kronos' spies on the edge of Sherwood would have caught wind of the storm. It was obviously supernatural, and indicative of a powerful magical being. They'll report back to Kronos that someone is hiding here, someone with the power to threaten him. From there, it won't be long before people start remembering the incident with Hades and Typhon in the market. You're no longer safe here. In fact, Sherwood City is terminated as the headquarters of the Cross of the Iron Phoenix, as of now." He stopped mid-stride, still as a statue, and Zeus saw his throat bob as he fought to keep down his emotion. "We're disbanding."

Zeus collapsed in a chair. Shock stole his ability to stand, his very ability to breathe. "Disbanding?" he whispered.

"Until we can find a new safe space, we have to ground all operatives. All missions are cancelled until further notice. Any spies who are out on an assignment will have to find their own way of extraction. Some of us will have to take on new identities, as our departure from the forest will be seen as odd. This sets us back years. Do you realize that? *Years.*" He shouted this last word, and Zeus found himself recoiling. His father had been angry with him before, but he'd never shouted.

Silence reigned once more. Zeus couldn't bring himself to meet anyone's eye. He stared at a knot in one of the floorboards, wishing that one of his brothers had the power to turn back time. He'd always been impulsive, and it had always gotten him in trouble. But never like this.

"Why did you do it?" Poseidon asked at last, and more gently than Zeus deserved. Zeus gathered the courage to look at him. His brother's aquamarine eyes were full of sorrow and confusion.

"I had to tell Leda. I…" It sounded so stupid, now that it was out in the open. "We don't keep secrets from each other."

"And you had to tell her like that?" Hades said, in a voice that flatly belied his disbelief.

"I wanted her to see for herself," Zeus said in a small voice.

Atlas threw up his hands. "Say it," he snarled. "You wanted to impress her. You've been in love with her for so long that you didn't even know how to say it like a normal person."

"That's not true," Zeus lashed back.

"No? Everyone's ready to admit it but you," Hades jumped in. His voice was so cold it sent a shiver down Zeus' body. "She's practically one of us already, Zeus. Did you think you could call up a little parlor trick and get her to swoon like everyone else you've ever fancied? You risked it all, and you failed, and I can't even understand why."

Zeus opened his mouth to answer—and closed it again. The truth was, he didn't know, either. He only knew that the man he'd been wasn't enough for Leda. So, he'd resolved to show her the man he could be.

He thought of her eyes, shining with fear the last time she'd seen him. Her shoulders as she turned her back and ran into the woods. *Great success,* he told himself bitterly. She'd never want to speak with him again, and to make matters worse his brothers were going to go into hiding, as well. He'd just lost everyone he'd ever cared about.

"I *will* make this right," he said, casting about for an answer. "I can give myself up, say I was acting alone—"

"You can't." Ethan threw his hands up. "Haven't you understood anything? Your destiny is tied to your brothers'. Do you truly think that Kronos won't investigate all of us if he finds you?"

Good point. Zeus swallowed. "Then what do I do?"

"You leave." Raven wiped a tear from her eye. "All you must leave. Your father said it once, and I won't make him say it again. The Cross is disbanded. You will head out of the forest, ostensibly seeking your fortunes. We can forge letters of employment for you as a last assignment. Then the best we can do is wait, all of us, for our chance to come around again."

\#\#\#

Zeus was the first to go. He deserved it, after all. He packed his bags, strapped his knives to his person, and took his staff. He'd grown to like the weapon, and it made a good walking tool. He shook each brother by the hand and kissed each sister-in-law on the cheek.

"I'm sorry," he said to each of them.

Hades wouldn't look at him, but Persephone gave him a tight hug. "We'll come see you in your new place," she whispered.

Ethan gripped his arm and pulled him into a hug, too. "Everyone makes mistakes," he said, and though he did not smile there was a sliver of compassion in his gaze. "The important thing is to learn. To be a better man today than you were yesterday. And keep training. Your power is deadly, but that's only useful if you can control it."

Zeus dipped his head. Then he turned to Raven. She handed him a forged letter of employment, which he tucked in his bag. He was going to be a member of the guard in Centennial City. "Your brothers are angry now, but don't let this drive a wedge between you forever," she said. "Write to them. Often."

"I'll try," Zeus said. Raven gave him a stern look and he choked on his laugh. What if this was the last time he saw her? What if it was his last chance to earn a look like that? "I'll write," he promised.

"We'll come see you when the baby's born," Atlas said. Zeus' jaw went slack. "Yes, yes. It's still early days, but we think we'll have a little one in the early spring." He flapped a hand. He still looked dour, but Zeus recognized the press of his lips. He was trying not to smile.

Ivy put a hand on her belly and smiled for them both, shyly. "And she'll have to know her fun uncle," she said.

"And if we're in luck, she'll share a birthday with her little cousin," Diana added. She exchanged a small smile with Poseidon. "Family is family, no matter what."

Family is family. And he'd torn his apart.

There wasn't much else to say. He swallowed the lump in his throat and headed down the stairs. He pulled on his new pair of boots, then opened the door, marveling at the way sunlight slanted through the crack and sent dust swirling through the air. He wondered what the air would look like in Centennial. This might be the last time he saw the clean, bright forest sunshine. This might be the last time he saw their front yard, their woven stick fence. It might be the last time he looked upon their cheerful red door, the door he'd repainted last year. It might be the last look he ever took of Sherwood City—

And it might be the last look he got at Leda, who stood right beyond the fence.

She was dressed practically, as usual, in brown and green, wool and leather. Her hair was wound about her head in dozens of tiny braids. She wore a short sword at her hip and a pack on her back.

"Where are we going?" she said.

This was too much. His whole world had been turned upside-down in the past few days, and now he had to confront his best friend. He hadn't seen Leda since the storm, and hadn't thought she wanted to see him. He'd been trying to come to terms with the fact that he'd never see her again. And now…

"I'm going to Centennial City," he replied. "Got a job." Maybe when he was settled, he could earn leave and visit his parents. Maybe Leda would come around then.

"Hm." She cocked her head and pursed her lips. "I don't know anything about Centennial City. Guess we'll have to learn by doing. Best way to do it."

Zeus reached for her hand, then tucked his own behind his back. There was no need to make things more awkward than they already were. He wanted no secrets, no dishonesty, no unfinished business between them when he left. "I'm sorry. I put your life in danger and I ruined everything because…because I thought I had to impress you. Now the Cross is disbanding because of me, and everyone has to move away, and… well, thank you for coming to say goodbye."

Leda was smiling at him. And it was her exasperated smile, her *you're being an idiot* smile. Against all odds, Zeus felt his heart lift. "What do you think all this is for?" She gestured to her pack. "Extended camping trip in the woods?"

"You can't possibly be dropping your whole life to come with me," Zeus said, incredulous. He kicked himself mentally, he should stop talking and let her come—but he couldn't. He'd promised her honesty, and she would get it. "You had to 'think about things'."

"I thought. And when your father told me the news, I

thought some more. And I realized that if I don't come with you to Centennial City, you're going to get yourself stabbed or married at sword point. Honestly, it's going to be exhausting looking after you."

Her smile had broadened. Her golden-brown eyes raked over him slyly and for the first time in a long time, Zeus blushed.

Chapter Thirteen: Everything Together

The baby girl wailed in Atlas' arms. He bounced her gently, blinking away the tears that stubbornly sprung to his eyes.

"Everything looks healthy," said Diana as she finished examining the baby. She smiled at him. "Congratulations. She's perfect."

She hobbled over to a chair, supporting her own swollen belly, and Poseidon leapt to assist her. Their child was due in a matter of days, but she'd still insisted on coming to Labyrinth City to assist Atlas and Ivy with the birth of their girl. Poseidon had to admit, he was glad. Atlas and Ivy knew precious few in Labyrinth, and he'd gotten lost every time he'd tried to go out into the city. He was also relieved that Atlas and Ivy had opened their home in anticipation for Diana's birth. Poseidon had found a house for them on the banks of the River of Life, and they didn't have many neighbors who could help them if something went wrong during labor.

There was plenty of time to worry later—not that he was worried. For now, he stroked his wife's glossy black hair and said, "Curfew is soon. Do we need anything from the market?"

Diana dictated a list as Atlas took his baby girl over to Ivy, then gave him a farewell kiss that lingered on his lips long after he left the apartment. Curfew had been imposed on Labyrinth City not long after the Cross had disbanded, and it was hard to shake the feeling that the two things were connected. Poseidon hadn't managed to visit Sherwood since moving away. Ethan and Raven came to them, once, and Ethan had warned him that Kronos had started the search for the four brothers. Perhaps it was this knowledge that had him slinking into every shadow as he headed down the high-walled streets of the city. Or perhaps it was the fact that he came across four members of the city guard in two blocks. They were big men, burly, and bristling with knives and spears. He spotted a crossbow on one man's back. He knew the guards were always strongly armed in Labyrinth City; they were nervous about the Minotaurs who lived in the bowels of the great maze. But he couldn't help but be reminded of Typhon, and the brutality he brought to Sherwood. What sort of world were they bringing this little girl into? A few years ago, their futures had been secure and bright and obvious. They were supposed to lead a grand resistance, face off against Kronos, and make a whole new Olympus.

But the Cross of the Iron Phoenix was all but disbanded. Nothing had happened for so long. And the more things stagnated, the more Poseidon wondered if he really wanted them to change. He had a perfect wife and a child on the way. Life on the banks of the River wasn't as wonderful as life in Sherwood had been, but they'd started making friends and engaging in trade on the waters. Their son or daughter would grow up swimming like a fish instead of climbing like a squirrel. And they weren't so far from his brothers. He could see himself growing old in his house, sitting on the pier while his children ran boats up and down the river, catching fish for dinner every night and hosting their cousins each week. Sure, taxes were high and pointless, and they turned out all the lights when an armed expedition forged the river once a month. They had to watch their mouths and be careful of their neighbors. But no life was perfect, and he had a feeling that this was as close as he was going to get.

He stopped in at the apothecary and bought willow bark and yarrow, earning a knowing look from the apothecary. Then he picked up rice, flour, some essentials, and a fat stack of honey cakes as a treat. As he shouldered his way back through the door of Atlas' tiny apartment, he couldn't help but grimace. He and Diana might live in the middle of nowhere, but at least he could stand up straight in his own house. He thought wistfully of their tree home in Sherwood, of its broad trunk, of all the space to run outside.

"Your girl's going to grow up short," he joked as he came into the kitchen. At the sight of Diana's pale face, he stopped. "What's wrong?"

She stood by the sink with a hand on her belly. "Just a bit of discomfort."

Poseidon knew better than to believe her. Diana never let a bit of discomfort show. "Is it the baby?" he asked in a low voice, leaning in.

She let out a strained laugh, dark eyes crinkling. "Which one?" she joked.

Atlas came out of the bedroom before Poseidon could pry further. His face was drawn, and there were deep circles under his eyes. "Tell me you brewed tea. And that we have something stronger to put in tea."

Diana nodded to the kitchen table, where a pot sat under a cloth. Atlas poured two cups and took one to Ivy. The second he doctored with a liberal splash of liquor, then sat with a sigh and leaned back. "You're certain she'll be all right?"

"Are you doubting my wife's abilities?" Poseidon bristled.

Diana waved him off. "Don't get touchy, dear. It's natural. Ivy's birth went very smoothly, even if it didn't look that way." Her mouth twisted and her hand went to her belly again.

Poseidon forced himself to take a deep breath. He imagined his irritation as the tide, going out, leaving peace in its wake. "What will you name her?" he asked.

"Maia." Atlas smiled fondly down at the table. "Little Maia. She has her mother's hair already."

"And your eyes," Diana added. Then she let out a strangled cry.

Poseidon was next to her in an instant. "What's wrong?"

She gripped his hand so hard he felt his bones grind together. "It's the baby."

"It's coming, isn't it?" he said. Diana nodded.

"Fetch a doctor," he told Atlas.

Diana shook her head. "It's nearly curfew—"

"The guard will have to let you through. It's an emergency!"

Diana was still protesting, but Atlas was already scraping his chair back and grabbing his coat. Poseidon nodded gratefully. He'd always been able to count on his brother. He helped Diana stand again. "Now, tell me what to do."

He spent the next hour collecting all the spare bedding in the house and putting it on their bed. Diana insisted on checking on Ivy one last time as he boiled rags and prepared raspberry leaf tea. And with every passing minute, his blood fizzed ever stronger. Where on Olympus was Atlas?

"Don't worry." Diana lay back on the pillows. "Fetch me a scissors. I can do it myself."

The big man dragged himself back through the door close to midnight. A bruise was starting to puff up on one dark cheek, and his knuckles were bloody. His green eyes flashed with anger as he shook his head. "No doctor," he spat.

"What?" Poseidon yelped. Then he stopped, coughed, and gently moved Atlas away from where Diana practiced her breathing exercises. "What do you mean, no doctor?" he continued in a low voice.

Atlas looked like he wanted to smash his fist on the table, but he settled for wiping his bloody hands on a rag. "The guard wouldn't let me through. Said there were no exceptions. I thought I could get past him anyway, but six of his cowardly friends jumped me." His lip curled. "They barely got away."

Poseidon's heart began to drum a frantic beat. "But what if something happens? What if she bleeds out? What if the baby won't...emerge?"

"Curfew lifts in six hours. I'll run for the doctor first thing.

How's Ivy?"

"I'm fine, and so's Maia." Ivy stood in the door to their bedroom, looking rumpled and rosy. Little Maia was tucked in a sling against her chest. "Let's all focus on Diana, all right?" She moved through the kitchen and over to Diana's side.

"You should keep exercise to a minimum," Diana murmured.

Ivy took her hand. "Hush, you. Now what were you telling me at this point?"

Diana was calm, though her nostrils flared with pain. She shooed Atlas away and directed Ivy as she brought her legs up in preparation. "Get ready," she told Poseidon.

He caught the child, a squalling, tan baby boy. The boy was laid on his mother's breast, and the umbilical cord was cut. Ivy bit her lip as she inspected Diana. "I don't think you're in danger," she said uncertainly.

"I'm fine," Diana replied. "We'll fetch the doctor in the morning. Here." She shifted the baby over to Poseidon. "Perseus, meet your father."

A tiny fist shook in the air. Poseidon caught it, and his son's tiny fingers wrapped around one of his own. His heart swelled like the sea. "Perseus," he murmured. Wonder shivered over him. "My boy."

He didn't think he could be more in love than he was in that moment. Emotion brimmed over in him. Tears welled in the corners of his eyes. He forgot the rebellion, he forgot his destiny. He forgot everything except the tiny figure in the crook of his arm. He heard a distant roar, and a moment later, a curse. Atlas shouted from the kitchen. "The fountain outside *exploded.*"

"Poseidon?" Diana was looking at him, a mix of wonder and worry on her face. "You're glowing."

###

The doctor came in the morning and professed Diana to be in excellent health. He looked irritated to have been dragged from his bed, but was quickly mollified by a cup of tea and a shot of mead that Poseidon had brewed before they set out. "It's the streets," he confessed when he was in a better mood. "They're teeming with people. It looks like every fountain in the city broke, all at once. What could do that?"

Atlas and Poseidon tried very hard not to look at each other.

"It's likely some new trick. Either that or an action against the Minotaurs that went terribly wrong." The doctor sighed and wiped his glasses on his coat. "Why we have to be at war with them is beyond me. I've lived here thirty-four years, and never once had a problem with a Minotaur. Well, except the ones that work for—ahem." He cut his eyes at the brothers, then nodded curtly. "I'll be going."

"We'll travel home as soon as we can," Poseidon promised when the doctor had gone.

"Why rush? We have the room," Atlas replied.

Poseidon snorted. He and Diana were sleeping on a

mattress in the living room, and the tiny kitchen was the only place they could socialize. Atlas barely fit in the kitchen all by himself. When all four of them were there, they literally rubbed shoulders. To say it was cozy was to willfully misread the situation. "Maybe you should come with us," Poseidon suggested. "Lie low after your scuffle with the guard."

Atlas waved him off. "It was hardly a scuffle."

"It was a full-on beating, seven to one." Poseidon snorted. "How many did you take down before they got you?"

Atlas grinned. "Seven. You know no one gets the better of me."

Ivy rolled her eyes as she moved between them, bouncing Maia up and down in a woven sling. "Honestly, you two. As though scrapping in the street like schoolboys is an honor."

"When it's for a good cause, it is an honor," Atlas replied. "You'll be glad of my scrapping skills when I'm teaching Maia how to beat up her bullies."

"*I'll* be teaching Maia how to beat up her bullies," Ivy said, wagging a finger. "From a distance, with a bow."

"She needs to be able to throw a good punch, too," Atlas argued.

"She'll never have to. People will be too afraid of her shooting to ever touch her." Ivy stroked her daughter's russet hair.

Poseidon had to laugh. With two such willful parents, Maia would be a force of nature.

Three quick raps sounded on their front door. The three of them exchanged worried glances. Had the doctor returned?

Was there bad news? Or perhaps the guard had tracked down the man who'd taken out half a patrol last night.

"Let me," Ivy said in a low voice. Still bouncing the baby, she went over to the door, opening it a crack. "She's sleeping," she began in a low voice. "Oh. Thank you."

She turned back as the door shut. "Mail," she explained, holding up an envelope.

It was the rough, undyed brown of paper made in Sherwood. And it had their father's handwriting on it.

Atlas opened the letter with a knife and began to read aloud. The letter was written in code, to account for the fact that Typhon had almost certainly had it opened and scanned for evidence of sedition.

Dearest Nephew,

I write to you with the hope of congratulating you on the birth of your child, though I have heard nothing yet. Your aunt and I very much look forward to meeting your new family and enjoying the spirit of a lively child.

We would love to invite you to visit our home —

"Perfect," said Ivy.

Atlas' brow furrowed. "I'm not so sure." He continued.

We would love to invite you to visit our home, so that we might discuss a new business opportunity. I have recently begun a sawmill operation and believe that transporting the lumber to Labyrinth City could be a lucrative contract.

Atlas looked up. "Operation Sawmill. That's the code for trouble."

"Big trouble." Poseidon's fingers tapped on the table. This was going to be a problem.

Ivy pulled Maia close. "What does that mean?" she asked.

Poseidon looked down at the table, tracing the whorls of wood with one finger. Atlas had made this table himself, carefully working through it with his magic so that it was stable and shone like gold in the soft light of morning. He'd built his whole life like he'd built this table: with care, precision and love.

"It means we go visit our father. It's about time we went back to Sherwood. We'll find out what's wrong, and how we can fix it."

Ivy buried her nose in her daughter's hair. Her blue eyes were solemn, swirling with a mix of fear and resolve. "All right." She kissed the top of Maia's head, and Poseidon saw a certain sorrow in her gaze.

"You shouldn't go," he said.

Ivy looked at him strangely. But Atlas was nodding in agreement. "You and Diana should stay. It's still too early to travel after the birth. And if something is wrong—"

"I can take care of myself," Ivy said, quickly and coldly.

"But who will take care of Maia?" Poseidon asked.

Her retort died on her lips. She'd clearly intended to go as a family, but why risk it? She turned to Atlas. "We go everywhere together. Ever since we met. We've been on assignments, on stakeouts…"

Atlas slipped one of her small hands between his two great ones. "I'll be back soon. You'll be responsible for making sure Diana is safe and comfortable, too. But if our father's in as much trouble as his letter suggests, we can't risk taking any innocents into the forest."

She took a deep breath, and for a moment Poseidon was certain she'd argue with him. Instead, she sighed. "You're right. But I don't like it. I don't want you running off into potential danger the week after you've become a father."

Atlas pressed his forehead to hers, and Poseidon took his leave.

Diana was much more practical than Ivy about it. "Of course, you have to go," she said when he explained the situation. She was looking well-rested and lovely. Color had returned to her cheeks and lips, and her dark eyes crinkled up at the corners as she looked at their son. He was sleeping peacefully, full of milk. "And of course, we have to stay. I'll give you a list of supplies that you can bring home from Sherwood."

Poseidon leaned into her. She smelled of sweat and blood, but her lips were sweet beneath his. "You won't even notice we're gone."

She smiled against his mouth. "Nonsense. I'll miss you every minute, and not only because I'll be changing diapers by myself."

Chapter Fourteen: Too Much To Lose

Atlas started seeing the signs of Kronos' cruelty as they came to the boundaries of Sherwood City two days later. The stones that had once neatly paved the streets were cracked and uneven. Some of them had been pulled up and no one had bothered to replace them, leaving gaping furrows in the ground that made for treacherous walking. He and Poseidon passed a torched house in what had obviously been a carefully controlled fire. The people of Sherwood no longer had greetings and cheer to spare; those they met on the road kept their heads down and their hands tucked before them, as if they were trying to make themselves smaller targets. When Atlas tried to greet an old acquaintance the man sped away from him, as if they'd never known each other and Atlas was some kind of hoodlum.

The main square was in total disarray. Half the shops were closed; one had a broken window and looked as though no one had been inside of it for weeks. There were no vendors on the square, nor anyone strolling around it. The stage had been repainted in red and black, the colors of the tyrant, Kronos. The usual riot of plants and flowers that lined the edge of the market were twisted and brown, despite the gorgeous spring weather.

Strange statues lined the square. They were marble, and they showed off people in various poses—most of them cowering, Atlas noted. Their faces were highly detailed and suffused with terror. Whoever had carved them had done an exquisite job. And had terrible taste.

But the worst was the sacred tree.

The tree's leaves had turned black as the void, and strange white berries clustered on their branches like pustules. Iron cages hung from the high, strong branches. And in those cages…

"What the…?" whispered Poseidon from beside him. Their sacred tree had been defiled and turned into a gibbet. Atlas saw a skeletal hand emerging from the bottom of one cage, as though its owner had died reaching for his freedom. Scraps of clothing fluttered in the wind, and a foul scent drifted down to them.

A long rope hung from each gibbet, and to that rope was attached a sign. Atlas came closer and examined the first one.

THE REMAINS OF THE TRAITOR AND OUTLAW BARDON SULLIE, read the sign. Cold washed over Atlas. He looked up. Nothing remained that could identify the man.

Poseidon nudged him. "Control yourself," he whispered. Atlas looked down. Frost spread around him in a sunburst pattern, spreading across the brown grass and curling up the edge of a pot that had once held geraniums. He huffed and spread warmth over the space, melting the frost and softening the ground. He let a carefully controlled dribble of power flow through his feet and spread throughout the square. In a few weeks' time, new grass would grow here, but it would be too late to connect it to the way he stood here today.

It was a start, but a poor one. It was almost nothing.

Atlas looked at every sign hanging from every gibbet. All the men were Outlaws, and strung up for the crimes of treason, thievery, and murder. Atlas had to wonder what had happened here. Harper O'Donovan had always had a strong policy against killing anyone.

"Let's go," Poseidon said in a low voice. "We're drawing attention to ourselves."

Indeed, a guard on the edge of the square watched, suspicion growing on his face. "Friends of yours?" he called.

Yes. Atlas' fists clenched. He could take one idiot guard. But Poseidon put a hand on his shoulder and squeezed in warning.

"We're new in town," Poseidon explained in his cheerful, friendly voice. "We wanted to see what sort of criminals we might have to deal with."

"None, anymore. Where are you staying?"

"We've got an uncle here," Poseidon replied.

"Well, get to your uncle. And don't let the boss catch you being too curious," he said.

"The boss?" Poseidon murmured as they started walking again. "Who do you think the Boss is?"

"Has to be Typhon." Typhon had been Kronos' representative for Sherwood City for as long as Atlas could remember. As a Chimeric Beast his lifespan was a bit of a mystery—he obviously had a longer one than the average Olympian, and Atlas had never noticed the usual signs of aging. Perhaps Chimeric Beasts lived until they got killed.

Maybe Atlas should have taken care of Typhon a long

time ago.

The road out of the square was lined with more terrible statues. When had they had time to put all these up? Atlas wondered. And how had they paid for it?

"Lord have mercy." Poseidon had stopped dead. Atlas bumped into him.

"What?" He reached for his sword before remembering he hadn't packed it. He had a knife strapped to his back, under his shirt, but chances were the guard was still watching them and drawing a weapon would blow their cover. He settled for making fists.

Poseidon stared at one of the statues. It was of a young man, recoiling, with his hands up before his face as though he could ward off whatever fate faced him. His mouth was open in a grimace and his eyes were wide. He was larger than most of the statues around here, almost as tall as Atlas himself.

Atlas looked again.

The boots were scuffed and worn in a way that true marble could never represent. Stray hair fluffed over part of the man's cheek, a spot he'd missed when shaving. And the expression in his eyes…no sculpture could master that. Not the greatest master on Olympus.

"This is no manmade statue," he realized.

"Let's go." Poseidon took his arm again and started to walk. "Whatever did that is *not* coming for us. Dad will fill us in."

Atlas could do nothing but follow, dumbstruck.

Hades opened the door to them as they came scurrying into the yard. "Quickly," he said, shutting the door so fast he nearly caught Atlas' finger in it. Once they'd taken off their packs and boots, he gave them each a brief but strong hug. "Zeus is already here," he said, face somber. "There's a lot to talk about."

The house still smelled of fresh bread, and despite the circumstances of their arrival, Atlas felt his body unwind. He could almost pretend he was a kid again, coming home from a long day of training to warm stew and happy company. Indeed, a big pot sat on the table, surrounded by bowls and looking untouched.

Ethan and Raven broke out into smiles and came forward to hug Atlas and Poseidon. Ethan's smile was lopsided, showing off a few broken teeth. Raven's was bittersweet. "We're glad you came," she said as they took their spots around the table. "Though we lament the circumstances."

"What happened to Sherwood?" Zeus said. "You said you'd tell us when we were all together, so let's hear it."

"Why don't we let your brothers settle in a bit?" Ethan suggested. "Drink off the dust of the road."

"I'm settled enough," Atlas replied. Poseidon looked like he wanted to argue, but he nodded instead.

Ethan looked from one boy to the other, sighing. He looked to be lost for words, a rare occasion for him. "Holding back will do nothing for us now," Hades prompted gently.

"We need to know what's going on."

Ethan looked helplessly at his wife. "Kronos is what's going on," Raven explained. Her voice was even, as though she were laying out a regular report for the Cross. "He identified Sherwood City as the most likely spot for you to be living not long after the four of you left. Typhon ransacked it, set a good number of houses on fire, and put the city under martial law. It's been that way ever since. We had to learn to keep our heads down and abide by curfews, but for a while that was it…until Kronos decided to test his newest peacekeeper on us."

"Her name is Medusa," Ethan said, finally getting his voice back. "She's an experiment, born out of the mind of Typhon and his chief alchemist, Echidna. She's…"

"Terrifying?" asked Hades.

"Horrible?" said Zeus.

"Monstrous?" suggested Atlas.

"Beautiful," Ethan replied. The brothers blinked at each other. "And therein is the problem. She's so beautiful that men can't help but look at her. And if she meets their gaze, she turns them to stone."

"With Medusa in the forest, we can do nothing," Raven said. "We can barely hunt to feed ourselves. Forget the idea of meeting to plan anything, or to try to escape, or to move what's left of the Cross's resources. Our efforts here have come to a standstill. No one wants to stick their neck out, because we've all seen what happens when we do. Almost half the city's been petrified."

"*Half?*" Atlas clutched his spoon so hard it bent over his thumb. "We didn't see anywhere near half on the way here. Where's she keeping them all?"

"The best-looking ones go to Novaris, where they line the road up to his palace." Ethan bared his teeth in a grim smile.

They were silent for a good while. Zeus puffed air out of his cheeks, sending a miniature whirlwind across the table. He felt different to Atlas, too—less boyish, more mature. The look in his eye was one of consideration. "So why did you call us all here?" he said.

Ethan and Raven exchanged a look. Raven stood up. "Your father and I can no longer effectively run the rebellion," she said. "It's time to pass the mantle."

Yes. The sense of despair that had infused all of Sherwood had tried to take hold of Atlas as well, but his mother's words helped to shake it off. There was a solution to all of this. There was a way. He nodded.

But as he looked around the table, he failed to see his enthusiasm reflected in the faces of his brothers. Hades was looking down at his bowl, frowning. Poseidon twirled his spoon on the table. Zeus was uncharacteristically still.

Hades had always been the leader. Surely he was just thinking of what to say. Atlas pushed down his words and forced himself to wait.

Hades sat with his own thoughts for several long moments. Then his maroon eyes flicked up to find every gaze at the table leveled on him. He flashed a brief, humorless smile.

"I have a son," he said.

Atlas blinked. "And? Ivy gave birth too, a few days ago. And Diana." He realized too late that perhaps he should have let Poseidon break that news. But Poseidon was nodding, a broad grin breaking out over his face.

"So, three of us have sons and daughters. Obligations in this world that are larger than ourselves."

Raven dropped her head. Ethan was nodding as though he understood, though he looked fifteen years older than he had at the start of this conversation. But disbelief simmered beneath Atlas' skin. For years they'd spoken of their destinies. Of the need for someone to do something, *anything* about Kronos, the dictator of Olympus. When Typhon roughed up the marketplace, they daydreamed of defeating him. When the tax wagons came through the forest and Harper O'Donovan had raided them, they'd marveled at all the money that had been stolen from the common man to build another great palace or another high wall. "We've *always* had obligations that are greater than ourselves," he said. His voice rose, impassioned, and even though Ethan shot him a warning look he couldn't control it. "We've always had this destiny. How long are we supposed to wait to fulfill it?"

"Things are different than when we were boys," Hades argued. "When I had no responsibilities, it was easy to play at being the hero. And if I'd died, I wouldn't have left behind a widow and a child."

"How many widows did that *hag* make when she came to Sherwood?" Atlas was standing now. "If we'd acted before now, we might have saved them. Does their deaths mean nothing to you?"

Hades pushed back from the table so hard he knocked his chair to the ground. "Don't you dare act like I don't care. I've seen friends, and noble people, and dedicated members of the Cross in those statues. And I hate that they died, but it wasn't my fault and nothing will bring them back. Do you think they'd want us to sacrifice ourselves for whatever remains of them?"

"Maybe they would have liked a little help first," Atlas snarled. Thorns burst all along the edge of the table. Zeus jerked back in alarm and Poseidon made a small noise as a thorn pierced his thumb.

"Enough!" Ethan clapped his hands together in a sudden, startling sound. "We've lost ordinary men and women, we've lost over half the Outlaws, and we've lost our way. Those members of the Cross who remained in Sherwood knew that they were taking a risk. More importantly, they had the choice to stay or go. I'm giving that choice to all of you. Our dreams of freedom are, perhaps, farther away than they've ever been. But they'll never die, not as long as even one person on Olympus longs to be free. If you're in, your mother and I will hand over what we have on Kronos and the Cross, and help you smuggle it out of the forest. If you're out, you may enjoy our company and our food and leave when you like. And you may always return. You are my sons, first and foremost."

Silence reigned. Atlas and Hades stared at each other. Animosity thickened the air between them. But at last Hades took a deep breath and opened his hands, wiggling his fingers. Atlas ran his finger along his side of the table, and the thorns vanished. Raven picked up the ladle and began to scoop soup into each bowl. "All right, then," she said. "Tell me about the babies. Boys or girls?"

The conversation was stilted and awkward at first. Atlas couldn't remember the last time he'd fought with his brother. He'd been more prone to arguments with Zeus, or physical fights with Poseidon. And most often it had been them against the world. But now…it was as though the world had ceased to make sense. Hades, so drawn to responsibility and duty, was turning away from the destiny he'd held close for years. Zeus had seen their destiny as a point of pride, a mark of what made them special. But he hadn't even looked at Atlas during their argument, much less backed him up. And Atlas knew that his almost-twin was thinking of his own boy back home, and wondering what sort of life Perseus would have if they took over leading the Cross in earnest.

Yet the lack of a coherent rebellion had made the situation in Sherwood what it was. If they'd still been strong, would they have been able to stop Typhon and Echidna before they hatched this monster? And how much worse would things get? What other horrid creatures did these two monstrosities have up their sleeves?

After lunch, Atlas went back to his old room. His bed was made up as if he'd only left it yesterday, his books and childhood toys neatly stacked on the dresser that had held his clothes. He picked up a wooden horse and sat on his bed. The mattress sagged beneath his weight. The horse had been carved by his father and the wood was worn smooth from years of play.

The door opened and his mother slipped in. Raven had gained a lot of gray hair since Atlas had moved away; her face was thinner and her mouth tended to turn down instead of up. But her dark eyes were as sharp as ever, and when she smiled it was the same motherly smile he'd always known.

"You're being hard on yourself," she said. "I can see it in your face."

He turned the horse over and over in his fingers. "I'm strong," he said. It might be a brag, but it was true. "I'm powerful. I'm destined for something great, and I want to achieve it. And what have I been doing for the past seven months? Sitting around. I work as a private guard in Labyrinth City and protect some fat merchant who does deals with all Kronos' generals and gets rich off the suffering of people like me."

"No one is like you, my son." Raven slipped an arm around his shoulders.

Atlas scrubbed at one eye. "The longer we wait, the more we'll suffer. And yes, Hades has a child. What sort of world does he want the boy to grow up in? A world where he could be turned to stone? A world where he could be killed for speaking his mind and calling out injustice?"

His mother lay her head on his shoulder. "I can't pretend I don't understand you. But I sympathize with Hades, too. When your father and I agreed to take you all in, we spoke about it at length, for many nights. You had a destiny, but you were so small. The best way to prepare you for your destiny was to raise you as members of the Cross, yet that meant putting you in constant danger. When your mother brought Zeus to us, we suddenly had four bright, brilliant sons. And I wanted to stop. Give up everything to do with the Cross of the Iron Phoenix and live as a normal family.

"That…doesn't seem like you." Atlas had never seen his mother unshakeable in her loyalty to the cause.

"Well, I said the same things your brother said. That our greatest duty was to our children, that we needed to be there for them. That others could get themselves killed, others who didn't have such a responsibility. For there is no responsibility greater than raising your daughter, Atlas." Her hand found his and squeezed it. "But your father was of your mind. He wanted to make the world a better place, and he wanted to make sure you had the tools to do it. Eventually, we chose to raise you as honored members of the Cross, as you know. In large part, it was because we knew your birth mother would have wanted it. And once the decision was made, I honored it."

"What would you do now?" Atlas asked. Now things were more dangerous, but that made action more urgent as well.

"I can't make your decisions for you. Neither can Hades. But remember that your brothers aren't bad just because they've changed their minds. They're struggling, as we did, with how to balance their lives as parents and warriors. Every choice you make requires sacrifice, and only you can decide whether a sacrifice is worth the reward."

He nodded. Raven squeezed him once more, then stood to leave him with his thoughts. "Maia's a nice name, by the way," she said gently. He nodded, but his thoughts were already far away. He barely heard her close the door.

\#\#\#

"We can always revisit the idea in a few years," Zeus said. It was later that evening, and the brothers sat in the living room with mugs of ale and a rare moment of peace. Ethan and Raven had retired for the night, perhaps to give them an extra chance to talk.

"A few years?" Atlas stared at him. "You can't even wait five minutes when you want something."

Zeus shrugged and smiled ruefully. "I know. But that's what made me realize how different things are now. I can't wait for my son to be born. I *can* wait to fulfil my destiny."

Son? "Leda's pregnant?" Poseidon said.

"Five months. I couldn't keep the news to myself, I told Hades and Mom and Dad as soon as we arrived."

"It was all he could talk about, really." Hades shot Zeus a fond but irritated look. "Your arrival saved us from a life-or-death conversation about what color to paint the nursery."

"You have room for a nursery?" Atlas was only a little jealous. Only a little. But he turned back to the matter at hand. He didn't think they could wait. "What is life going to look like in a few years?" he asked.

Hades shrugged. "Another child, maybe. Work." Poseidon and Zeus were nodding.

"We have work. And what if life in Lumina ends up like life in Sherwood? With people too afraid to go outside or meet their friends? With human statues, everywhere you turn?" Atlas' blood was starting to sing again. His brothers simply didn't get it.

Hades drained his cup, then looked frankly at Atlas. "Let me ask you a question. What will happen to Ivy and Maia if you die?"

Atlas looked down at his knees. "Ivy's a hunter, she can take care of herself—"

"And Maia? Do you want your daughter to grow up with no memory of you?"

"We're strong, and we're powerful. We've never met an enemy we couldn't defeat, *especially* if we work together," Atlas argued.

"We've never taken on enemies like these, either," Poseidon pointed out. He cringed under Atlas' furious glare. "Sorry."

"We're not invincible, Atlas. Stop acting like you are," Hades told him. "Think about your wife. Does she want you dead in some hare-brained scheme to bring down a tyrant we've never even been able to get close to? When you married her, you swore to love and protect her. Could you really disappoint her like that? Leave her grieving like that?"

Atlas clenched his jaw. "That's low," he told his brother.

He couldn't imagine Ivy in grief. The hours she'd spent

in pain in childbirth had been some of the worst hours of his life. And if he were the cause of her pain…a cause that wouldn't go away, but would strike at her again and again, for years if not forever…was anything worth it? Even the cause?

"The Cross needs us," he said to his cup, for he couldn't stand to look into his brothers' eyes.

"Everyone needs us, for one thing or another. Your family needs you most," Hades said. "Stay with them. Too much has changed, and we don't have the strength to fight it. Zeus is right: in a few years we can see where we are, and whether we're ready."

There was a moment of silence. Then Zeus said, "Hang on, hang on. Repeat that. I'm *right?*"

Atlas and Poseidon left again two days later. Both of them were eager to get back to their new families, but Atlas couldn't help feeling like a disappointment as he hugged his father goodbye. "I'm sorry," he said into Ethan's ear.

"You have nothing to be sorry for," Ethan replied gruffly. His smile didn't reach his eyes, though.

They headed back out of town on foot, the way they'd come in. Atlas had to remember to step carefully over the road, and as they walked, he saw more evidence of destruction: trees had been hewn down, houses burnt out, fences destroyed. Every so often they came upon another statue, someone who'd caught the wrath of Medusa and had been too unimportant to be moved from where they were petrified.

At the edge of the city Poseidon sucked in a breath. "Trouble," he whispered.

Atlas looked up from the stones. A gaggle of guards stood at the edge of town, looking edgy. At the sight of the two travelers, they formed up smartly to either side of the road. And between them, Atlas got his first look at Medusa.

She was a tall creature, lithe-limbed and muscular. Her skin was an odd grayish color, like a pale corpse left to bloat in the river. Atlas found himself admiring the sculpt of her arms and calves, eye drawn toward her face. That face was more sharply beautiful than anything an artist might have designed: sharp cheeks, full lips, a proud nose. And above that face was a black head of coiled hair.

Then one of her coils unraveled and looked at him.

The coils were black snakes. And now that Atlas had noticed them, they took an interest in him: they lifted away from her skull by the dozens, twisting their little heads around and flicking out pink forked tongues.

"Don't look her in the eye," Poseidon said in a low voice. "Keep your head down and keep your temper, too."

"I know," Atlas murmured. Then he had to look down to make sure his legs hadn't turned to stone already. They refused to carry him forward. He took a deep breath and forced himself to take a step. They were two innocent travelers. Here for a visit with their uncle and aunt, now leaving after an unproductive attempt to work out a deal on his uncle's sawmill operation.

"Name and business?" said a guard as they approached.

Poseidon gave their fake names and handed over their fake papers. The guard gave them a cursory glance before handing them back. "How long were you staying?" he asked.

"A few days," Poseidon said.

A susurrus hiss filled the air. Atlas' eyes flicked to Medusa, and he felt heat and terror crawl over his body in equal measure. He quickly looked away. But her snakes had taken even more interest in them.

"Be specific," she said. She had a surprisingly low, musical voice. It somehow promised sensuousness and bloodshed at the same time.

"Three—uh, four days?" Poseidon said, licking his lips. He'd gone pale and sweat beaded at his brow.

"Three days," Atlas corrected, hoping to be firm.

"It's a long travel for three days," said the guard. "From Labyrinth City and the River of Life?"

"It's for business. And we've got family at home. You know how it is," Poseidon's cheery manner was back, though Atlas could tell he was forcing it.

"Family," pondered Medusa, and Atlas' heart began to pound. "I *don't* know how that is." Her booted feet came into view, then the bottom of her black snakeskin tunic. "Do you love your families?"

"More than anything," Poseidon admitted.

"Do you think they'd miss you if you never returned?" One grayish finger touched Atlas' arm. Her nail was as black as the snakes on her head, and as sharp as their fangs. A thin line of blood welled up as she drew her finger down to his elbow. "I'm curious, you see. I have no family. I…struggle to understand love."

In any other woman's mouth that would be an invitation. And perhaps it was for her, too. *Don't look.* Looking would be his death. All he wanted was to get home to Ivy and Maia. If he got out of this he'd stop being so disparaging of the normal life and appreciate what he had.

The fingernail moved to his chin. She was going to force his chin up. Atlas set his jaw.

"The big boss is scheduled to conduct his checkup," said a new voice. Atlas tensed. Then he eyed the speaker—a nervous-looking recruit. Wait a moment, he recognized that man. He'd seen him at the market, selling leather at his father's stall. He was a local. And he'd joined Kronos' men? Sherwood truly had fallen.

"That's marvelous," said Medusa. Her rich lips pursed in thought. "He always enjoys my demonstrations."

"I've heard he's in a horrid temper," the recruit said. "Enraged and looking for targets. And we haven't cleared up the blockage on the south side yet…"

"You make your point." A snake dipped into his line of vision to hiss at him. Then Medusa turned away. "Work can be so dull, and I'm not allowed to petrify anyone in uniform. Can't you at least give me a break?"

"Move along," muttered the recruit. He caught Atlas' eye and nodded slightly. He'd recognized them, too.

Atlas nodded back, relief surging through him. The recruit must have joined to make the best of things. To help out wherever he could. Or maybe he was part of whatever was left of the local rebellion.

There were still people dedicated to the cause here, and willing to put their lives on the line. All wasn't lost, Atlas thought as he and Poseidon hurried away.

And if others hadn't given up, he wasn't going to give up, either.

Chapter Fifteen: Inside Man

Atlas kissed little Maia on her sleeping head. One chubby leg kicked fitfully and she made a tiny grumbling noise. His heart squeezed. He suddenly found it difficult to swallow.

"Maybe this is a bad idea," he said as he quietly shut the door to their room. Ivy sat at the kitchen table, red-eyed, with a sack next to her stuffed with food. He couldn't remember the last time he'd made his beautiful wife cry. The feeling of guilt swelled. He should sit down with her, cover her hand with his, and promise never to leave. They could drink tea like they did every morning; she would work on her new bow while he whittled a whistle for Maia. Watch the sunrise swell in wild pinks and oranges outside their window. It could be a day like any other.

"I won't push you out the door," Ivy said in a wobbly voice, cracking a brave smile. "But if you say it's important, it's important."

Atlas sat heavily, pain shooting through his heart. It *was* important. His brothers could ignore the cause for the lives they had, but someone out there was suffering at the hands of Kronos tonight. And someone else would tomorrow. He thought of the statues petrified in Sherwood City's main square. Surely some of them had been married. They had families that would grieve them forever. Or maybe it was even worse: maybe those families would starve without an extra pair of hands to help put food on the table.

Ivy wiped her eyes and looked at him, proud and wistful at once. She'd watched her mother die a completely preventable death because of the cruelty of Kronos and his minions. Now, when he imagined the scene, he saw dark, tight curls and light brown skin. Maia's grass-green eyes.

He wasn't going to wait around for Kronos to take everything he loved from him. He was going to strike first. For Olympus, for the people. For his daughter's future.

"I know that look," Ivy said. She tied up the sack. "If you leave now, you'll make it to the gates by the time they open. You can get a good day of traveling in and you'll reach Lumina by tomorrow evening. Greet your brother for me."

Atlas didn't want to stop in on Hades. He didn't want his brother to have another opportunity to talk him out of this. Besides, the Cross had trained Atlas how to talk to other members outside of a mission. He couldn't. It could compromise the entire network. And even if Hades wouldn't continue the work, Atlas didn't want to put him at risk. If he were captured, he couldn't be traced back to anyone else.

But he didn't want to worry Ivy, so he leaned in for one last kiss. She twined her arms about his neck and pressed against him, deepening their kiss with a little gasp that sounded too close to a sob. Her body was warm and soft, and even in Labyrinth City she smelled of roses and cream and fresh soil, all the scents of home. Longing swelled in him. He could stay here, take her back to bed, work on giving Maia a little brother—

She pulled away. Fresh tears adorned her eyelashes.

"Come back to me," she whispered.

Atlas nodded once, a solemn promise. Then he picked up his pack, and the sack of food, and he slipped into the high streets of the city.

He was dressed as a traveling laborer. If anyone asked, he was a woodworker headed toward new prospects in the capitol. Nothing on him suggested that he was a highly-trained member of the Cross: his sword and bow were at home, waiting for the day he would reclaim them. All he had with him were a set of knives that completed his cover and a long, elegant staff.

The city air was still cold from the night, though dew was already beginning to evaporate in the morning sun. A few people wandered the streets: doctors, hurrying to or away from some emergency, lamplighters to extinguish the streetlamps, callers who went from house to house, waking the inhabitants with a sharp rap or a stone tossed against a window. At the city gates Atlas presented his papers and his story and was waved through without a second thought. No one really cared about those leaving Labyrinth city. He headed down the steep mountain road, sticking to the side as carts began their arduous ascent, carrying merchants eager to reach the Labyrinth markets.

At the base of the mountain he turned back and bestowed one final look upon his home. The sun was turning the red-brown walls of Labyrinth City to a sparkling bronze. From a distance, the city was a wonder: snaking paths and high buildings strung with hanging gardens, looking at once impenetrable and unknowable. A marvel and a testament to the creatures that lived there and their ability to build.

Twice he'd been driven from his home by the threat of Kronos. There would not be a third time.

The Honorable Gentleman Wizard's Club was a tall stone building in Novaris's city center, adorned with sculptures of chimeras and gorgons and important, studious-looking men. The white stone sparkled in the sunlight, when there was any; today it was raining, as it had every day this week. Atlas grumbled a curse at the weather and shoved himself deeper into the alcove across the street from the club. He'd stolen a fine suit over a week ago and he was getting tired of wearing it day after day, only to cancel his mission for some reason or other. Word had recently reached him of a riot in Lumina. Over a dozen men hanged for daring to protest the rising cost of bread. He didn't have all the time in the world; he had to act.

He took a moment to get into character. Shoulders back, head up. Walk as though the rain meant nothing to someone as important as he. He briefly considered drawing out a broad leaf he could use as an umbrella, but that sort of flashy magic was best saved for his mark. Instead, he stepped nimbly over a puddle and made his way to the front door. He kept his nose in the air and his lip curled faintly back, as though nothing he saw here could impress him.

It was hard to keep the haughty expression on his face. The moment he entered he found himself in a cozy foyer paneled in dark wood. The wood here was carved as well, this time in swirling symbols that he recognized from the few alchemy textbooks his father had tried to make him read when he was younger. The tiles beneath his feet were laid in a herringbone pattern, and as he looked he caught flashes of silver threading through them in similar curving patterns. Wards, maybe?

Beyond this foyer was a broad staircase leading up to offices and a second floor. Next to the staircase, directly across from Atlas, sat a door. Atlas had found out from nine months of scouting and developing his network that the higher up a mage went in the building, the more powerful he was. And Atlas wanted to meet the most powerful mages he could—they were the ones in Kronos' employ. They were the ones that could get him face-to-face with his enemy.

But he had to work his way up. And to work his way up, he had to work his way *in.*

A skinny, small man stood behind a desk made from the same dark wood that paneled the walls. Even though he was at least a head and a half shorter than Atlas, he managed to look down his nose at the big man. He had a thatch of hair so red it was nearly scarlet, and pale skin dotted with freckles. "May I help you with something, sir? Perhaps you're lost?"

Atlas remembered his cover and adopted a cultured accent. "I am not. I am here to join the club."

The little man coughed as though trying to conceal a

laugh. "Waiting for your sponsor, then?" he said. "Or did you think that you could rent a suit and pass the test with some two-penny magic tricks?"

Atlas had known about the sponsor. He'd also known that cultivating a relationship with a mage who could get him into the club would take months more. So even though showing off his magic was dangerous, it was the best way to get in quickly. And it was the best way to catch the attention of his mark, too. "I'll take the test," he said easily. He leaned forward, his sneer becoming more pronounced. "And when I pass, I'll have you disciplined for your tongue."

"Yes, yes. How bruised your ego must be." The doorman's mouth turned up in a faint smile. "You'll be glad of it when you're a member and I assist you in keeping out the riffraff, *good sir.*" Still chuckling, he turned to his desk and rang a little bell. He obviously had no faith in Atlas. The thought rankled the big man, even though he knew it was normal. After all, what sort of magic had he used to prove himself?

The door at the end of the hall opened and a woman poked her head out. Her dark hair was pulled back in a messy bun, and she wore thin spectacles. She clutched a stack of papers and she glared at the doorman as though he'd interrupted her at some very important work.

"We have another vagabond intent on humiliating himself this morning," the doorman said.

She transferred her glare to Atlas. "Come on, then," she said ungraciously. She beckoned.

The club held tests once a quarter, and anyone could submit their name. Those who did were subjected to a barrage of invasive magic as the club board sought to break mental defenses and peer into their entrant's mind. According to Atlas' contacts, most entrants didn't last longer than two minutes before they had to be carried away. Those who did withstand the first test were offered the chance to show off their own magic and win their membership. And the more impressive their magic, the more doors they opened.

"You can still back out," said the woman as Atlas passed her. "The mind test will break you."

Atlas laughed, forgetting for a moment that he was playing the part of a cold and correct gentleman. She jumped at the boom of his voice. Then she shrugged, as if to say, *your funeral.*

She led him first to a small room stuffed with papers. She found one for him to sign, asserting that he had entered the club of his own free will, and agreed to partake in the test with no coercion from any other party. He also absolved the club of responsibility for any mental anguish he might suffer as a result of the test. Cheerful stuff. Still, he signed without a second thought. Then he followed her through to the main hall.

The main hall looked like the library of Ivy's dreams. The wooden floor shone warmly from the light of dozens of hanging lamps. All around the edges of the room, books glowed in their leather spines. Desks sat in neat rows, perfect for study. Today, all of them were empty. On a dais at the front of the room sat three other entrants on fine wood-and-brocade chairs. In a gallery above the hall stood a small crowd. Those were the masters and the mages who would be judging them today.

"Take a seat. You arrived last, so you test last," the woman said. Then she turned and stalked over to the side of the stage, flopping down in a bad temper.

"Thanks," Atlas muttered sarcastically. He took his seat next to a fidgeting, pimply youth. The boy eyed him with obvious terror. "Relax," he said in a low voice. "I'm not going to be the one testing you."

A clear chime rang out over the hall. A man stepped forward, holding a little silver bell. "Welcome, entrants," he said. He sounded coldly amused. "You have petitioned, one and all, to join the Gentleman Wizard's club. Should you be accepted amongst our ranks, you will have access to the finest magic and highest knowledge our profession can provide. Should you fail, you will be cast out, and you may not apply again. Wizards rely on mental strength and moral fortitude to cast our spells, and so the first test will be a test of your mind. You will all undergo it together; should any of you pass, we will proceed to the next phase of the test." He put a slight emphasis on the word *should.*

He glanced at his fellow wizards, and it was all the warning Atlas had before he was slammed with pain. It was as though someone had stuck invisible fingers inside his head and was sifting through his brain. His life began to flash before him: his first broken arm in the training yard, facing off against some guards in a Cross mission gone wrong, holding Ivy's hand as she screamed on the birthing bed. He struggled to breathe. He couldn't let this test defeat him. But he couldn't let the wizards see his true purpose, either.

He focused on Maia. On her brilliant eyes, on the way she giggled when her mother splashed her in the bath. He focused on her chubby feet as she took her first steps, and on the curl of her hair. His child. He would live to see his child, and he wouldn't do it as a sniveling simpleton broken by magic. The pain split his head. He thought he caught the scent of burning hair. He dug his fingernails into his palms and focused on that pain, so tiny in comparison.

But little by little, the pain in his palm increased, and the pounding in his head diminished. At last he dared open his eyes. His vision swam and, for a moment, he couldn't understand where he was. Then he realized his cheek lay against the stage floor, and the sea of desks were at eye level. He'd fallen out of his chair.

He uncurled his hands. One of his fingernails had sliced through the skin of his hand and a bright dot of red beaded up in its place. He found a handkerchief in his pocket and dabbed at the blood as he got to his feet.

Around him, the other entrants lay on the floor as well. Unlike Atlas, however, none of them were getting back up. One frothed at the mouth. The pimply kid who'd been so scared of him looked dazed. His eyes crossed and uncrossed.

"Are you all right?" Atlas bent down and touched his shoulder.

The kid began to sing a lullaby.

"No touching the other entrants," said the man in the gallery. He rang his silver bell again and figures hurried forward to drag the rest of them away. A minute later, Atlas was alone on stage.

"Your name?" the man asked. He sounded annoyed. As though Atlas had ruined his plans by passing the first test.

"Harper O'Donovan," he said, sending out a silent apology to the other man. Hopefully, Harper wouldn't mind Atlas using his name for a good cause.

"And you think you can impress us?" the man said.

Atlas let a cocky grin spread over his face. He reached for his power, the power of Olympus. "I do."

"Begin, then," said the man.

He didn't realize that Atlas had begun already.

Atlas used the first swell of power to clear away his headache as though it were nothing more than a few dusty cobwebs in the room of his mind. With his second swell, he looked around. The room was fairly austere, but there was a small apple tree in a pot to one side of the stage. Atlas turned toward it. *Grow,* he thought, and sent his magic rumbling through the floor.

The apple tree shot upward. Its roots broke through the clay pot with a crack and its branches unfurled like fingers beckoning. Atlas cocked his head. It wasn't enough. He reached down into the well of his power and made a picture in his mind as he breathed in. Then he breathed out.

The masters gasped. Each leaf was now veined with tiny

ribbons of silver.

It still wasn't enough. Atlas didn't want to merely impress these men. He wanted to blow them away. He wanted a key to the top floor. He inhaled the fresh scent of apple blossoms and another idea formed in his mind. At his next exhale, the tree swelled with fruit. The apples grew plump and sweet-scented. Their skin was of purest gold.

One apple fell to the ground with a *thunk* far too heavy to be fruit. Atlas stilled his hands and his power. In the utter silence that followed, he walked over to the apple, his fine stolen shoes clicking on the wood floor. He picked it up and dusted off the dirt that clung to it with his handkerchief. Then he turned and walked back to the edge of the stage to present it to the spectacled-woman who'd shown him in. She stared at the apple in open shock.

"My compliments," he said.

She took it hesitantly. Her fingers were cool against his. Her palm dropped at its weight. She sniffed it, then set her teeth against it. "It's real gold," she gasped.

The gallery exploded.

"How—"

"What…"

"—*see* that?"

The man in charge tried in vain to ring his little silver bell, but the chatter became more animated. Someone shouted "Harper!" and in his elation, Atlas almost forgot that was the name he'd given.

At last, the wizard with the bell pulled forth a wand and

fired three bright sparks into the air. At this, his colleagues remembered themselves. They smoothed the edges of their smoking jackets and righted themselves, though they still murmured, agitated, cutting excited looks down into the gallery.

"We will adjourn to discuss the status of your application," the wizard told Atlas. "You may wait in the foyer."

Atlas gave a small half-bow, as gentlemen were wont to do. He didn't bother trying to control his smile. He knew as well as anyone: he was in.

###

He waited for over an hour.

By the time someone came to fetch him, Atlas' glee had turned sour and uncertain. Perhaps they thought he'd cheated. Or perhaps they were so intimidated by his ability that they didn't want him to join their club. Had he overdone it in his need to impress? He'd never been like Zeus, obsessed with looking flashy. But he had always been confident of his power, and perhaps he'd taken that confidence too far.

At last, the door opened and a wizard from the gallery came through. "O'Donovan?"

"That's me," Atlas said, as much to remind himself as anything.

"Come. Our most illustrious members would like to meet you."

At last. He stood and shook off the last of his uncertainty. They'd obviously been debating what level of access to give him.

The wizard led him up three flights of stairs. With every flight Atlas' heart grew lighter and lighter, until he was so elated, he almost forgot to listen to his guide. "We had to thoroughly examine the tree. We thought it was a top-level illusion, but you actually *grew* a tree. And an apple made of gold!" He chuckled, shaking his head. "Impossible."

Impossible for some. Atlas smiled.

His guide stepped off the staircase at the third floor and opened the door on a large, stately room. Chairs had been arranged in a circle, and in those chairs sat the wizards Atlas sought to join.

And most importantly, his mark sat in the center chair.

The mark was a younger man than Atlas had expected— as the son of the famous Merlin he'd anticipated a man at least his father's age. Yet the boy was certainly no older than Atlas himself. He wondered if the mark used youth spells. They were a dark magic, but what else could he expect from Kronos' top wizard?

"We'd like to examine your wand," the mark said. His eyes were cold and calculating, thoughtful. The other wizards looked at him with something very much like fear, when they looked at him at all.

Atlas spread his arms. "I have no wand."

The wizards murmured amongst themselves.

The mark merely raised his eyebrows. "Your book of

spells, then."

"I have no book of spells," Atlas replied. The murmuring intensified.

"No wand, no book of spells, and no spells hidden about your person? Then how, pray tell, did you do your magic?" The mark drew lips back in a disbelieving sneer as he brought out his wand. It was a long and elegant thing, made of a dark wood with a crystal embedded in the hilt. It stank of necromancy and dark magic. Atlas could feel it at odds with his own life-giving power.

The ghost of his father's voice ran through his mind. He was to keep his magic a secret. He was not to reveal himself. Yet how else could he get close to Kronos? How else could he bring Olympus' great tyrant down?

No, Father had stepped down as the leader of the Cross. He'd left the choice in Atlas' hands. Only Atlas could decide what was best now.

"I draw my power from the very source of all power and life," he said, drawing himself up to his full, impressive height.

"Impossible," said a man at the end of the row. "No one can draw power from Olympus herself, not without a medium to act as a vessel. And even if you could find a way to connect to that power, you'd burn yourself up."

"You're saying what, exactly?" Atlas put on a sneer that could rival his mark. "That I cheated?"

"Did you cheat?" the mark asked, fixing his gaze on Atlas. His eyes were dark, but something like black fire seemed to flicker within his pupils. A shiver scurried down Atlas' spine as the man twirled his wand between his fingers.

"No," he said, trying to sound firm rather than desperate. If they didn't believe him, they'd turn him out and he'd never get closer to his mark than he was right now. "I'll prove it to you. I have the magic of Olympus. Any sort of growing magic you want, I'll give it to you."

Whispers rustled through the room like a river. The mark did not partake, however, nor did he move his eyes from Atlas.

Then he cocked his head and said, "How about this?" He moved his wand in a lazy circle.

A grayish figure dropped from the tip of his wand to the ground. It had four limbs, straggly black hair and a dirty loincloth. Its ribs poked through mottled gray-green skin. Its arms and legs were sinewy and thin, spread like an animal's, and its fingers and toes were adorned with blackened nails. All around, the other wizards gasped.

The creature looked up. It reeked of death. Its eyes were black pits, its mouth snarling and stuffed with rotting, sharpened teeth. Atlas took a step backward out of reflex.

But he'd faced worse monsters than this, and without the help of his powers. He thought of Medusa. How he wished he'd had the courage to use his powers on her. Might he have been able to free Sherwood then and there?

There was no time for speculation. The creature leapt at him. The air erupted with shouts of panic.

Atlas stepped aside and worked without thinking. The wizard who'd led him up still stood behind him. He screamed.

The undead creature opened its maw wide, eager to close it around living human flesh.

Then it jerked back. Its mouth closed on empty air, a few scant inches from his guide's face. It fell to the floor, a thick vine wound about its throat. Its black-nailed fingers scrabbled at the vines, but Atlas moved his hand in a circle, closing his finger into a fist, and more vines sprang from the edges of the chairs. They wrapped around the creature's arms and legs. It screamed in fury. A leaf unfurled from the vine at its neck and flattened against its mouth, creating an effective gag.

The wizards' shouts turned to a flurry of astonished whispers. "Is it real?" one of them said.

Atlas' mark stood, then. He was taller than Atlas had expected, but where Atlas was bulky with a lifetime of training, the mark was slim, with birdlike limbs and fingers well suited to drawing magic circles.

He approached his own creature without fear. It raged and snapped, but he simply ran his finger along the length of one vine. One long fingernail split the vine's flesh. He put his finger to the wet sap within. Smelled it. Tasted it.

"It is real," he confirmed. He turned to look at Atlas, and for the first time Atlas saw something in those cold eyes: respect. And perhaps an ounce of fear. "I can capture summoned creatures in my wand and give the illusion of creating something. But you simply…made something out of nothing, didn't you?"

Atlas dipped his head.

The mark waved his wand, and Atlas' vines went slack.

The creature had been dismissed.

"Welcome to the Honorable Gentlemen Wizard's club," the mark said, and extended his hand. "My name is Tom Ambrose."

###

Tom Ambrose respected power. It was the first thing Atlas had learned about him, when he'd arrived in Novaris and was looking for a way into Kronos' inner circle. The problem, he kept getting told, was that Tom was the most powerful wizard on Olympus, with the exception of his father. And Tom didn't speak with his father, who was a proud opponent of Kronos and his rule.

Well, now Tom Ambrose was the *third* most powerful wizard on Olympus. While Tom had the book learning to be a great wizard, he couldn't compete with the natural power that was Atlas' birthright. Atlas hoped that Tom would be intrigued by this power and the chance to shape the man behind it. But it would be all too easy to make Tom jealous or afraid. And so, when Tom invited Atlas to dine with him, Atlas was careful to paint the picture of a gentleman's son from Sherwood City, a city so far out of the way that Kronos never bothered to go there himself. A city without more than half a dozen books on magic, and a backwards opinion on the craft as well. Atlas spoke of a father that had flatly forbidden him from learning magic and had forced him into the merchant trade. He was powerful, but woefully ignorant in the ways of spellcasting. It wasn't so far from the truth, really. Atlas had only been able to practice when they were certain no one would interrupt them, and his magic wasn't the sort that ordinary wizards had access to. As his brothers had different powers than he did, no one had been able to provide much guidance on the specifics of his abilities. But Tom might be able to help him. And Tom might want the power that came from having influence over Atlas.

Atlas found out more about Tom, as well. He learned that the man was a twin, though Tom disliked talking about his brother for some reason. Tom liked good wine, and as sweet as he could get it. He liked reading any book on magic he could find, and could quote books that no one else even knew existed. Atlas learned that whenever Tom shot him that calculating look, it was because he was rethinking something he thought he knew about Atlas. He asked Atlas to do countless spells and Atlas tried his best, earning a bout of 'hmmms' and 'interestings' as he grew plants, changed the colors on roses, and made trees sprout from between cobblestones.

But it wasn't until three weeks in that Atlas was certain Tom actually liked him.

Tom had invited him up to his private study, a little room with a balcony overlooking a market square. He poured out two glasses of fine wine and sat, letting the orange and pink hues of sunset wash over his pale skin.

"You look sickly," Atlas informed him, taking a seat across from him on the balcony.

"Not all of us are blessed with your worldly beauty," Tom said, flapping a hand. "And I've been up all night. My father left some books with some—" an odd look came over his face, and he cleared his throat. "Tricky spells. We've been trying to perfect them without much luck."

"Anything I can do?" Atlas said.

"They're not exactly related to horticulture," Tom replied. "And anyway, I didn't bring you up here to talk about work."

Atlas buried his frown in his wine glass. Work was all Tom ever talked about.

"You know how to talk to women, right?" Tom said abruptly.

Atlas almost dropped the wine glass in surprise. Was Tom fishing for information? Did he realize Atlas had a wife and child? That he wasn't who he said he was? "I…have some experience," he hedged.

"I knew it." Tom leaned forward and put his wine glass on the little table between them. "Women must have been all over you in Sherwood."

"They tended toward my brother. He was infamous." Atlas let out a rueful chuckle.

"Look, I like women. But none of them want to come near me. And every so often I find someone who maybe does, but then it turns out she's only interested in the power or she wants to ask me for a favor or she was too scared to say no in the first place, or—" He threw his hands up. "You get the idea."

Atlas thought for a moment. The best way to play this was to be sincere. So he said, "Everyone wants to feel special. What could you do to make a girl feel special?"

"Magic. I can do magic. It's all I can do." Tom barked a laugh and slouched back in his chair. "It's all that keeps me useful." He got an odd, hollow look in his eye. "But that's the problem. My last lady friend only wanted me to show off how powerful I was. The one before that was afraid I'd turn her into a rabbit or something, so she ran away in the middle of the night instead of breaking up with me. Her whole family disappeared."

"Why a rabbit?" The wine was making Atlas feel sleepy and silly.

"Who knows?" Tom flapped a hand. Lace frothed from his sleeves, making a lazy arc in the air as he moved his arm.

"Maybe the problem is that your magic made her feel that *you're* special. You have to do something to make her feel like *she's* the special one to you." He thought of Ivy and chuckled. "Or you could wait for a girl to declare herself."

"You're no help," Tom grumbled.

"I could grow you a nice bouquet of flowers," Atlas offered. He squinted, reaching for his power. The wine was interfering with his concentration, making it hard to pull on his power. And it was distracting. The noise of the market square drifted up and invaded his thoughts.

"Eggs! Fresh eggs…"

"…hothouse tomatoes, you know they're rubbish…"

"Roses for the lovely ladies! Fresh roses, the perfect gift!"

Atlas focused on the rose seller. He missed roses, growing wild, tangling up the sides of houses and shops and bursting with cheerful color. In Labyrinth City, fine houses with gardens cost a fortune, so Atlas had been forced to settle for fresh flowers in a bowl on the table every morning. He missed the fresh scent of soil, the natural perfume of the flowers.

"Roses! Glorious—*augh!*" the rose seller screamed.

The air filled with shocked cries. Atlas opened his eyes. A rosebud the size of his little fingernail twined around his wine glass. Tom was peering over the edge of the balcony, his face alight with wonder. "What did you *do?*" he said.

Atlas stood and joined him. Below, the market was fast disappearing under a canopy of green. Branches and brambles wove together to create a broad roof, and from that roof bloomed dozens of roses, in every size and color. They grew up, and up, scaling the side of the building like slithering snakes, until one stem wound around the rail of the balcony and presented a perfect yellow rose to Tom.

Tom eyed him. "You are such a show off."

Atlas laughed, a deep belly-rumble of a laugh. "That wasn't something you knew?"

"At least you're entertaining." Tom shook his head, smiling ruefully, and sat again. "I'm certainly not keeping you around for your advice about women."

"My girl advice is…fine," Atlas grumbled. He knew what Zeus would say about it. Tom rolled his eyes.

The black fire in his pupils was gone, Atlas realized. That coldness and cruelty that separated him from his fellow wizards was a guard, a wall that kept him separate from the others. And he'd dismantled that wall for Atlas. He might not even realize that he'd done it.

Now might be the time to act.

"About your father's spells," he said as Tom poured them another glass each. "I'd like to help, if I can. It's what friends do for each other."

"And that's what we are? Friends?" Tom gave him another sharp look, as though asking a question in his mind and searching Atlas' face for the answer. The walls were starting to go back up.

"Aren't we?" *Play it cool,* he told himself. "I've been nothing but open with you. I came here to do something with my talents, strengthen my abilities. You've helped me with that. It's only natural I should want to help you."

"Yeah. Everyone wants to help me. I should have a hundred friends." Tom laughed an ugly laugh. "So eager. Eager to get themselves an audience with my master, or worm their way into my father's old library."

Atlas refused to show any emotion. There was no law that said he couldn't be Tom's friend and use him, too. Besides, why should he care if he used the man? Tom was on the wrong side of this war. He was probably responsible for the deaths of thousands of innocents.

"I bet you never thought you'd rise this high, did you?" Tom glared out the window. "A Sherwood bumpkin rubbing elbows with the top wizards of Olympus. You probably think you've got it made. Only you have no idea. Do you know why everyone else at the Gentleman Wizard's Club is afraid of me? Why *they're* not my friends, giving me bad advice about women and helping with spells?"

"Because they're power-hungry imbeciles?" Atlas guessed.

"Because their predecessors died trying to use me," Tom replied fiercely. "They all got what they wanted: proximity to Kronos. The chance to show off. But Kronos doesn't tolerate failure. And if he thinks you're anything but completely devoted, he'll kill you. He won't even think twice. It makes no difference to him, and even if he could have used you later, so what? There are so few disposable people in his world that he doesn't even care. I'm only protected because of who my father is. Because my father might actually be a threat to Kronos, and I am the one man who knows him best in the world." Tom shook his head. His mouth turned down as he swallowed the last of his wine. "And the moment I stop being useful, I'm dead. You don't want to cross Kronos, Harper O'Donovan. Not to help me, and not to help yourself."

"Kronos couldn't kill you, surely. You're the second most powerful wizard in the world," Atlas said. *Third most powerful,* he amended silently.

"Third most powerful," Tom corrected, drawing a knee up and propping his arm across it. Atlas raised an eyebrow. "My father has the greatest command over the magic we humans understand. And Kronos, of course, has more power yet. He can bring monsters out of thin air, monsters that have never walked this planet. No one else can summon something from nothing." Tom blinked, and his expression turned thoughtful. "No one but you."

Atlas felt his pulse quicken. "Do you think Kronos and I might share the same source of power? Have I...tapped into it somehow? Do you think anyone could?"

Tom snorted. "Not likely. And don't talk like that. You're spouting treason. I can forgive you because you're a country bumpkin and you're excited, but if you go around the streets discussing the source of Kronos' power, you'll be in chains before you can blink."

Atlas had to make a split-second decision. If he pressed on, he might blow his cover. But Tom trusted him, and was a bit drunk, and tomorrow he would certainly regret this conversation. This might be Atlas' only chance to pry.

He'd do it. "Why? What's the great secret behind Kronos' power?" He said it as though he were joking, as though he didn't believe there was any great secret at all.

"Nothing. But Gods don't like people going around town spreading the idea that there might be other Gods."

"Kronos is no God," Atlas said before he could stop himself. "Gods can't be defeated. He'd never have to worry about uprisings or rebellions or...any of the stuff he's worried about."

"Harper," hissed Tom, leaping to his feet. He stormed to the edge of the balcony and looked out, to both sides and up, before shoving Atlas through the balcony door and closing it behind them. Then he opened the study door and peered down the hall.

When he shut it again, he was shaking his head. "You really must be my friend. You're too stupid to climb the political ladder."

"Thanks?" Atlas guessed.

Tom shoved a hand through his brown hair and started to pace. "You can't say this sort of thing to me. Because if you do I have to decide whether to be more loyal to him or to you, and I'm too much of a coward to betray him."

"Sorry." Atlas put his hands out. "I'm sorry. I was—I guess I got excited. Remember, my own powers are a mystery to me. My father and mother hated that I had them and all of Sherwood avoided me. Maybe I thought that if I knew where *his* came from…you know I'm loyal. To you and to the empire." He'd practiced that lie so many times he could say it in his sleep.

"Yes, well, your power is a mystery," Tom allowed. He'd stopped pacing at least. "Before you, I thought that only a god could do what Kronos does. And I thought that Kronos was the only god." He fixed Atlas with his shrewd, thoughtful expression.

Atlas was so close. So close to understanding the source of Kronos' power. And to think, it might be the same as his own— "What makes you so certain Kronos is a god?" he asked, trying to imbue his voice with the perfect amount of skepticism.

Tom told him.

###

Atlas threw open the door to his rented room, slamming it behind him and weaving vines over the handle to prevent anyone from coming in. His hands shook and his breath came in ragged gasps. He started throwing everything he saw into his bag. He had to leave, now.

He should never have asked Tom about Kronos. His cover was blown. Worse, his world was shattered.

Everything he'd ever known about himself was a lie. His birth, his nature, his destiny—

And he didn't have time to think about that, because the door shook with an almighty blow.

"City watch! Open up!"

He'd known Tom would send minions after him. Tom had admitted as much when he'd said he was a coward. He'd always choose his master's side. The betrayal still stung, though, and Atlas flinched as the door crashed again.

He closed his eyes and breathed deep. He needed to think like a seasoned member of the Cross now. His first plan was an emergency extraction. He flicked a hand toward the door, and a few more vines curled up at the threshold, waiting.

The lock splintered and the door cracked open. Vines reached through the crack like arms, winding tight about the guard. Atlas heard a scream, but he had no time to stop and watch his magic at work. He shoved the window over his bed open.

He was halfway through the window when someone intoned a word from the other side of the door. Fire burst over his vines. The air filled with the scent of burning sap and singed hair. Atlas tried to smother the fire, but water manipulation had always been his brother's strong suit. He tumbled out of the window and hit the cobblestones, hard.

A gloved hand landed grabbed his pack and hauled it up, and him with it. "We hoped you'd run," growled a low, guttural voice. Atlas looked up into a helmed face. The golden crest on the helm was stamped with the image of a scythe. Kronos' symbol. Another guard smirked behind him, while a third stepped forward and backhanded Atlas across the face.

Atlas roared defiantly. Power burst from the stones beneath him and pale roots twined around the guards' feet, pulling them against the ground. A tree branch whipped down and slapped the guard who'd dared lay a hand on him in violence. Atlas slid free of the pack and his captors and dealt each of them swift blows as he ran past them, down the moonlight-soaked street and into the city. Behind him, warning bells mixed with the crackle of flames. *Fire in the city.* Smoke followed him as he raced around a corner. Ducking into an alley, he paused for a breath to run through his options.

He'd lost everything. He had no weapons, no money, no papers. Even if he could get out of Novaris and into the wild, he had nothing to help him survive. And the city gate would be closed and heavily guarded until daybreak. His best chance was to find somewhere to lie low until he could slip out of the city with a caravan or crowd, but where would that be?

He pressed against the wall as he heard a clanking, and a whole regiment of men in palace guard uniforms trotted past, pikes up. His stomach flipped unpleasantly. Had Tom already told Kronos everything? Had he been feeding Kronos information all along?

A figure stopped at the end of the alley. Its armor had been modified to fit its massive frame. Greaves were strapped over hairy legs and arms, and a powerful, animal musk rolled toward Atlas. In the moonlight, two slender horns curved toward the sky. A Minotaur guard.

Atlas clenched his fist. An idea had just occurred to him.

The Minotaur swung his head down the alley. He could smell the smoke on Atlas' clothes, perhaps, or the stench of his fear. Atlas breathed deep and pulled on his power.

The Minotaur growled. His hoof sparked on the stones as he stamped. Then he charged.

Atlas let loose. The city rumbled as trees sprouted new branches and roots, as vines flowed over the top of the alley. The vines wrapped around the Minotaur's mouth and nose, pulling him to the wall. He flailed, ripping at the foliage, but for every branch he snapped or vine he ripped, two more took their place. He howled in panic. Then, after three long minutes, he stilled.

Atlas checked to make sure he was still breathing, then got to work. He stripped the Minotaur and pulled the armor on over his clothing. Even though Atlas was much too large for a regular man's armor, the Minotaur's breastplate hung loose on him. He tightened everything as best he could, picked up the Minotaur's pike, then headed out to the street.

He trotted up to the back of a golden-plated crowd. People ahead of them were shouting. Their captain, a man with a red plume on his helmet instead of the standard white, turned around.

"Block off Temple Street near the square," he barked. "No one in, no one out."

Atlas followed the others as they hastened to obey.

The noise of the night had turned to pandemonium. His boarding house was ablaze and while a few guards had joined the bucket chain to put it out, far more were interfering— shouldering through the line, interrogating its members.

"Come on." The man next to Atlas nudged him with the end of his pike. "I'm not going to stay here to get screamed at. Let's hit Temple Street."

Atlas trudged after him, trying to keep his eyes averted.

The city was quiet only a few blocks from the fire, though he spotted more than one frightened face peering through the window. The residents would be punished if they left their homes during curfew, but they had to be ready to flee in case the fire came to them. More than one of the looks he got was laced with a hate that made him shiver. This was why he had to overthrow Kronos. Yet he couldn't do that by hiding like a coward. But what exactly *could* he do?

He had the night to figure it out.

They clanked over to Temple Street and took up their posts. The square was a broad space, neatly paved, with an arch in the middle that celebrated Kronos' rule over Olympus.

A statue of him stood at the top, benevolent and commanding, stretching out his hand as if to gesture at all that he owned.

"What's wrong with you?" Atlas' guard partner asked, and Atlas realized that he'd been glaring at the statue, hands in a fist at his side.

"Nothing," he said, forcing his hands to loosen. Beneath him he felt the ground tremble a little.

More soldiers appeared on the intersecting streets, enough to make the square bristle with steel. What was happening?

A rumble interrupted his thoughts. Next to him, the other guard stood at strict attention. Atlas followed suit. Across the square, the line of guards that crowded a street parted, lifting their pikes in salute. A moment later, a carriage came down the road between them.

It was the largest carriage Atlas had ever seen, wide enough to carry a dozen men at least. It was high, too, supported by wheels almost as large as a man, and drawn by four angry, red-eyed beasts in cruel-looking harnesses. They tossed their eagle heads and scratched at the ground with their lion claws. Griffins. Their wings had been bound to their sides and black plumes were attached to their heads. In fact, the whole carriage was black, blacker than the night around them, adorned only with a single golden sickle.

The carriage driver stopped in the middle of the square, directly in front of the the arch of Kronos. He hurried around to the side and opened the door, then threw himself to the ground as a tall figure stepped out.

The figure wore stylized black armor that fitted his slim frame like a second skin. Spines jutted from the shoulders and down the back. His steel-toed boots clicked on the stones as he took a few steps away from the carriage. Moonlight glowed off the pale planes of his face, which were as sharp as his armor. His eyes were sunken in his face, two pits that Atlas couldn't divine.

Kronos held out a hand, and a ghastly grey arm emerged from the carriage to take it. Atlas' breath hitched at the sight of the snakeskin tunic, the gold belt. The hair that writhed and hissed. As she looked around, heads dropped all around the square. Evidently, the people of Novaris had some experience with the creature Medusa.

"We have a traitor in our midst," Kronos announced to the silent square. "A man who would destroy me. A man who thinks he has the power of a God." As he spoke, Medusa left his side. She stalked to one edge of the square and began to walk along it. The guard next to Atlas began to tremble. Atlas wouldn't let himself be moved. He'd survived this gorgon once; he could do it again.

"This man was allowed to escape earlier tonight. He's at large, in your city, and you have failed so far to find him. Such laziness and incompetence is not to be borne. Are you not the finest Olympus has to offer?" Down the row, a man sobbed as Medusa swayed past. "Have I not reason to be proud of my guard? My wizards say I could replace all of you with demons who would do my bidding." Kronos looked over his shoulder into the carriage. His inner circle must be within. Maybe even

Tom was there. Would he recognize Atlas from a distance, in his disguise? "Perhaps I should. Perhaps none of you are fit to be anything but decoration. And if you are to be decoration, you might as well decorate my palace without needing food or pay."

A gray-green figure stopped in front of Atlas. He kept his gaze smartly averted, standing tall.

One black-nailed hand rose up to his cheek. He steeled himself, remembering the last time she'd touched him. But Medusa was uninterested in his skin today. Instead she toyed with the strap of his helmet. He swallowed, eyes catching on her full, sensuous, terrifying lips.

Those lips curved into a cruel smile. "Odd for a man to be wearing a Minotaur's helmet," she said, and with a flick of her nail, severed the leather strap. The helmet tumbled from Atlas' head. She stuck her finger through a hole made for a Minotaur's horn and waggled it. "Had to borrow some armor in a hurry?"

He was made.

Before he could think of what to do Medusa turned and seized his partner's chin. She forced the man's head up until their eyes met. "No," the man gasped. He tried to push her off, but her fingers dug in. Blood trickled blackly between them. "Please, no, I didn't know, I swear I didn't know—" Then he could say no more. Gray flaked up his face like shale. His voice died with a grating like a stone tongue against stone teeth. His arms froze and his uniform faded in color, until he was entirely gray, entirely still.

Medusa pulled away. She licked one long finger and crooked it towards Atlas. "Come with me, or meet the same fate."

"What is this?" Kronos called from the middle of the square.

"The imposter was *here*," Medusa hissed. "And the imbecile next to him didn't even realize." She tossed the helmet toward Kronos. It *clanged* on the square.

Atlas came forward. There was no point in hiding himself now. Instead of trying to make himself look small and insignificant, he unfurled to his full height, pushing back his shoulders, letting the moonlight show how big he was. "Greetings, Tyrant," he said.

"You say Tyrant like it's a bad thing," Kronos replied coldly. He turned to face Atlas, and as he drew closer Atlas could see how sickly he looked. His jaw was so sharp it could cut glass. His cheeks were sunken like a dead man's. His fingers were spindly and long-nailed like claws. "And I suspect you're being a little hypocritical. You see, I think you want something I have: *power.* Do you deny it?"

"I want the world to be free of you," Atlas said truthfully.

"Free of me, and bound to another. This world needs direction. It needs someone who will shepherd it, who will watch over it. After all, a child abandoned is a child who suffers." For the first time Atlas saw a flash of something in the deep sockets where Kronos' eyes should be. "Tell me, why do you think *you* can stop me?"

Atlas knew better than to answer. He only had to wait for

his moment. Olympus longed to obey him. But he couldn't take on every single soldier in the square at once.

Kronos cocked his head. "I think it has something to do with what that boy said. Boy. *Boy!*"

There was a shuffling from within the coach, then a thump. Tom scurried out and bowed low to Kronos, rising only when Kronos waved an imperious hand. He looked disheveled and red-eyed, and he directed his gaze everywhere but at Atlas as he replied. "He has the power to summon something from nothing. It is a power I have witnessed in no one, except for you."

Atlas couldn't even find it in himself to hate Tom. Tom was like his brothers—dedicated to his own safety. He'd simply been born on the wrong side of things.

"Yes. The ability to create something from nothing. The ability to grow a tree with silver leaves and golden apples. A marvel that had my wizards talking for weeks. I thought nothing of it until I learned who you thought you were."

"And who am I?" asked Atlas, fury and defiance rising within him. This fool thought so little of him, he hadn't even tied him up. "Aside from the man who will take you down?"

"How did you get this gift?" Kronos asked. He sounded almost conversational. "From your mother, perhaps?"

"It came to me," Atlas replied. "When I was a young man. Neither my mother nor my father have any magic."

"I know you're lying," Kronos said. "I know who your mother is. I've spent your whole life tracking her, in fact. She's an interesting woman, with powers quite similar to your own.

A woman who has the tendency to drop her children and leave them in the first convenient spot she finds. Who would rather spit out another brat than try to raise the one she had. And do you know…She evaded me twenty-five years ago, when I suspected her to be with child. I think that child…is you."

"Well, you're wrong," Atlas replied. He swallowed again, but the truth of his words settled in his bones. The woman and man who'd raised him, who'd taught him right from wrong, they were his parents. And they were no more magical than the next common man.

Medusa leaned in and whispered something in Kronos' ear. He cocked his head, thinking. "Well, I suppose there's one way to find out. I'll simply burn down the little forest you grew up in. I'll round up the survivors and have them all turned to stone. Unless, of course, they'd like to betray you."

Memory struck, of the burned-out sacred trees, of abandoned houses, of the square full of stone. "Leave Sherwood be," Atlas snarled. Something *twanged*, like a root growing too fast.

"Tell me the truth, then. Who are you, really?" Kronos snarled.

"I'm the man who will take you down," Atlas repeated.

Kronos smiled, revealing sharpened, yellowing teeth. His chuckle was dark and cold enough to send shivers down Atlas' spine. "But I have one advantage you don't have, boy." He gestured to Medusa. She stalked around and seized Tom by the throat. "I have no friends to protect. Only tools." Tom gasped. "Turn him to stone."

"*No*," Atlas burst out. Roots threaded through the cobblestones and pulled Medusa away from Tom.

"Don't," gasped Tom, leaping for him. But a vine snatched him out of the air and pulled him back. He surged with power, fueled by anger. As the carriage driver drew his sword, a branch swept down to slap it neatly out of his hand. More vines burst from the walls around the square. The tree branches waved without a wind.

Part of him wondered why he was doing this, why he was sticking his neck out for Tom after the man had betrayed him. Maybe it was because he wanted to prove that they truly *were* friends, that he cared about Tom as a person. Or maybe it was because he understood Tom better than he wished he did, and he wanted to create the kind of world where people didn't need to be sorted between friends and tools. Or perhaps it was simply because dying at the hands of Kronos' pet gorgon was a fate too despicable to be contemplated.

Plus, he was getting another idea.

"You want to know where my power comes from? Fine. I'll tell you. In fact, I'll show you." He raised his voice. "I challenge you to single combat."

Kronos looked unimpressed. "Why would I take you up on that?"

"Because you want to see what I'm capable of. You want to prove who's most powerful. So, prove it to me. The winner takes the throne."

Kronos made a show of examining his fingers. "I already have the throne. That leaves me with much to lose and little to gain. What do I get if I win?" A slow smile split his face, and a wave of foreboding washed over Atlas. He could almost hear Hades' voice in the back of his mind. *This is a dangerous idea. Turn back now.*

Of course, Hades had already turned back. Like a coward. That wasn't Atlas' way.

"I accept your challenge," he called to the crowd. "Under one condition. The winner takes the throne…and the loser loses his soul." His voice dropped. "And with it, your powers. Do you accept?"

"I accept," Atlas said. He'd never lost a fight hand to hand, and he wasn't about to break his streak.

Chapter Sixteen: The Weight of the World

Kronos' palace was a high, black-walled keep bristling with guards in golden armor. Atlas was led beneath a wickedly sharp portcullis, through a dark courtyard, and into a small, windowless room with a bed and a bucket. Tom prodded him inside with his wand. "It's better than the dungeon, so don't try to get out," he said. His voice was hollow, emotionless.

Atlas turned toward him. "I—"

The door slammed shut, and he heard several bolts slide into place, despite the fact that the door had only one.

He was never going to sleep. The contest was scheduled for daybreak, so he paced the room, going through his forms. He called and dismissed trees and flowers and mounds of dirt. Kronos had had longer to practice his magical combat. But who would he have practiced against? His power must be great, but he hadn't had occasion to use it in years, if not longer.

He'll try to cheat, Atlas thought. With so much at stake, and so little honor to him, that was a given. And Atlas could do nothing but practice, and think about why he must win.

When dawn pinked the sky outside, a servant came to fetch him and bring him down to the front of the palace. She did not speak to him, and he did not try to speak to her. She left him at the entrance to the courtyard and scurried away before he could even thank her.

Tom waited for him in the early morning gloom. The air

was brisk and cold and smelled of sulfur. "You need a squire to help you with your armor," he said dully. "Kronos thought it would be amusing if it were me."

Atlas wondered what fate lay in store for Tom when the fight was over. Would Kronos reward him for betraying Atlas? Or would he punish Tom for letting Atlas get so close? And if Atlas won, would he forgive Tom? Or would he make the wizard pay for all the suffering he'd caused, even if it had been to save his own life?

"Well, thank you," he said as Tom fitted a breastplate over his chest.

Tom was shaking his head. "Why?" he asked softly. He held up a greave and Atlas slotted his hand through.

"This is my destiny," Atlas replied, just as softly.

"Your 'destiny' is a fool's errand," Tom bit out in a low, quick voice. "Kronos will use this to crush morale and make people suffer even more. I know you think you have a chance, but you don't. You never did."

"I certainly don't have any chance I don't take," Atlas said, tightening the greaves on his arms before moving to the ones on his legs. "And I'd rather try than give up. If I have to die, I'll die for a cause."

Tom sighed. "You really were too stupid for politics." He finished tying the last strap and tried to step back.

Atlas caught his arm before he could disappear. "You don't have to be like this," he murmured, leaning in. "I was your friend. I can still help you."

Tom laughed hollowly. "You can't even help yourself.

You're a dead man walking, *Harper O'Donovan.*" His lip curled and he wrenched his arm free.

Sunlight edged over the top of the courtyard wall. It was time.

Kronos stood in the middle of the courtyard, waiting. It looked as though he'd invited all his cronies to come and observe the fight: the walls were packed with Minotaurs, Trolls, Goblins, and Dwarves. And men, of course. People who had benefited from Kronos' evil ways by following in his footsteps, by using cruelty to extract submission.

Well, they were all about to find out how dangerous such practices were. As the sun slid down the palace walls like molten gold, Kronos held out an open hand. The responding roar was deafening. Everyone stamped their feet, clapped their hands, screamed.

Kronos closed his hand into a fist, and at the signal, silence fell. In a cold, clear voice he began. "You have been called here to witness a one-on-one combat between myself and a pretender. This man thinks he speaks for the world when he challenges me."

"I do speak for the world," Atlas snarled, unable to let Kronos continue. "You are a tyrant, and we have suffered you for too long."

Kronos laughed. "You will bear witness to this day, and when you return to your lands, your cities, you will tell the world what happens when you defy me. Let the games begin!"

He turned toward Atlas, smiling, expectant. He didn't even move to defend, much less attack.

Death to tyrants.

Atlas came on hard and fast. Vines burst like ropes from the very walls, causing the mortar to crumble and more than one onlooker to scream. Plants sprouted from the ground, seeds that had lain dormant beneath the stones finally prompted to action. Soon the courtyard resembled a lush meadow.

Then the thorns began to grow.

He raised the bushes high, a sharp and dense wall that surrounded his prey. Kronos looked at them with disinterest. They rippled inward, drawing closer and closer to the tyrant. Kronos smiled, showing off his yellow teeth. Why wasn't he trying anything? Why wasn't he fighting back?

Why didn't he look scared?

No matter. Atlas focused on the thorns, sharpening them until their points were as deadly as daggers. He gave the thicket another push with his mind, and the thorns surged in. They glistened with dew as they reached for Kronos' pale throat.

One thorn scratched at the tyrant's earlobe. His smile grew. He shrugged, and the whole thing crumbled to dust.

Atlas gaped. His hands fell to his side. Never had he seen such power. Not when three of his brothers teamed up against a fourth. It was as though his powers had been child's play. It was as though Kronos considered this a game.

Kronos moved. Atlas threw his power down into the dirt, bringing the courtyard stones up to fashion a wall that kept him from his foe. He had to buy himself time to think. Every fighter had a weakness; Kronos' would be that he wouldn't take this seriously. He wouldn't fight for his life, because he didn't think he had to. But Atlas knew now. He was fighting for the fate of the world, for his own *soul*—and if he didn't do things perfectly, he was done for.

The wall burst apart. Kronos strode forward, purpose in every step. He flicked his hand and a whip of smoke and shadow materialized in his fingers. He cracked it once and Atlas was thrown back into the courtyard wall. He slipped down to the ground. His vision swam but he struggled to his feet. He couldn't lose concentration, not for a moment. He brought a tree made of iron and grabbed a branch, shearing it off with his thoughts. It lengthened in his grasp, becoming a staff. He swung the staff toward Kronos. But Kronos cracked the whip again, and the iron staff went flying. At a third crack, the whip curled up his arm. It burned like fire; it burned like ice. Atlas wrenched his arm away. There was a ringing in his ears. Too late he realized it was his own voice, screaming.

He raised more iron trees. The second held five-pointed leaves that he broke off and threw like stars; Kronos waved his hand and summoned a wind to bat them away. He made himself a sword; the whip shattered it at a touch. The crowd jeered him and Kronos egged them on, waving for more. Atlas' arm was beginning to go numb where the whip had touched it.

The crowd was distracting Kronos, Atlas realized. He was playing it up, trying to make a good story that they could take home to tell their own lackeys and messengers. Atlas could use that cockiness. He stumbled, pretending fatigue and barely missing a lash from the whip. He thought of the tree he'd grown in the Gentleman Wizard's Club. He could do this. He could turn the fight.

He let the next whiplash catch him in the back and went down. He didn't have to fake agony as he rolled over, hissing at the pain that crawled over his spine and ribs. The unforgiving sun glared at him, judgmental. Then a shadow blocked it out.

"Poor child. To think you were my match. To think, after all these years, I couldn't defend my throne. Did you suppose you were the first would-be usurper?" He raised his whip high and lifted his skeletal head. The crowd around them chanted his name.

"No. But I will be the last," Atlas said, and attacked.

His vines snaked all the way up Kronos' body. They were threaded with silver and gold and iron, mobile enough to twist his arms behind his back before they set. Flowers made of uncut gems burst forth, weighing him down. He staggered under the weight. Atlas leapt to his feet. He was ready to finish this. He brought his hands apart for one last attack—

And the vines burst. The whip came down, and his arms were pinned to his sides. Fire raced up one side of his body and down the other. He tried to pull free, but shadow spread over him, wrapping him like a cocoon.

Kronos leaned in, and for the first time Atlas saw the eyes that glinted in the depths of that skull. They were the yellow of an animal, the yellow of sickness. They were enraged and cold and clear. In that moment Atlas knew: he'd been playing up his weakness, using it as a ruse to draw Atlas into a false plan. And Atlas had fallen for it. He'd doomed himself.

He'd lost his soul.

###

For three days Atlas was on display outside of the palace, chained to a post. Everyone could come and see him, and they did. Some wore pitying looks, while others jeered and spat on him. Others shook their heads at the folly of it all. *Prideful,* he heard. *Arrogant.*

And he couldn't deny it.

He'd wanted to save the world. He'd wanted to be known as a man who made a difference. He should have given up when his brothers did; the destiny was one they'd shared, after all. And now he languished in chains that had been manufactured to sap the magic from his being, chains that were too thick for even him to break. All alone. He didn't know whether he hoped his brothers would come, or hoped they'd stay away.

Tom came to him on the second day. He brought a hard roll and a bit of water, and when Atlas' honor guard asked him what he was doing he snapped, "Being human."

He tipped the cup to Atlas' mouth. A good half of the water sloshed over his chin, but Atlas didn't care. The sun had been a harsh companion, burning his neck and shoulders, and the cool water felt good. And the bread was something to do, at least.

"Why?" Atlas asked. His voice sounded like the chop of a rusty axe after a day and a half without food or water.

Tom understood the real question. "I'm not here to rescue you, if that's what you're asking," he said. "I'm here for the opposite reason, actually. You're going to die, and I'll never see you again. And you were a damned fool, but you had amazing power. It's a pity it'll be gone from the world."

Atlas surprised himself with a chuckle. The chuckle became a laugh. The laugh sounded like a squeaky hinge, but once he started, he couldn't stop himself. Perhaps he was too exhausted to stop.

"What?" said Tom, sounding annoyed.

Atlas moved his tongue around in his mouth. It was fat and tasted foul, but he managed to say, "That's…what you…think."

A wrinkle appeared between Tom's brows. "What?"

"That's enough chat, sir." The guard sounded apologetic, but firm. "We were to allow no one through."

"I'm not your average bystander," Tom said coldly. "I'm the one who brought this usurper to our lord." He stood up and cast one final look down at Atlas. "Goodbye, *friend.*"

On the third day, Atlas was visited by Kronos himself.

Kronos had shed his armor in favor of a loose black robe that made him look even more like death than usual. One skeletal hand tilted Atlas' chin up. "Citizen," he said, voice dripping with false pity. "How you must suffer. Then again, you seem to want to take the weight of the world onto your shoulders."

He smiled, revealing those sharp yellow teeth. With one hand he made a wide sweeping motion. There was an answering rumble from the mountain. He drew in a boulder the size of a Minotaur, swirling his hand around and around. As he swirled, the excess stone chipped away from it until it was a perfect globe. His eyes narrowed. Atlas got the feeling of great power rushing beneath his feet, a power he longed to access. That power flowed through Kronos and into the rock suspended above them.

Then the boulder dropped.

It smashed into his back, knocking him flat to the ground. The crowd gasped. He couldn't breathe. He couldn't move. He would suffocate here, among the soil that had always served him.

Something scraped the ground, and Kronos' voice drew near. "Now you *can* carry the weight of the world on your shoulders. Insofar as you can carry anything at all." He laughed, a high, cold sound.

But Atlas was feeling something: a trickle of power. He groaned and reached for it reflexively.

And it came to him.

The chains. They must have been damaged in Kronos' great display. Summoning every remaining piece of strength, Atlas drew from the ground. The power flowed into him, renewed him. The sun became a warming life-giver, not that hot blaze of death. His roots went deep and made him strong. Trees could bring down buildings, tear up mountains, take back all the world. And perhaps they could bear it, too.

He pressed his hands into Olympus herself and surged up. The boulder was impossibly heavy. His arms shook. But the answering gasp of the crowd, a shouted, *"Look!"* gave him another swell of determination.

He saw the robe of Kronos swish as the tyrant ruler turned around.

He took a deep breath and summoned all his strength, and the strength of all the life around him. He lifted his arms from the ground, steadying the boulder on his back. With another breath, he pushed up to one knee. He lifted his head and met the god's eye. *Stronger than you think,* he said to himself.

The same thought was reflected in Kronos' eyes. He knelt so that he and Atlas could look frankly upon each other. "You don't quit," he said, and there was something admiring in his tone. "You'd have made a good right-hand man for me."

"Never," Atlas gasped.

"Never," Kronos agreed. "For your soul is mine. Medusa."

She came at his call, kneeling beside him. Kronos put his hand on Atlas' chest. "Kill him," he said, and removed his hand with a flourish.

It felt as though Atlas' heart had exploded and pulled through his chest in a thousand razor-sharp fragments. Atlas choked on his scream. He wouldn't be like the statues of Sherwood, frozen in shock and horror. He would control what he could of his death. He gritted his teeth, and swallowed his pain, and raised his eyes until they met hers.

Her eyes were as lovely as the rest of her face: long-lashed, dark, and deep as wells. Something dark turned within them, a swirling of black, poisonous waters. They drew him in, and in, and he couldn't break away even as he felt his legs cramp up.

Ivy, he thought, fighting to remember the red-gold of her hair, the wildness of her laugh. He wanted her to be the last thing on his mind when he died.

The three brothers met at the gates of Novaris. Hades had pulled a hood over his head to disguise his maroon eyes and grayish skin, while Zeus had rubbed ash in his hair to give it a darker cast. The normally cheerful Poseidon looked bedraggled and wan, with sunken eyes and wrinkled clothing. His curly hair was matted and dull. He barely responded when Hades wrapped him in a fierce hug.

"If there's anything we can do, we'll do it," Zeus said. "And we *will* find something we can do."

Poseidon's nod was sluggish and far away.

They'd received word only a few days ago. Hades had been at the Lumina fish market when he'd spotted the woodcut, pasted to a wall outside a guardhouse. *EXECUTED FOR TREASON*, the bulletin had proclaimed. He'd recognized his brother by the fierceness of his gaze, by the sheer strength of will outlined in every muscle of his body. He'd stopped still, so shocked even his heart skipped a beat.

"Are you all right?" said a tentative voice, and only then had Hades realized his body was hot, so hot that steam rose from his shoulders. He'd hurried home and wept into his wife's shoulders as their son looked on, confused and concerned.

He'd left Persephone and Achilles in Lumina. He didn't want her anywhere near Kronos. He couldn't face the guilt if she somehow got hurt. His brother had already gotten himself into terrible trouble, or worse, and it was Hades' fault. He'd refused to continue with the Cross, refused to fulfil his destiny. He'd refused to do anything about the scourge that terrorized Olympus. He'd been too content to sit in his little house with his wife and his son. If Atlas had had someone to work with, perhaps he wouldn't be…gone…now.

Now he stood at the city gates, wondering if he truly had the courage to face up to his failure.

A tap-tapping sounded from behind them. A man and woman came up the road, dressed in plain traveling clothes. The man leaned on a hard wood staff. For a moment Hades didn't recognize them. Then, with a shock, he said, "*Dad?*"

Ethan's hair had turned white, and his weathered face was deeply wrinkled. Next to him Raven had a few deep lines at her mouth and eyes. But her hair was flushed over with gray. Ethan didn't use his staff as a mere prop—he leaned on it, favoring his left leg. Hades swallowed a sudden, new grief. When had his parents become old?

Ethan said nothing. He held out his arms. One by one, the boys came to him. He didn't even try to disguise his tears; he let them flow freely over his face. His liver-spotted arms were still strong, though sinewy, and they nearly crushed Hades when it was his turn.

"I'm so sorry, Dad," he whispered. His nose filled with the scent of hot ash.

"I suspect we all are," Ethan replied in a hoarse voice. He pulled back and opened the leather satchel at his waist. "Papers for everyone. They'll get us in and out of the city without too much trouble. I had to use up my last favor to get them, but it was worth it."

They went up to the gate. The day was cloudy, and a cold wind blew down the mountain, but Hades felt no chill. He kept his tears in check as they handed their papers to the guard and got waved through. Then Ethan took the lead, pushing through the crowd up Fisher Street. As they walked Hades took his mother's arm, helping to guide her through the throng. "Does Ivy know?" he asked in a low voice.

Raven nodded. "We brought her somewhere safe. And the rest of you will be joining us there. It's too dangerous to go back to your old lives. There's too much connecting your brother and you."

His old life. The life he'd chosen over the Cross and the path for which he'd been destined. That life was over anyway. He was such a fool.

The crowd grew only thicker as they made their way toward the palace district. The shops here were fancier than those by the gate: the tailors sold dresses and suits of silk and velvet, and the markets here traded in delicacies Hades had never even heard of. The blacksmith touted armor with gold threading and swirling patterns in light and dark steel. At least the travelers didn't look out of place: people of all sorts thronged the street. And like Hades and his family, they were moving toward the palace.

The road up to the palace was long and neatly paved in slick and shining black stone. Hades felt it thrum strangely beneath his feet, as though the stone itself reached out to him.

As though it recognized a kindred spirit. It was obsidian, he realized. Volcanic glass. Voices grew quieter on this road, as though the people were almost afraid to speak. They hadn't gone far when Hades realized why. Marble figures lined the road, frozen in various expressions of terror. He spotted a young and beautiful bride, the flower garland in her hair so delicate it looked as though a stiff breeze would blow it off her head. He saw a musician, standing tall with his harp, mouth set in defiance even as his eyes shone with fear. Dozens of them, perhaps over a hundred, the most beautiful of Kronos' stone-turned subjects and a grim reminder of what awaited those who crossed him. Some of the people who walked past stared in open morbid fascination, while others kept their eyes averted, as though they were too afraid to look on their fellow countrymen.

The throng was thickest outside of the palace gates. Six guards, dressed in the armor of Kronos with his sickle on their breastplates, looked on stoically as people pressed against the bars. Hades kept tight hold of his mother's arm as people pushed on them from all sides. They muttered as they did so. "Heard he could grow a tree of gold and silver…" said one.

"Poor fool could've made himself rich," replied his friend. "Now look at him." They both turned away, shaking their heads at the waste.

"Heard he nearly got him," whispered someone else.

They were promptly hushed. "That's treason talk. You want to end up lining the palace road?"

Gradually Hades was pushed forward, towards the high iron bars of the gate, until at last he was pressed up against them.

He could no longer hold out hope or make potential excuses. Atlas' face was a stone rictus of defiance, mouth set in a grim and stubborn line. His chiseled eyes still gleamed with certainty—the certainty that he was right, that he would win. His broad shoulders buckled under the weight of the boulder he carried, but his legs were steady, dedicated to the burden.

Every inch of it was him. And it was also stone. He was unquestionably dead.

Next to Hades, Raven let out a mangled sob.

"You there," snapped a guard. He was looking at Raven. Hades put a protective arm around her. "What upsets you so? This traitor received his due."

Hades felt his mother's fingers dig into his arm. He tried not to wince. "My mother's a sensitive soul," he called back. "She lost a son of her own not too long ago."

The guard was still looking at him strangely. "Clear out," he snarled.

Hades looked at Atlas one last time before turning away. The cold wind would never bother his brother, nor the beat of the sun on his brow. Never again would he leap from the woods, swords out, to fight like a madman. Never again would he laugh as he told a joke or looked upon his little girl. Hades' skin grew hot, and a glowing magma tear slipped from his eye. He blinked the rest of his tears quickly away, wiping his face. By the time he and Raven had fought their way to the edge of the crowd again, the tear was nothing more than ash flaking away from his face.

###

"This is my fault," Ethan said heavily. "And I'm sorry for it."

The family had gathered at a hideout not far from Poseidon and Diana's little house on the River. Poseidon had found an uninhabited island here, and unbeknownst to Hades, he'd been building a safe house there. More than a safehouse, in fact: he'd built an entire town. Several buildings surrounded a fire pit, and chickens scratched and clucked in a little yard. It was almost as though he'd tried to recreate Sherwood City in miniature for them. Once everyone was on the island, Poseidon raised the waters and turned the River into a churning menace. His blue eyes blazed with the only purpose he'd shown since the discovery of Atlas' capture. Now the adults sat around the firepit while their children played between the houses.

"No," Hades said. He sat next to Persephone, holding her hand as though it were the only thing keeping him tethered to this world. Ethan looked like a broken man, and Hades hated to see it. Especially when he was responsible. "It's my fault. I was the one who refused to face my destiny, and Atlas took it upon himself to face it for me."

"All of us refused," Poseidon said in a voice hardly louder

than a whisper. "All of us share in the blame." But Hades knew that was untrue. As the oldest brother, he'd always been the one to lead the pack. To tell his brothers when to train more and when to stop. When Hades had told the others what was right and what was wrong, they listened. Only Atlas had had the courage to ignore him and follow his own path.

"None of you are at fault," said Ivy. Her eyes were nearly as red as her hair, and she held on to Maia as though the little girl were the last precious thing on Olympus. For her part Maia was quiet, clinging to her mother and staring uneasily at the rest of them. But Ivy sounded angry. "Atlas would never have gone to Novaris if we hadn't had a tyrant ruling this world. If he didn't revel in causing pain and suffering. His minions let my mother die because they thought it would teach me a lesson, and it did." She stood and pressed Maia to her chest. "It taught me that some people aren't fit to rule. Some people are meant to be brought down, at all costs. Even if they're not people at all. I don't care if you call it justice or revenge, but I want him dead. He needs to pay for what he's done. To everyone."

"Vengeance." The word tasted strangely sweet in Hades' mouth. He looked around. Zeus' eyes were ablaze and crackling with electric energy. Poseidon sat straight for the first time since he'd heard of his brother. He looked over at Persephone. Her dark eyes were trusting, and she nodded once. "Yes," he said.

"Vengeance can be a bitter fruit," Ethan cautioned.

"I don't care," Ivy said.

"And…they do say it's a dish best served cold," Raven added. Ivy only glared at her.

Persephone squeezed Hades' hand. *Do something.* "We need a plan," he said. "Something that takes into account Kronos' movements, his power, his defenses and his weaknesses. If we can build a case and catch him out in the open—"

"I'm not going to wait for him to kill someone else's love," Ivy blazed. "He needs to be destroyed *now.*"

"And how do you propose we do that?" Hades snapped. Persephone's fingers dug into the flesh of his wrist. He'd gone too far. Ivy whirled to face him, tight-lipped with fury. "Atlas had been infiltrating Kronos' inner circle for a long time. He'd had time to prepare and scout out his options. If we don't do at least as much, we'll be throwing our lives away. We won't be avenging him, we'll be joining him." Hades turned to his father. "How many people are still members of the Cross of the Iron Phoenix? Would anyone rejoin the cause?"

"Once you're in the Cross, you're never really out," Ethan said. He heaved a sigh. "I know a few I could reach for certain. Friends who would not hesitate to come." He didn't look happy to be admitting it, but he didn't argue, either.

"Let's gather our forces and plan our attack," Hades said. "For Atlas. Make sure that when we really take Kronos down, he stays down."

Ivy stared at him for a long moment. Her hand came up to stroke the back of Maia's head. Maia lay her head against Ivy's shoulder, her little fists clutching Ivy's tunic tight. "All right," she conceded grudgingly. "But if I think things aren't moving fast enough, I'll take matters into my own hands. Kronos is an animal, and any animal can die by the bow." She turned and stalked into one of the treehouses nearby.

"I'd better get to work," Ethan said, pushing to his feet with a groan. "I really am too old for this."

"But if this works, we'll win. No more rebellion," Zeus said. "You can retire."

Ethan smiled humorlessly at the ground. "Wouldn't that be something."

###

The next few days were a flurry of activity as everyone worked to make the island inhabitable for dozens of people. Raven and Persephone coached the children as they built more shelters for the visiting Cross members to sleep in. Ethan wrote message after message, tying it to the flock of pigeons Poseidon had brought to the island and sending them out to his contacts. Hades and his brothers set up a training ground and discussed what they knew of Novaris and Lumina. If they attacked Kronos in his capitol city, there were bound to be threats to the local population. And as much as Hades wanted to defeat Kronos once and for all, he couldn't kill innocents in his quest to do it.

On the fourth day, the Cross of the Iron Phoenix began to arrive.

The first members were Centaurs, bedraggled and

foaming from a hasty trip through the plains. Their leader, a mare named Livia, bowed to Ethan and flipped a mane of dark brown hair over her brown shoulder. She had a sharp face, with a long jaw and large teeth that she bared in a smile. She led a dozen soldiers, fitted with bows and hunting knives.

"I'm glad you could make it," Ethan said.

"We have despised and resisted Kronos since he ascended the throne of Olympus," Livia replied. "We will do anything in our power to bring him down. You have the might of the Centaurs of Etna behind you."

"And the others in Etna?" Raven said, coming up beside Ethan and crossing her arms.

Livia bowed in turn to her. "They have ever distanced themselves from the conflicts of Kronos and the outside world."

"In other words, cowards," muttered Ivy from where she tossed grain to the chickens.

Livia stamped her hooves on the ground. Pebbles flew from beneath them. "Whether it is cowardice or wisdom, I cannot say. But we have made our choice."

"We appreciate that." Hades strode forward. If he was to lead this rebellion, the least he could do was act like it. He led the Centaur party to an area that had been built like a stable, offering them food and refreshments. Centaurs were capable archers, and their hooves were deadly melee weapons. His father had won the resistance a great victory when he'd gained the trust of the Centaurs, and Hades couldn't afford to lose it.

No sooner had the Centaurs been settled that another

boat came across the river. This held the broad, furry shape of three Minotaurs. Hades tensed. Minotaurs were dangerous and formidable, and often unpredictable. He bowed. "May your horns be sharp, and your bones strong."

The largest of the Minotaurs bowed back. He had a golden ring through his nose, and the hair on his curly beard and around his nose had turned white with age. His horns curved around in three coils on his head. "We of Labyrinth City come to offer our aid," he rumbled in a deep bass voice. "I helped to deliver your brother, and I felt the mourning of Olympus at his passing."

Hades ducked his head to hide a sudden onslaught of sorrow. "Thank you," he said gruffly.

More people trickled in by ones and twos—some old friends from Sherwood, the Outlaws, contacts that Ethan had cultivated in Lumina and Novaris and Labyrinth City. They paid their respects to Atlas' widow and child and got to work building up the island and sharpening their weapons. Harper O'Donovan arrived on the third day and enveloped Hades in a fierce hug.

"He was a good warrior," Hades' old friend said. "Anything we can do, we will."

Hades drew back. Harper's face was more lined than the last time Hades had seen him, and the carefree glint in his eye was gone. His chin was rough with stubble, his clothes tattered. He looked like he'd been sleeping outside for months. He saw Hades take it all in and smiled without humor. "Life in Sherwood is a lot different than it used to be.

Just remember this, in case you ever thought I was only in it for the glory."

By the end of the fifth day, Ethan came up to where Hades looked out over the River of Life. Night was falling and the other side of the River was clear. "If we wait, more will come," he said quietly.

"How many more?" Hades asked. The island air buzzed with a nervous eagerness. He didn't want to lose that energy, nor give people a chance to remember why the Cross had been disbanded in the first place.

"The longer we wait, the more will show. But there are two in particular that may need time to slip away from their duties. And without them, I fear this plan will never move forward."

"Who are they?" Hades asked.

"I'd rather you see for yourself," Ethan replied. As if in answer, lightning flashed down, hitting the center of the island. A thunderclap answered, making Hades and Ethan duck instinctively.

A black cloud had gathered over the island, too suddenly to be a natural phenomenon. Hades groaned. What had Zeus done now? He turned and crashed through the trees that still ringed the island and gave them some semblance of privacy.

He burst into the little square. All members of the Cross had gathered, weapons drawn and aimed at the two figures in the middle. Zeus held a crackling lightning bolt, Leda held a spear, Ivy her bow and Poseidon a shard of ice as sharp as a sword. The Minotaurs held short swords, the Centaurs small bows. The Outlaws were ready with slings and knives. And in the middle stood two men. One had a white beard long enough to tuck into his belt and wore the blue robes of a master wizard. The other was young, with the simple brown robes of an apprentice. A thatch of red hair flopped over his sharp face.

"Merlin," said Ethan with evident relief. "Stand down, everyone."

Over a dozen faces turned to him in shock.

"*Merlin?*" Poseidon dropped his blade. It broke neatly in two as it hit the dirt.

"The master wizard?" Timotheus put his sword away and folded his arms. "This smells like a story."

Ethan motioned for two Outlaws to step aside and went into the middle of the circle. Then he hugged Merlin tight, clapping him on the back. "You old dramatic fool. I told you to take the boat."

"You know my feelings on boats. And I think I've rather made a good point. Your security is criminally poor," said Merlin, the master wizard, in a wobbling voice. He brought a wand out from a robe pocket and waved it with a gnarled hand. Around him a circle of runes blazed in the dirt, then faded. "Not a single security ward. And your godling there has a tendency to shoot first and ask questions later." Merlin *tsked.*

"Of course I shot first," Zeus muttered, turning pink.

"I've been waiting for the opportunity to take Kronos down for over fifty years," said Merlin. "I've known for a long time that you three were my best shot. Have you got a plan for luring him away from his city?"

"Uh." Hades glanced around. Now all eyes were on him. "It's coming together."

Merlin snorted. "Come on. I knew I'd have to be the brains of the operation. Livia, you'd better join us." He turned with Ethan and they began to walk toward the shelter that had been turned into the war room.

Hades hesitated on the edge of the square, bristling with a mix of resentment and embarrassment. He *did* have a plan. Maybe it was rough around the edges, but that didn't mean he needed Merlin to sweep in and redo everything.

A cool hand landed on his arm and Persephone looked up at him through her dark lashes. "Let him say his piece," she suggested quietly. "You know you could use the help."

"I wish he'd said it more quietly," Hades grumbled. But his wife was right; she always was. He leaned down for a quick kiss, pressing his nose against hers. Then he strode to the shelter.

It held quite a crowd: Poseidon and Zeus, Leda and Ivy, Ethan and Merlin. Hades shouldered his way past his younger brothers, and Zeus reluctantly made way for Livia, who stamped one steel-shod foot impatiently until space was made for her. As night fell in earnest, the air turned chilly, and behind them someone started a bonfire in the middle of the square.

Ivy crossed her arms and glared as Merlin calmly lit a lamp and suspended it with a wave of his wand. "So what's this plan, old man?"

"I have a man on the inside, you see." Merlin began to roll up the map of Novaris that lay on the table. "My son, Tom. He's a powerful wizard, but the approval he craved led him in the…wrong direction. He's part of Kronos' inner circle, not least because Kronos likes to spy on me." He cackled, rubbing his wizened hands together.

"So your son reports on you…which means we can feed him false information," Hades guessed.

"Indeed. We need to tell Tom something that's important enough to draw Kronos out personally. That'll mean dealing with his army, but if you want to destroy him now, there's no getting around that."

"So, what would that important thing be?" asked Leda, cocking her head.

"Why, that I'm joining the fight." Merlin smiled brightly. "He's always suspected I had ties to a resistance movement, but he's never known for certain. And he's never been able to find me when I've hidden myself. Once Merlin sets a ward, the ward cannot be broken." He tapped his chin with his wand. "I will write to him, begging him to reconsider his allegiances one last time. I'll write it with Dragon's blood ink, which is only made in the great city of Etna. I'll let slip that we've turned the Centaurs of Etna to our side. Tom will take the letter to Kronos."

"Kronos has been eager for any excuse to attack Etna," Livia acknowledged. "But your scheming would bring us into open war. You would make enemies of the people living there.”

“Not if the fight never gets inside.” Merlin pulled a fold of paper from his robe and smoothed it out on the table over the map. Mount Etna had been crudely drawn and dotted with little notes and slashes. He used his wand to point as he spoke. “We will be on the mountain, concealed by my magic and by whatever natural cover we can find. As Kronos approaches, before he can enter the mountain itself, we will reveal ourselves and begin the fight. We’ll have the high ground. Timotheus and his Minotaurs will hide in the tunnels and ambush any soldiers who try to sneak in. Livia, you and your Centaurs will perform a flanking maneuver from the other side of the mountain.”

“It’s risky,” Livia said.

“Any move against Kronos is risky.” Merlin flapped his hand impatiently. “Are we dedicated, or not?”

“We are,” said Ivy quickly, and glared at Hades as if daring him to contradict her.

Hades turned to his father instead. “You’ve been the leader of the Cross of the Iron Phoenix for a long time. What say you?”

Ethan looked at the map. He seemed to dislike the question. He took a deep breath and said, “We’re all here. And we’ll probably never be as many as we are right now. I say this plan is the best we’ve come up with so far.”

Merlin clapped his hands together. “Then I shall write the letter. We will have tonight, and tomorrow we must move. It won’t take Kronos long to assemble his army, not if he thinks time is of the essence."

They disbanded to spread the news and hand out assignments. Hades stayed at the table, peering over the map. This mountain felt familiar somehow. It tugged at him, the way the volcanic glass in the palace had done. Even though he'd never been to Mount Etna, he was comforted by the fact that their last stand would be there, somehow.

"Think this'll work?" he asked his father as the other man returned to the table. Ethan held a bottle of wine. He took a slug straight from it before passing it over to Hades.

"It had better. I don't intend to lose any more sons." Ethan sat heavily. Tears glistened on his cheeks and Hades found himself sitting beside him. "All this time I trained you, I knew it was possible you would fail. I knew it was possible one of you would die. But I simply…never allowed myself to think about it. Maybe if I had, I'd have quit while I could. Your brother could have had a normal, happy life."

"In Sherwood? Terrorized by Medusa?" Hades pointed out. He shook his head and took a quick sip from the bottle. "I have a feeling that we'd be here no matter what."

Ethan's shoulders shook with silent sobs.

All over the island, little parties broke out. Someone started on a drum they brought, and someone else broke out a harp. Harper produced a set of wooden pipes and soon there was dancing. People laughed, and kissed, and wagered who would walk the furthest tomorrow or kill the most in battle. Timotheus got into a wrestling contest with five Outlaws and took them all down, roaring in triumph. And Hades went around to every single person, thanking them. Looking them in the eye. They were all scared, but they were all dedicated, too. They were ready to take their own lives back.

It was close to three in the morning when he was finished, and the party was still going strong. A slim, olive-skinned arm slipped through his and his wife pulled him around. "Finished with your duties yet, O mighty resistance leader?" she teased.

"Where's Achilles?" Hades asked. Persephone pointed. The boy had fallen asleep across a Minotaur's chest, back rising and falling as he snored contentedly. The Minotaur in question was also snoring, great rattling breaths that would have broken glass, had there been any on the island.

The drum took on a slower beat, and the sound of the pipes turned mournful. Hades pulled Persephone close, inhaling the scent of her hair. He still marveled at the warmth of her skin all these years later, as though she'd just come in from the sun and was still blessed by it. She lay her head against his chest and smiled against him. "Your heart's racing," she said.

"Always, when you're near," Hades replied. He propped his chin on her head. Together they swayed, until the fire died down and the last of the revelers chased each other inside.

###

The next day was a day of headaches and arguments. Only children and those unfit to fight were staying on the island, and in the rush to pack Hades had to break up countless arguments about which comb was whose, who had lost who's sword, and who'd snored loudest the night before.

When they got to the edge of the river even more bickering ensued as they tried to sort out who should go first. In the end Poseidon waved an irritated hand, sweeping the water aside as though it were dust. "Hurry up," he grumbled. "My head is killing me." Diana patted him as she went by.

Hades crossed last, after checking that no warriors had been left behind. As he stepped into the muddy river bottom footsteps echoed behind him. He turned as Ivy trotted down the steep side of the bank. "I thought you were staying with Maia," he said, arching an eyebrow in surprise. "I thought you and my father agreed."

Ivy gave him a hard look. "Your father agreed with himself. I *will* avenge my husband. Raven can look after the children better than I, anyway." She flipped her red hair over her shoulder and marched ahead of him.

Hades decided not to engage in a battle he was going to lose. It might set a bad precedent.

From the other side of the bank, they walked. They ate as they did so and cut across fields and through woodlands, avoiding the paths that would take them through towns. Several times Merlin stopped, and considered, and brought out his wand to run a few spells before waving them onward. No one complained, to their credit, and in the afternoon a few people were feeling cheerful enough to break into song. Hades shushed them with regret. Who knew when they'd be able to sing again?

They met up with more of Timotheus' Minotaurs and camped for the night on the edge of a lesser forest, making shelters out of branches and blankets and eating dried meat and fruit. They couldn't afford to give themselves away with campfires, but Hades went from group to group, heating stones with his hands so that they could benefit from a bit of warmth, at least. Talk was quiet and most kept to themselves, thanking Hades with a brief word or nod before falling silent. Hades returned to the little circle of stones he shared with Persephone, his brothers, and their wives.

"How are they?" Persephone gave him a gentle smile. She could always tell his mood, and right now it was pensive.

"They're afraid," Hades replied.

Zeus snorted. "Why would they be?" Leda nodded next to him, eyes on the stone, which glowed like a dying coal.

"Why wouldn't they be?" Poseidon countered. "Some of us will die tomorrow, and I think we all have reason to remember that no one here is invincible."

His eyes flicked to Ivy. She stood up abruptly. "I'm going for a walk."

Hades reached for her wrist. "I don't think that's a good idea—"

"I'll go with her," Diana said quickly, and shook her head minutely at Hades. Together, she and Ivy went off into the forest. Hades sighed. He didn't doubt that Ivy and Diana could take care of themselves, but they didn't need to attract extra attention, either.

"We need a plan for Kronos himself," Poseidon said. "I

know none of us want to talk this way, but Atlas wasn't a match for him on his own. I can draw on the River, as long as we're not too far from it."

"We can draw Kronos to the south side of the mountain." Zeus leaned forward. "Hades, you're the strongest of us. Kronos will naturally look to defeat you. And while he's distracted, I'll take care of him with these." A little zip of lightning shot from his thumb to his pinky.

Leda smacked him. "Don't show off. You're going to burn this whole place down, and then where will we be?"

Hades tossed fitfully that night. The night was cold, despite his heated stones. Even the sounds of the forest, so familiar to him throughout his childhood, couldn't lull him to sleep. He rose near dawn and made his way to a shallow stream, where he splashed his face and neck to wake himself up.

"Here, love." His wife's cool hands pulled up his shirt and she dipped a rag into the stream, washing his back.

He shivered. "Thank you. I didn't mean to wake you."

"You didn't wake me." She laughed. Even when she was being quiet it sounded like tiny wind chimes. "I was already awake. When you can't sleep, I can't sleep."

"Sounds like a curse," Hades said.

Persephone wiped him dry and helped him with his shirt again. "You will prevail," she said softly, lacing up the front of his shirt.

Hades caught her fingers in his. "How do you know?"

She smiled, teeth pale against the dark of her mouth in

the gloomy morning. "I've seen how you act to protect those you love. There's no one I'd rather have fighting for me."

Hades dipped his head and kissed her. It might be the last opportunity he had for a long time.

Chapter Eighteen: Missing Heart

Mount Etna gleamed in the morning sun. Its steep mountain face was lush with moss and the ragtag army ascended carefully, trying not to leave too much evidence of their passage. A few mountain goats ran bleating from the Minotaurs, but they ignored the men and Centaurs. The mountain herself was quiet today. No quakes, no trickling smoke. In fact, it felt as though she was waiting. Like Hades.

The Minotaurs disappeared into the mountain passageways to hide, while the Centaurs trotted around the back of the mountain's base. Merlin and his son Harry went with them first, constructing careful illusions that would keep Kronos' scouts from spotting the Centaurs and giving away their crucial advantage. Then Merlin wove a spell over the city within the mountain, a sort of gentle time loop that would keep those who dwelt there inside, tending to their own selves. By the time he was finished, Merlin was starting to get out of breath.

"It's not easy, being the greatest wizard in the world at my age," he puffed. "Harry! More water." As his son hastened to find his canteen, the old man leaned against a boulder.

"Are you sure you can do this?" Hades asked. "Because the rest of us can do without the concealing spells—"

"Don't condescend to me, young man." Merlin poked him in the chest. "I've been weaving master enchantments since before you were born. You focus on your crude military tactics, and I'll focus on the noble art of magic."

"Right." Hades tried not to roll his eyes as he walked away.

He found an obsidian outcropping that would provide good cover for Persephone, Diana and himself, and chased away the goat that had taken refuge from the Minotaurs there. Poseidon, they'd decided, would immerse himself in the river, while Zeus would find shelter on the other side of the mountain. If Kronos thought there was only one brother, the chances of defeating him were greater. Hades watched as one by one the others scoured the mountain, finding rocks or small trees to use as cover. Some of the Outlaws, versed in the art of camouflage, even covered themselves until they blended perfectly with the landscape. Merlin even stepped on someone's hand as he prowled up to investigate a different group.

And then they had nothing to do but wait. The sun beat down, scorching the back of Hades' neck. Then it slipped over the horizon. Persephone shivered.

"You're cold?" Hades said, surprised. All he felt was relief that the sun had gone.

"Of course we're cold," Diana answered for her. "We're without shelter here." She tossed him a derisive look and set about rubbing Persephone's shoulders vigorously.

Hades set his fingers to the ground. He felt so at home here, it hadn't even occurred to him that others might be cold. He breathed deep and sent his consciousness out into the mountain. He was instantly was aware of every life on the mountain's surface, from the tallest Minotaur to a crawling ant. With a gentle exhale, he sent warmth radiating out over the mountain's surface. His army should be comfortable now.

Persephone touched his arm. "Thank you." She lay down, reaching out to him, and he snuggled into the crook of her arm.

He heard the army before he saw them.

The rumble began at dawn. The enemy's footsteps and voices combined to roar over the plain as they advanced. Hades lifted his head and focused on the horizon.

At first, all he could see was a mass of black dots, appearing at the edge of the world. It looked like ants swarming over a honey sweet. More appeared, then more still. Thousands upon thousands.

He was shaking. He would face Kronos today.

"How close do you think they'll get?" Diana murmured. "Before he realizes something's not right."

Hades didn't answer. He watched the army draw closer. Humans and Minotaurs made up the bulk of it, though there were a few Centaurs in their cavalry, and Griffins pulled chariots and wagons stuffed with war machines. Kronos' forces must be ten times as large as their own, at least. Sunlight flashed off armor and pikes and swords.

"There, at the back." Diana pointed. Hades followed her finger. In the distance, Kronos' carriage of war rumbled over the ground. That carriage—the man within it—was his goal.

The army stopped at last at the base of the mountain. The front line of soldiers stood still and looked straight ahead, waiting. Behind them, men worked in a flurry of activity, unloading one of the wagons. They were putting something together. Hades held his breath.

A voice boomed out over the field. "I know you're there." It was deep, and coldly amused, and it wormed its way down Hades' spine like a shiver. "Come out and face me, old man."

Old man. *Merlin.* The ruse was working so far.

Merlin's voice replied, magically amplified. "I'm disappointed in you, Tom. I'd hoped you would choose the right side, for once. As for you, Kronos—come and get me, if you can."

There was a long pause. Below, the men had finished setting up their gear. They began handing out gigantic bows to the Minotaurs, bows that would take two or more men to load. The arrows were capped with a small clay pot instead of the usual arrowhead.

"I don't think I will come and get you," said Kronos.

The Minotaurs fired.

Bolts arced up the mountain side. The ground around them exploded, sprouting pockets of fire. Hades hissed as one of the hidden Outlaws screamed. The bows were armed with incendiaries.

A second volley was already coming their way. The air

filled with dirt and smoke and the smell of burning foliage. "Archers," Hades shouted, cursing himself. The chances of them hearing him were next to nothing, and the smoky air would obscure him.

"Your powers," Persephone whispered to him.

Hades hesitated. Revealing his powers might give Kronos too much information. But he'd have no chance of defeating the dictator if he lost his entire army. He slammed his hand on the ground and watched it ripple like a rug from beneath him. It spread to the base of the mountain, tossing the front line of Kronos' army into the air like toys. A signal if ever there was one.

Around him, Outlaws popped up and bent their bows back. The battle was officially underway.

Hades grabbed Persephone's hand. "We need to get rid of those big bows. Could you run to Zeus?"

She nodded. Her face was pale with fear, but the set of her mouth was firm. She pressed a quick kiss to his lips, then dashed away.

Hades began to walk down the mountain, putting power into every step. The ground trembled before him, growing in force as it rumbled toward the army. While their captains screamed, red-faced, for them to advance, they could hardly gain purchase on the slope of Mount Etna before they were thrown off again. The Minotaurs took refuge behind a shield wall, aiming high with their powerful bolts.

As he descended, Hades saw the door of the black coach open. A tall figure emerged and unfolded himself, then turned toward the battle. Toward Hades.

The figure's eyes found him. Something electric and angry hummed through Hades' body, hate and vengefulness and righteousness all wrapped up with power. He brought his foot down hard, scattering men before him. The figure in black began to stride his way.

A sword whistled into his view. He brought his own sword up to counter it and shoved the man with his other hand. The man went flying. Heat radiated from Hades in waves, and he didn't bother to hide it. Let them see his power now.

The black-robed, skeletal figure of Kronos drew closer. Behind him strode his great weapon Medusa, and Hades felt a thrill of hatred. With any luck he would kill two monsters today.

###

Poseidon waited at the bottom of the River of Life.

His powers allowed him to breathe water. When he'd ducked beneath the surface of the River last night, the water had been teeming with fish; at the approach of the army, they'd disappeared in flashes of silver and black. And now it was only he, waiting for his brother's signal. In one hand he held a shining obsidian pebble.

His thoughts strayed to his wife. Diana shouldn't be here. He'd begged her not to be here. She'd looked at him with her cool dark eyes and said, "What sort of medical relief do you have?" When he had no answer, she nodded. "A midwife is better than no one."

She would stay out of harm's way, he told himself, creating a tiny underwater whirlpool to keep his fingers occupied. She was there to heal, not to hurt.

The first of the bodies plunged into the river. It was one of Kronos' soldiers, stuck through with an arrow. Red clouded around him in the water.

The obsidian pebble grew hot in Poseidon's hand. He dropped it to the silty river bottom where it sank, glowing, into the ground. It was time.

\#\#\#

Foot soldiers charged down the hill in front of Hades and the armies met in a clash of shields and pikes and swords. Hades sent out a tremor that knocked down the first shield row of Kronos' army, feeling a grim satisfaction at the screams of the fallen. Little by little, he would even the odds. Even so, he kept his eyes on the tall figure of Kronos and his serpentine lieutenant as they approached.

A whip of smoke and shadow lashed toward Hades. He raised his hands and a black spike jutted from the ground in front of his face. The whip wrapped around it, shattering it. Kronos chuckled darkly. "Another pretender." He let the whip drop from his hands. It disappeared in a wisp of black on the wind. "I enjoyed destroying your brother—I assume he was your brother. I think I'll enjoy destroying you just as much."

He drew a long black sword from the scabbard at his side. This was real steel, Hades saw immediately, but it was still wreathed with shadow. Hades drew his own sword and reached down with his power. A large patch of the mountain cleared around them. Both armies knew better than to interfere. The ground beneath Hades rumbled and swirled with magma, all his to command. He was the son of a God, and his power was mighty.

Their blades met in a clash that vibrated the bone all the way up to Hades' shoulder. He gritted his teeth. Kronos looked like a man half-dead, but his strength was not to be underestimated. Hades lunged with an attack that Kronos easily turned aside.

"Master," Medusa hissed. Her snakes rattled eagerly. "Master, let me kill him for you."

"This one's mine," Kronos snarled. "Don't interfere."

An arrow missed Hades' shoulder by a scant inch. Above him, another explosion rocked the mountain as the Minotaurs loosed another volley of explosives. Hades cursed silently as he blocked a swing, then a thrust. Where was Zeus? Had Diana reached him?

He didn't have time to wait. He needed the arrows gone. And for that, he needed his other brother. He fumbled a smooth obsidian stone out of his pocket as he clumsily blocked another swing, then kicked dirt up toward Kronos. As it flew, the obsidian shards sharpened to needle points, embedding in the God's skin. Kronos snarled and leapt back.

Hades felt the stone flash warm. He slipped it back in his

pocket. He could only hope that Zeus felt his stone and understood.

Before him, Kronos' face ran with tiny red rivulets. "You do bleed," Hades said.

Kronos' lip pulled back in a wordless snarl. He brought his hands together over the hilt of his sword—and when he brought them apart again, he held two swords.

"Brilliant," Hades muttered. Then he had no time to say anything at all. The swords moved in a swift and deadly dance, and he had to focus his whole being on staying alive. He blocked, skipped back, and called up obsidian that flattened into scales and fitted over his leather greaves as he brought his arms up in defense. The scales shattered as Kronos' sword came down on them. But at least the sword had missed Hades' head.

Screams sounded from the plain. It started with a few on the edge of the River, but the sound grew like a flood. Griffins shrieked and Minotaurs bellowed, and fear rolled over Kronos' army like a stink. For a moment they were both distracted, turning to look.

Funnels of water had emerged from the river like tentacles, whipping back and forth, lashing at his men. Some were knocked to the ground, bleeding. Others were picked up and carried back to the river. The army boiled and surged as everyone abandoned their right flank and fought to flee the River's influence. Hades heard distant thunder—hooves from the other side of the mountain. The Centaurs were coming to attack the left flank in the confusion.

Hades recovered himself and lunged again. Kronos growled and turned his swords to block. "Take care of that," he snarled to Medusa. She hissed in reply and slithered away.

Kronos looked rattled. Things were going well so far. Now all Hades needed was for Zeus to do his part.

###

Diana ran up to Zeus, panting, as the battle began. "Those arrows," she said.

"I see them." Zeus frowned at Leda. "I can aim for a man, but aiming for a man's bow? I'd need to be closer."

"But the closer you are, the more likely we give the game away." Leda smiled, a feral challenge. "Well, I've never backed down from a fight. Today won't be my first time."

They began to pick their way down the mountain, taking shelter behind what trees and rocks they could find. As they approached little pockets of fire where the explosives had caught on to shrubbery and moss, Zeus conjured a tiny storm to put the fire out. The Minotaurs had aimed for many of the trees the Outlaws and other archers had hidden behind, and the air was thick with the stink of burning skin and hair.

A man groaned as he brought down a cooling rain. His shirt had burned off. The skin beneath his leather cuirass was bubbled and bloody. Diana hissed a breath in. She bent and put a finger to his pulse.

"I need to get him to the River," she said. Its healing properties would stop the burn.

Leda pressed her hand. "Be careful." Zeus nodded. He and Leda helped lift the man, propping him against Diana's hip. They watched as she made her way down the mountain.

"I don't like it," Zeus said. "She's not a fighter like us."

"She's strong. She'll be fine." Leda shook a lock of hair out of her face. "Let's win this."

###

The battle had passed them now, with Kronos' army storming up the side of the mountain. The enemy was taking heavy casualties, and the air was thick with the stink of blood. Nevertheless, their captains screamed and egged them on. The wave of Men and Minotaurs seemed endless. They disappeared into caves and entrances into Etna, and nothing but their screams came out. Timotheus and his Minotaurs were defending the close quarters with ease. Around Hades and Kronos the battle raged, but still, no one tried to interfere. They knew better.

Kronos struck with the fury of a man whose plan has fallen apart. His blows nearly knocked the sword from Hades' hand and it was all Hades could do to avoid being skewered. He had yet to unleash his full power, and he'd been hoping to keep it reined in…but he might have no choice.

He swung up to block an overhead swing from both Kronos' swords. Their dark aura blazed and Hades heard a *crack.* Suddenly, he was left holding only a hilt. His blade fell to the ground in three smoking pieces.

"Who are you?" Kronos snarled. Hades scrambled back. "Who sent you? Was it *her*?"

Hades fell back onto the mountain slope, scrambling for any weapon. His fingers closed around a stone and he hurled it, shaping it as it flew so that it sharpened to a point. Kronos smacked it away with the flat of one sword. "Tell me," he growled through clenched teeth. "Tell me, and perhaps I'll make your death swift and merciful."

Hades dug his fingers into the dirt. If he could throw up a wall, maybe he could get enough time to make a new sword—

A massive shape blocked out the sun. Hades looked up. The horned outline of a Minotaur loomed above him. The Minotaur raised a double-headed ax with blades the size of Hades' torso. He roared in rage. Then in pain. Hades rolled to the side as the brute collapsed, right where he'd been lying. The ax landed in the dirt.

Persephone gripped her sword with two hands and pulled the blade free.

Hades scrambled to his feet and grabbed the ax, bringing it up in time to block the next blow from Kronos. "What are you doing here?" He'd put her at the back of the line, safe from the action.

"I'm keeping you in one piece," Persephone replied grimly, parrying another soldier's swing and kicking him in the chest. He tumbled, screaming, down the mountain.

"You need to get back with the others," Hades told her.

Persephone snorted. "And leave you to get stabbed from

behind? Not likely."

The ax was heavy, but it was more effective than his swords had been for blocking Kronos. Still, he was panting as he pulled away from another clash. He needed to find a way to end this. He needed more help.

He touched the stone in his pocket again, sending out another second signal. *Please let Zeus respond. Please...*

Thunder clapped overhead as a string of electricity fizzed from bow to bow in the firing line at the bottom of the mountain. The Minotaurs screamed and dropped their bows. Flames licked along bowstrings and shafts.

Hades ran a finger along the edge of his ax blades. They began to glow the angry red of smelting iron. He caught Kronos' next swing, sending sparks along the edge of the black blade. Kronos twisted away. "We end this. Today," he snarled.

Poseidon stood waist-deep in the water. With every wave of his arms it sprayed out over the plain, wrapping around enemy soldiers and throwing them across the land. Minotaurs and Men fled to the other flank, which was a boil of panic. Their Centaur allies wreaked havoc with hoof and bow. Meanwhile, the bank close to Poseidon was empty. Safe. Their own men could reach the River and take advantage of its healing properties. As he kept Kronos' army at bay his men limped to the water, holding on to each other and gasping in relief as they waded in.

He noticed her as she gently lowered a patient below the surface. "Diana?"

Her eyes met Poseidon's as her patient's chest submerged. They were filled with anguish. She cupped water in one hand and poured it over the man's burned face. He waded over to her, freeing one arm to cup her cheek.

"It's horrible," she whispered. Her eyes shimmered with tears.

"You can go into the mountain," Poseidon urged. "Through the tunnel entrance there." He nodded to where the River emerged from the mountainside. "Stay there until the fighting's done."

"And let someone die by my inaction?" She gave him a sad smile. "You vowed not to do that. And I vowed to stay by you, always."

Poseidon held her gaze, and felt a new energy swelling in him. Diana had always known what was right, and how to do it. He smiled briefly, and his heart lifted at her answering smile. Then she turned and waded through the water, headed back up the mountain for more casualties. He turned his attention to the plain again. He smashed a trebuchet and created a whirlpool on the edge of the river where a few soldiers were attempting to slip in and sneak up on him. He summoned a current to deposit them far downstream, at the edge of the Brown Swamp. He sent a wave crashing toward Kronos' black coach, lifting it off the ground and smashing its axle as it tumbled.

He was so focused on what he could do at a distance that he forgot to check his own flank. A scream snapped his attention back to the riverbank.

Diana was on her knees, hands around her throat. She scratched at a scaly, green-gray arm. Her eyes were wide with fear, hard with defiance. Poseidon's gaze traveled the length of that arm to the head of snakes, the striking cheeks, the black tunic. Medusa was smeared with mud, and blood trickled sluggishly from a cut on her shoulder. Her lips were pulled back in a sharp, triumphant smile.

"No!" he screamed. Diana's shoulders shook as she fought to pull away, but she was trapped in Medusa's gaze. Gray flushed over the top of her head.

Poseidon lashed out. A wave surged forward, lifting Medusa and flinging her like a rag doll. She soared through the air with a shriek.

Poseidon didn't see where she landed, and he didn't care. He dove beneath the surface and swam to the river's edge. This couldn't be happening. Splashing up to the bank, he raced over to Diana, slipping to his knees in the mud.

"No," he whispered. Her eyes were already grayed over, her mouth frozen in the act of saying his name. He grabbed her hand, her living hand, and squeezed as hard as he could. Funneling water, he wrapped it around her, gentle as a blanket. "Come back," he begged. It was the River of Life, couldn't it stop this?

But the River only healed what was not yet dead.

"Please." He wrapped himself around Diana, yearning

for the warm, yielding body. For the soft hair, the gentle rise and fall of her chest. But she was cold, and hard, and still.

Thunder crashed. Across the plain a group of enemies fired off a volley of arrows at Poseidon. He flicked a hand and a funnel of water smashed into them, cracking their bows and sending them to the ground.

Poseidon got to his feet, leaving his love on her knees. His mind was a haze of grief and anger, but one thought pierced it: they were still in a war. And in this war, he would have his vengeance.

Hades spotted the waterspout from the corner of his eye. It reached for the dark clouds that rapidly spread over the plain as it stabilized. Then it left the muddy riverbank and started to crawl over the plains.

He swung the ax. His last blow had cut through one of Kronos' swords, leaving nothing but a melting stump. Now the God was on the defensive.

"So, there are three of you now," Kronos said. "I'll admit, you've given me more trouble than the big one. But I've yet to break a sweat."

Hades shifted his ax. He needed to focus, he knew that, but part of his mind was fixated on Persephone, who was working with Leda to keep the rest of Kronos' men out of his way.

"You should be sweating," he said, and swung. Kronos

dodged easily. The whip appeared in his hand again. *"Now!"*

The sky broke. People screamed. A bolt of lightning arced down to strike Kronos on the arm. He screamed. The whip evaporated. Hades swung again. But the God was quick, even when clutching his arm. He rolled away and came up panting. His eyes flicked to Zeus.

"Two on one?" he sneered. "How honorable of you."

"We're after justice. We don't much care how we get it," Zeus said. A ball of white crackled between his fingers.

Hades and Zeus exchanged a glance. *Now.* Hades reached down, finding his power in the mountain, in the magma. The ground shook and two giant obsidian hands erupted at Kronos' feet. They seized him at the calves, warming and solidifying in an instant. He snarled like a caged animal. His eyes flicked from Hades to Zeus, to behind them. For a moment, real panic shone from him.

Zeus lifted his hand, shaping the lightning into a long spear. "I'd say pray to your Gods, but I don't think that's going to work out for you, somehow."

Kronos smiled.

His whip appeared in his uninjured hand. He lashed out, but wide—far too wide. He'd missed Hades by a good two feet.

There was a soft gasp from behind him. Kronos yanked.

He realized too late what the God had planned. He lunged forward as Kronos pulled Persephone tight against his chest. "Stop!" he screamed, to Kronos, to Zeus, to the world. But it was too late.

The lightning bolt struck true, piercing Persephone's chest. She stiffened. White fizzled over her body. Her eyes rolled back in her head.

Then she went slack.

Kronos threw her limp form to the side. Hades flung himself on the ground next to her. Her skin steamed. Her lips were parted, her eyes lifeless. Hades put two fingers frantically to her neck, turning his cheek to her mouth.

She had no pulse. She had no breath.

He heard a distant crack as Kronos burst free of his stone shackles. It echoed the roar within him. The world trembled and blurred. Noise faded to distant and unimportant sounds: his brother screaming, Kronos laughing. The mountain cracking open. The air filled with a bitter and poisonous smoke.

A long-fingered, black-gloved hand grabbed him by the arm and hauled him upright. Kronos' yellow eyes blazed as he backhanded Hades. Hades fell to the ground.

Get up, whispered a voice in his head. Her voice. But she was gone, and he had nothing to get up for anymore.

Kronos lifted him by one arm. Sweat slicked his face. The mountain roared and spewed. Kronos hit him again. He brought a boot down, hard, on Hades' sword hand. Hades felt the crack of bones and stared at his fingers, uncomprehending. Kronos' hand closed around his throat.

"God or not, you're no match for me," he snarled.

Then he dropped Hades and leapt back. A white lightning bolt sizzled into the ground at his feet. Zeus stumbled next to Hades, one hand covering his mouth and nose. He was shaking and coughing, but he raised his free hand and hurled another lightning bolt. As if in answer, a volley of arrows sailed over them, forcing Kronos back even further.

Two arms hooked under Hades' armpits. "Get up," she whispered again. Only the arms were dark as soil, not olive-tan. Hades shook his head. He couldn't leave her. "Get *up.*" Leda dragged him backward, leaving furrows in the dirt. He couldn't even fight back.

"Persephone," he mumbled. Behind him, someone shouted, *Retreat!* "I can't." He couldn't leave her. He'd rather die together.

Leda paused to have a coughing fit. "Hades, the mountain," she gasped. "Can you control it? *Hades?*"

But Hades couldn't control anything. His mind was slipping into deep, peaceful oblivion.

Chapter Nineteen: What Do We Do?

Hades woke to the scent of fresh air and birdsong and newly-turned soil. He lay on his mattress at the training camp in the middle of the River. For one glorious moment he thought he'd dreamed it all—the battle, the fight with Kronos, the loss. Then he lifted his bandaged hand, and reality slammed back in.

It had all really happened. Persephone was dead.

He felt his will to move sap away. He let his head fall back on the pillow and stared at the hastily-made roof above his head, wondering if he could lie here until he died. Now that he'd noticed his hand, he could feel it throbbing. His tongue was thick and dry.

Maybe I'll contrive to die of thirst before anyone realizes I'm awake, he thought.

Then a small and impossibly perfect head popped into view. "Papa?" said his son.

Hades couldn't speak. He wrapped his good arm around Achilles and brought the boy in, squeezing until he squealed and wriggled free. "Papa? Why crying?" he asked.

Hades wondered if anyone had told the boy that his mother wouldn't be back.

His tears flowed thick, singeing the bedsheets as they fell in pearlescent, glowing drops. His life truly was over. Everything he'd sought to preserve and defend when he'd married Persephone—it was simply gone. And if memory served, they hadn't even killed Kronos.

What had it all been for?

His child reached out and touched one burning tear. He watched it slide, red, down his finger, leaving his skin untouched. The boy. Hades had wanted him to grow up free and happy.

And now what? He wouldn't grow up free, he'd only grow up motherless. Hades swallowed a sudden surge of self-loathing. He might as well die, too, and spare the boy more pain at his hand.

No, whispered a voice that he knew to be his wife's. Little Achilles needed him more than ever. And maybe he needed the boy, too.

Hades pushed himself up and looked around. It looked as though three beds had been in use here, but his brothers were nowhere to be seen. There was a table at the far side of the room, pushed up against the wall, and a pitcher of water on it. Hades struggled to his feet and, holding his son's hand, trudged over to it. There were no cups, so he drank straight from the pitcher.

"Mama says need cup," Achilles informed him seriously.

At the sound of the child's voice, footsteps sounded outside the room. Hades turned in time to see his mother.

Raven's hands came up to her mouth. Her eyes brimmed, then spilled over. "He's awake," she called, and ran forward.

She threw her arms around Hades and squeezed him so hard he coughed. More feet scraped outside as his brothers and their children ran in. By the time Raven had pulled away, the room was full.

Hades barely had time to draw breath. Poseidon leaned down and embraced him, covering Hades' thin frame with his own broad one. "I'm sorry, brother," he whispered hoarsely, squeezing tight. When he pulled away there was a hollow light in his eye, a light that Hades understood too well.

"Is she...?" Hades said. He couldn't bring himself to ask it. Was Diana dead?

Poseidon nodded once in confirmation. Then he sat heavily in the chair next to Hades, gripping his hand so hard that Hades was convinced the rest of his fingers would break, too.

Ivy knelt and put a hand on his shoulder. She still held Maia, balancing her on one thigh as she leaned in. "I'm sorry," she said. "She was so good..."

Leda hugged him, then little Perseus and baby Hercules. Then Ethan, who convulsed against him with a single sob. "My boy," he murmured.

It was too much for Hades. It was as though their grief doubled down on his. He buried his face in his father's shoulder. His body wracked with sobs so fierce he could barely breathe. With every word, with every look, reality set in more. The knife of her absence plunged deeper.

He wept until he could weep no more. When he was reduced to nothing but hitching breaths, his mother's hand appeared with a cup of water and she murmured gentle encouragement as he drank.

"You still need to rest," she said when he handed the cup

back. "I'll get you some soup, and *everyone else* can assist with island chores." She looked around the room, daring any of them to disagree with her.

"I…" Hades swallowed. "I need to speak with my brother."

Zeus stood behind the rest of them, looking wretched. His white-blond hair was greasy, his eyes red. He looked like he hadn't slept since the battle.

He also looked more terrified than Hades had ever seen him.

Raven's mouth turned down, but she rose and began to shoo the others away. "Out, everyone. There are chickens to be fed and eulogies to be written and heroes to be honored. This is one of the most difficult days of our lives, but life does go on."

At that last, she cast a final, steady look at Hades. He nodded slowly. *Life goes on.* For other people, maybe.

Then he was alone with Zeus. His brother took one hesitant step forward, then another. Hades couldn't meet his eye. He focused instead on his chest, the plain wool shirt and the frame beneath it.

"Hades…" Zeus said.

Hades surprised himself. "It's all right."

Zeus fell to his knees in front of his brother, grabbing his arm, and Hades couldn't avoid his gaze any longer. His electric blue eyes shimmered with desperation. "I'm so sorry, I'd bring her back if I could, I didn't know he'd do it…I know you'll hate me for it, but I *am* sorry, I'm so sorry…"

"I don't hate you," he said. His brain was still fogged by disbelief, by devastation, but he knew what Persephone would want—perhaps, more importantly, he knew what she *wouldn't* want. "Persephone wouldn't hate you for it. And she wouldn't want me to lose another brother because of her." He found the strength to put his good hand on Zeus' shoulder and squeeze. "You followed the plan. I can't be angry with you for that." It wasn't his brother's fault that it had all gone wrong.

Zeus let out a single dry sob of relief. He flung his arms around Hades and let out a dry sob.

Raven came back in with soup a few minutes later. "I think that's enough socializing for now," she said, setting the bowl on the table. The soup was accompanied by half a loaf of bread.

Hades sighed and picked up the bread, dunking it into the broth. "I want to know the details," he said.

"You need to rest," Raven tried to coax him.

"How long have I been resting?" Hades put down the loaf to scrub at his chin. He had the makings of a fine beard there.

"Three days," Raven admitted. "But you needed it."

"And now I need to know the truth. What did we accomplish?" *What did we buy, with the death of my wife?* "We didn't kill him, did we?"

"Kronos' death was not the only way to gain victory," Raven said. "Eat your soup, and I'll fetch your father."

The soup tasted of ashes and mud. Hades forced himself to eat, thinking of his son with each bite. He couldn't starve;

he had Achilles. He couldn't waste away; he was obliged to his boy. The soup had been reduced to a few slices of carrot at the bottom of the bowl by the time Raven returned, Ethan in tow, and Hades got the full picture of the battle.

They'd decimated Kronos' men, and in cities all over Olympus people whispered that it was a great victory. In the end, Etna herself had driven the tyrant away, sending out rivers of fire to chase them across the plain. Nevertheless, the Cross needed a place to regroup, so they returned to the island, to swim in the River of Life and plan their next move. The brothers had slept for days, exhausted by the use of their powers and the grief of their loss.

"Kronos may not be dead, but he's weakened," Ethan said. Even though he looked serious, Hades recognized the spark of hope in his eye. "We've proven him vulnerable. I know things look bad, but...we've given people all over Olympus hope again. The name of the Cross is being whispered all over the world. Resistance is reborn."

Hades sopped up the last of his soup. Despite his father's words, he felt bitter and empty. Resistance might be reborn, but he still wished he was dead.

\#\#\#

He slept, he ate, he rested. He tried to remember what he had to live for. He read to Achilles and watched the boy run at barrels with sticks. The child already showed an aptitude for the fight, but Hades found he could not rejoice in that.

What would fighting get him, besides a life of lost comrades? Around him, survivors tended their wounds with pitchers from the River of Life and worked on turning the island into a more dedicated training camp. They tore down the ramshackle structures and replaced them with real houses. The lean-to that had been their strategizing headquarters was replaced with a real house, and Ethan and Raven moved the boys in. The Cross put up fences that could hold gardens and pig sties, and someone built a real coop for the chickens. The people around him were settling into a routine. On some level, Hades knew that a routine would be good for him, too. He simply didn't know how to find it. What sort of routine awaited him with Persephone gone?

Sometimes Poseidon came and sat beside him. And sometimes Ivy joined them both. They sat in an understanding silence. They didn't need to talk, to exchange platitudes or assure each other that it would get better. They all knew that it wouldn't.

Hades wasn't sure how much time passed before she came. All he knew was that one morning, he woke to a strange scent on the air. Wildflowers at once exotic and familiar, a smell that stirred a strange and particular longing in him. For a moment he was five again, lying in his Sherwood bed and watching the fireflies bob outside his window.

Poseidon sat up on his other side. "What is that?" he said, in a voice rough from sleep.

Hades rose and pulled on his trousers, then Poseidon helped him into a jacket. Together they left their shared room.

A brown-skinned woman stood next to their father's table in a vibrant green dress. She was waiting. She was no member of the Cross—in fact, Hades hadn't seen her in a very long time.

"Mother?" he whispered.

She turned at the sound of his voice. Her eyes were the same deep green that Atlas' had been, and a sharp pain shot through Hades' heart. As though she felt that pain, a lily bloomed and wilted on the shoulder of her dress. It was made of vines, Hades realized now.

"You'd better sit," Ethan said heavily. "Zeus will be here in a moment."

Hades sat at the table, opposite the brown-skinned woman. Poseidon settled onto the bench next to him. "What did you mean just now?" he muttered.

The door opened, and Raven came in. Zeus followed behind, saying, "But why—?" He stopped when he caught sight of the newcomer.

"Boys, this is Gaia," Ethan said. "Your mother."

"Our…" Zeus' mouth fell open. He blinked.

"My sons," she said, in a deep and vibrating voice. The voice was full of sorrow, and compassion, and love.

And suddenly, it was too much for Hades. He buried his head in his arms and cried. The numbness that had swallowed him for the past days stripped away, leaving him with nothing but the truth. He was alone.

"My sons," Gaia said again. She knelt at the end of the table and wrapped Poseidon in her arms. Hades heard him sob into her shoulder.

When Poseidon's shaking subsided, she moved on to Hades. Her scent enveloped him, bringing him back to Sherwood City, to home. And beneath that, he thought he smelled smoke and ash and fire.

He was hugging his mother for the first time. His blood family was together again, except—they'd never truly be together again. Atlas was gone, sacrificed to a cause that might yet fail. And Hades would never be whole again. He turned and buried his face in his mother's green dress and he wept until he had no more tears to give.

She stood and made her way to Zeus, bringing him into her chest. Hades had to admit he felt…better, somehow. The sadness was still there, but it felt as though his mother had drawn out the poison that twined through his grief.

He stood, and went over to Zeus. The brothers linked hands. Raven brought in fresh bread, boiled eggs, cheese and butter, and Ethan filled their cups from a pitcher of River water.

"Sit," Ethan said. Hades obeyed, though he did not touch the food.

Gaia made no move to eat, either. She folded her hands in front of her and looked from brother to brother. "You know I am the woman who birthed you," she said at last in her deep voice, "Though I would not presume to call myself your mother. You have a true mother for that." She nodded her thanks to Raven, who had the grace to nod back. "However, you did emerge from my body, and as you did, you emerged from the depths of Olympus itself. You are the children of Olympus and sky. And you were born and raised to defeat the tyrant Kronos."

"We know of this destiny," Hades said.

"Is it…even possible to fulfil now?" Zeus said. A shard of pain sliced at Hades' heart. Zeus had never before been uncertain, especially of his own skill. "Atlas is gone, after all. Were we not to defeat him together?"

Gaia considered his words carefully. "I believe you can. Kronos may be the most powerful being on Olympus. He might even be the most powerful being in the universe. But the three of you, when working together, may be stronger even than he. I believe you have failed so far because there is one thing you do not know about him." She rose, and began to pace. "It's my fault. I should have told your father long ago. Perhaps I should even have come here, before, and told you myself." She stopped and looked down at her hands, and sorrow filled her to the brim.

Hades leaned forward. "What is it?"

"Tell us," Zeus urged.

Gaia smiled sadly. "You all know that I gave birth to four boys, who were raised together as brothers. What you do not know is that my sons total five."

Hades felt his heart drop into his stomach. His words died on his tongue. *No.*

She met his eye and nodded, as if she could read her thoughts. "Kronos is also my son."

Hades couldn't tear his gaze away. "Which makes

him…” he whispered.

“Your brother.”

TO BE CONTINUED.

About the Author

Joseph Bell hails from the quaint town of Pittsfield, Maine, where he grew up amidst the playful chaos of four younger brothers. Such an environment, rich with adventures and mischief, nurtured in him an expansive imagination that only deepened over the years, particularly as he transitioned into the roles of husband and father.

Today, Joseph is the proud parent of two wonderful children, Ethan and Livia. The whimsical stories he spun for his son, inspired by the intricate artwork tattooed on his arm, became the seed for the captivating narrative you hold in your hands. As he navigated the joys and challenges of parenthood, Joseph recognized the profound impact of childhood memories. From beloved stuffed animals to bedtime tales, these moments shape who we become. It's this nostalgia and desire to craft a lasting memory for his own children that spurred him to put pen to paper.

In "The Cosmic World of Olympus: Battle for the Throne", Joseph has woven together the threads of his personal experiences, his children's wonder, and the tales behind his tattoos. He invites you into this world with the hope that you'll find as much joy in reading his story as he found in writing it.

ACKNOWLEDGMENTS

First and foremost, my deepest gratitude goes to Joe Mansir. Without him, this journey into storytelling and the vision for "The Cosmic World of Olympus" might have remained an unrealized dream. To my mother, Cheryl Mansir, who has been and always will be my most steadfast champion, believing that no vision or dream is ever too vast to pursue. Thank you both for your unwavering support and belief in me.

To my beloved wife, Ivy, who stood by me, nurturing the dream of creating something that would transcend beyond just me. And to my children, who serve as the guiding light and inspiration, reminding me daily of the boundless possibilities this universe holds. Your belief in what this can be and will become fuels my passion and dedication.

I must also extend my appreciation to the individuals from whom I sought advice and guidance in the pursuit of not just writing my first book but an entire series. Each of you has left an indelible mark on this journey, playing a pivotal role in shaping the Cosmic World of Olympus. You all know who you are, and the depth of gratitude I feel for your contributions is beyond words. Know that you hold a cherished place in the heart of the Cosmic World of Olympus family.